W9-CRM-560

NO NAME

Center Point
Large Print

Also by Richard S. Wheeler and available from
Center Point Large Print:

The Business of Dying

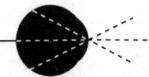

**This Large Print Book carries the
Seal of Approval of N.A.V.H.**

NO NAME

The Story of a Ghost Town

Richard S. Wheeler

CENTER POINT LARGE PRINT
THORNDIKE, MAINE

This Center Point Large Print edition
is published in the year 2020 by arrangement with
Golden West Literary Agency.

The text of this Large Print edition is unabridged.
In other aspects, this book may vary
from the original edition.
Printed in the United States of America
on permanent paper.
Set in 16-point Times New Roman type.

ISBN: 978-1-64358-575-8

The Library of Congress has cataloged this record under
Library of Congress Control Number: 2019957007

To all those who heartened me,
lifted me up when I fell,
and showed me a good world.

CHAPTER ONE

They were fixing to hang No Name at dawn, but No Name did not intend to be the guest of honor. A scaffold a few yards away awaited him. The town of Throatlatch hanged people so often they did not bother to dismantle the scaffold, and there it sat, a monument to the upright.

Westbound people came through Throatlatch, which sat on the bank of the North Platte river, waiting to empty pockets of travelers. No Name had heard that the town put its scaffold to use fifteen or twenty times a year.

No Name had no name. Or, as sometimes happened, he had every name. He was a young, skinny brown-haired cipher, instantly ignored, someone who drew no attention to himself. He could remember little of his early past and not much of his recent past. He was an oddity, someone who didn't seem to be there.

The sheriff of Wellbred County, Clyde Clemson, had questioned No Name closely.

"Everyone has a name. Why are you hiding yours? It won't get you anywhere with the law."

"Something happened on the Oregon Trail

when I was three or four. I don't know what. My parents vanished. I was handed to others, who handed me to others, who abandoned me at campgrounds. I had no name, so they all gave me one. I was Bob, Tom, Kid, Paleface, Brown-Eyes. Finally an old sheepherder took me in. He called me No Name, and that was that."

"You could have taken a name. Why didn't you?"

"I'd come to enjoy being No Name."

"Why?"

"Invisible. People don't see me."

"Plenty people saw you steal the judge's horses."

"They think they did."

"Doesn't matter. Horse thieving's a hanging offense in this Territory."

"What kind of horses?"

Sheriff Clemson eyed him. "Cut that out."

"Whose horses?"

"Cut that out."

"The judge's from Kentucky and says those horses are worth the price of half a dozen oxen."

They had convicted No Name in a few minutes. He thought it was orderly. Two witnesses said they saw No Name ride away with the horses, and a jury sentenced him to the noose. The jurymen were all dressed up real nice, with cravats and gold watches on fobs. No one in town knew who they were. They weren't the local grocer or baker or blacksmith. But there they were, doling out life or death.

Throatlatch was the county seat. Its office consisted of a clapboard building that had an all-purpose room, some offices, and two iron-barred cells. An outhouse stood behind the building, and the sheriff routinely took prisoners there because a pail in a cell stunk up the whole building.

On this fateful night, the room was occupied by three citizens. The sheriff, his deputy Gus Glory, who would keep the condemned man safe from angry mobs, and Majestic Skinner, the jailer and hangman who kept perfect records about who was sentenced to die, and how and when. The lawmen of Throatlatch played Rummy by the light of a kerosene lamp while waiting for dawn.

"You gonna give me a last meal?" No Name asked.

"Waste of tax money," Clemson said.

"Would you take me to the outhouse?"

"Use the bucket," Glory said.

"Still trying to bust out," the sheriff added.

"Deal," said Skinner.

Glory dealt seven grimy Bicycle cards to each man, set down the remainder of the deck, turned one over—a two of spades—to start the discard pile.

"Mind if I play?" No Name asked.

"What would you do with your winnings?" Glory asked.

9

"They won't stay in your pants tomorrow," the sheriff said.

"Let me play. You can put a leg iron on," No Name said. "I won't be going anywhere."

"You got nothing to bet," Glory said.

"You're afraid of losing to a dead man," No Name said.

That irked the sheriff. He hauled himself out of the chair, yanked a brass key from a ring at his waist, unlocked the cell door, grabbed No Name by the neck, and sat him at the table. Glory whipped seven cards off the deck and handed them to No Name.

"You can be King Midas for all I care," said Glory.

No Name had bad cards. Not a run, not a pair, not a meld in sight.

The kerosene lamp glowed steadily. No Name saw no light out the one window. Maybe some starlight. No moon. The front door was locked, the bolt thrown. The sheriff was taking no chances.

He was oddly well dressed, with black pinstripe pants and vest, a brass star pinned to his chest. He wore a small Smith and Wesson, thirty-two caliber, in a black holster that complemented his suit. He was smart not to haul around pounds of extra iron. The others weren't armed, but were a step away from a wall rack with several long weapons, including a shotgun.

Glory soon melded, and dealt a new hand. They were using poker chips as chits. No Name owed a dime.

"Just maybe gonna have some bad debt around here," Glory said. His brand of humor.

No Name's new hand was promising. If he could get a five and six of any suit he would meld with a mixed-suit run of seven cards. The lamp burned quietly, its chimney clouded by neglect. No Name had heard that the town was doomed. In a month or two, when the railroad came through, Throatlatch would have no more reason to exist. It survived now because of its rickety bridge across the North Platte. That was probably the reason no one had put a spare nickel into this court house.

No Name liked Clyde Clemson, and couldn't say why. They were opposites. The sheriff liked to be noticed, and dressed to make an impression. No Name liked to be invisible, and often was. The gazes of others slid past him, not noticing the young man with no name. There was safety in it. After years of knocking around unnoticed, it became comfortable. But now it had worked against him. He would hang tomorrow mostly because he had no name and wouldn't be missed. He would hang for reasons he didn't understand, perhaps for someone else's crime.

He drew a five of clubs and discarded a jack of diamonds. He was getting closer.

Skinner picked up the jack and discarded a six, which No Name ached to grab, but couldn't, and soon it would be buried.

Glory drew a card and smiled. He discarded a deuce. The sheriff pondered that, and finally drew a card, and discarded a six of hearts.

No Name eyed the door.

He plucked the six from the discards, unloaded a queen, and laid out a mixed-suit run.

"Well, aren't you full of beans," Glory said, not happy.

He tossed a chip in No Name's direction, and grinned. "Guess I'll get it back soon."

Clemson smiled, and paid up. Majestic Skinner did the same.

"Gives a man heartburn," Skinner said.

No Name wondered what it was that gave Skinner heartburn. Some people said mysterious things, and never explained their meaning.

No Name slid the chair back a foot, reached out to collect his winnings, but his hands didn't stop there. One hand grasped the lamp, the other hand dialed down the wick, which retreated into its cowling as its flame blued out. The room went black.

No Name headed toward the door, which was exactly where it should be, rotated the lock, slid the bolt back, and slipped into an inky night, lit only by a few stars peeking from layered clouds. He couldn't see a thing, but neither could the others. He heard a few shouts, and finally some-one in there scratched a match to life and lit the lamp. The others reached the door, and peered into nothingness.

No Name took stock. It was too dark to travel. The courthouse, if it could be called that, stood on the main street that ran north and south. If he headed south, he would soon reach the wobbly bridge that was the town's reason to exist. He could cross the North Platte, and find him-self in a vast wilderness, mostly prairie, barely mapped. He could be trapped trying to cross that arid wasteland. Or he could go north, drift into Montana Territory. Or he could stay. But until there was a bit of light, he could only wander aimlessly.

Somewhere across the dirt street stood a tonsorial parlor. Not a bad place to wait for dawn. Maybe a place to scrape away the rat's nest of hair on his face and head. Not that cleaning up would conceal him.

He waited for his eyes to adjust to the inky world, but they didn't. He couldn't see a thing. But the lit interior of the building behind him did provide some sense of direction. The sheriff and his men were making a dutiful tour of the grounds, but the blackness was as much their enemy as No Name's shield. He stumbled into the rutted road, smelled some horse droppings, moved away from the jailhouse, bumped hard into a building which he could only assume was the barbershop, and worked his way around to the back, where there might be an open door, or at least shelter from a suddenly-lit lantern.

"Well, you slipped out," said a quiet voice.

No Name froze.

"I got good night eyes. Come in if you like. I was expecting to see you hang this morning, but this is better. Maybe there's a little justice in the world."

CHAPTER TWO

The barber locked the door behind them. The shop was even darker than outside, if that was possible. But from a window, No Name could see that the sheriff was not giving up. He and Glory and Skinner emerged from the public building armed with handguns and bull's eye lanterns, and were starting a systematic search.

"He's half way to Denver," one of them said.

"No, he can't see either," someone said.

No Name thought it was the sheriff.

One of the searchers circled the barber shop, rattled the doors, and moved on.

"You'll want to look different," the barber said. "I can shave in the dark."

"And what happens when the straight-edge reaches my throat?"

The barber didn't reply, but No Name heard him bustling about, and then the barber touched his shoulder.

"Do this," he said.

No Name found a mug and brush in one hand, and a razor in the other.

"I'll trust you, and thank you," No Name said, returning the stuff.

"I am Mitgang Schuster. Come. It was said you have no name."

No Name felt himself being led to a chair beside the sole window, and he eased into it.

Somehow, powered by the distant stars, Schuster brushed lather into No Name's scraggly face, and gently scraped away grimy hair, so slowly and carefully that No Name felt not the smallest nick. A damp cloth wiped away the residue. He started to rise, but the barber pressed him down, and began to scissor his hair.

How that would turn out in pitch black night was a good question, but the barber's fingers clipped away layers of hair, all by touch. No Name marveled.

"When there's light, I'll fix it," Schuster said.

Across the rutted road, the searchers were drifting back.

The barber found a broom and dustpan and swept, still working blindly.

"In case they stop here," he said. "We have more to do. A suit, shoes, a hat."

"I'll just slip out when I can see."

"You'll be caught. We will make you someone else."

There was something to it. "Why are you helping? I'm a convict."

Schuster didn't answer for a bit. "Justice," he said at last. "There are more graves now, and for what? To prove something."

16

"Prove what?"

No Name heard the barber clean and restore his instruments. "It is complicated," he said.

"I can go to Montana."

"You think so, do you? With paid informants on every trail?"

No Name rubbed his smooth cheek, and marveled. He ran fingers through his disciplined hair, and could barely imagine how it happened.

"When the railroad comes. Throatlatch is doomed," Schuster said. "So is Wellbred County. So are the officials and merchants who've made a good living soaking gold and greenbacks out of travelers. But some of them have a little plan going. The Wyoming legislature is about to authorize a state prison. Maybe here, if Throatlatch has all the qualifications."

Those graves and his hanging, all began to make sense to No Name.

"Innocent men died?"

"Are you innocent?"

"I was accused of stealing horses. The judge's horses, I think. Witnesses said they saw me. I wasn't even here. I walked in the next day. I had no horse. I never stole a horse. I wouldn't know the judge's horses. I don't think he had a right to try the case. I . . . just don't know."

"I'm a barber. Know what that means? I'm on all sides. I hear it all and agree with it all. I'm a Confederate. I'm an abolitionist. I'm a Democrat.

17

I'm a Lincoln man. I am a Catholic. A Lutheran. A bible thumper. A Mormon. I hate children. I like children. That's because I got people in the barber chair. I got a razor. I got a till and keep lots of dimes in it. Know what I mean? Jones, he hates his wife, so I do too, right?"

"You're like me," No Name said.

"I'm gonna tell you something you won't like. These people, they just tried to hang you, so they're all bad, right? No, not right. They're like the rest of us. They mean well. Good times for Throatlatch. But they cut a corner here, forget something there, and then they're not so good any more. They hang strangers, right?"

No Name didn't like that. "Look, I'm getting out of here. Thanks for your help."

"Get caught in one day."

No Name shook his head.

"Your pants and shirt. They've seen you, shaved or not."

"No one sees me. That's the story of my life."

He slid out the door, avoiding the barber's protests, and felt night cold bite him. The black world had lightened a shade. The dawn of his hanging was not far away. He had barely slipped a few yards when a dog barked. And again. So the sheriff had left a snare after all. No Name sensed he was far from alone in that predawn. The sheriff had guessed right. There were soft movements nearby. No Name knew he was too

18

late. The noose might tighten this dawn after all. He wanted to run.

Maybe the noose was his fate. A man with no name was a man with no self. And no life. A drifter. He had drifted for years, almost a hobo.

He headed straight across the road, toward the county building with its burning lamp.

The dog barked.

"Who's that?"

"Mit."

"Who?"

"Mit the barber."

"Well, he's around here somewhere. He couldn't go anywhere."

"I'll check in," No Name said.

He reached the county building. No one was inside. A candle flame wavered. There were no long guns in the racks. That put a dozen men out there looking for him.

Clothing hung on pegs, tempting No Name. But that was a fast way to be identified. He carried the candle into the sheriff's own cubicle at the back. A lot of clothing hung from pegs at the rear. The sheriff was a dandy. No Name tried on a suit coat. A little too large. He gauged the matching pants to be a bit short. None of the other stuff worked well either. On another wall he found winter stuff. A sheepskin-lined coat. Wool britches. Boots too large. He slipped the coat on. It was too warm for April, but it would do. He discovered several hats but none was right. He blew out the candle and headed for the doorway, faintly visible in the hanging dawn.

"Who's that?" someone asked.

"Clyde," No Name replied.

"That drifter's around here somewhere, sheriff. When day breaks he'll pop out like a wood-pecker."

No Name wondered how a woodpecker popped out.

"How'd you get your name, Majestic? I always wanted to know."

"My ma named me for her woodstove. Best heater made, Majestic."

"We'll hang him in an hour, I'm thinking."

"No one's crossed the bridge. Not with three men watching."

"He's here, somewhere."

No Name was out of time, and the black was softening. Trails along the river or crossing it were guarded. He eyed the vague bluffs that would take him out of the river bottoms, and started in a easterly direction, guided by the Big Dipper and North Star, still vivid. He left the town behind. No dog barked. He was hungry. He worked through open brush, heading east even as the stars faded. He scared up some horses, which approached, snorted, and then stopped. They were tame. He did not intend to take one. A gray haze lay over the land, which still slumbered in the predawn. A barn loomed nearby, a dark edifice that startled him. He could not see a house or the rest of the outfit. But a barn might do. He felt his way around it, finding a double door on the other side. He loved the smell of horse barns, acrid, pleasant, a haven for owners even more than for horses. He stepped into gloom, looking for a wooden bin, which he soon found. He lifted the lid slowly, making sure to make no noise. He pushed his hand into a heap of whole oats. He knew the feel of them, even if he could not see them. Barley felt different, harder. He wished they had been rolled, but they would do. He hoped the owner would not begrudge him a few oats. He wished he could find something to grind with, but he found nothing in the darkness.

No time. He slipped away with a few oats in hand. He stuffed them in his mouth and let his saliva begin to work on them, but it would be a while before he had anything that could be called food. But it was a start. He'd been in worse fixes during his drifting life. That had to change now. The nameless days had led him into a noose. Off beyond the horizon somewhere, a railroad was working its way along the river bottom. He intended to find it.

CHAPTER THREE

Back on the two-rut road, he drifted away from
Throatlatch. It didn't matter where. He had an
odd way of making the best of things. Instead of
anxiously plotting out his next moves, he tended
to live entirely in the moment and make good use
of whatever he saw.

And in the dusky haze before dawn, he discovered a buggy approaching him, its driver in
a hurry. The well-dressed man was startled to
discover a stranger on this back road. He tugged
the reins.

"You have business here, fella?"

"Lost my way. This the way to Throatlatch?"

"Nope. Ranch road. You missed the way. It's
back some. You want a lift?"

"That'd be welcome."

Thus it happened that No Name found himself
settling in the buggy beside the judge who had
sentenced him to hang that very dawn. The judge
snapped the reins, and the trotter trotted.

"What do you need in Throatlatch. I might
help."

"Railroad coming through. I'm a crew foreman."

"Not for a while yet. Three months away still."

The judge snapped the reins again as dawn brightened. "I'm a little behind," he said.

"You start your day early."

"This day, you bet. We've got a good hanging coming along, and I preside. It's an entertainment."

"What you hanging? A side of beef?"

The judge chuckled. "Beef's worth something. This horse thief's not, except for a little diversion. There's nothing like a good show, and we get most of the town to see the sights."

"Yep, a cracked neck, a shudder, and it's all over. That's a sight, all right."

"You've seen a few?"

"I'm a railroad foreman."

"Yeah, you've seen a few. String 'em up."

It was bright enough so No Name could see the merry judge, who was at the same time, assessing his passenger, the clean-shaven and groomed face and clean coat.

"You have some baggage somewhere?" he asked.

"It was shipped to Throatlatch."

"Well, then. Express office."

"Come along to the hanging, and then we'll get you straightened away."

"I love a good hanging," No Name said.

"This'll be a corker."

"How so?"

"The younger, the more entertaining. Not much fun in hanging someone who's old as the hills. But take a kid, wild-eyed and evil, and it fills the saloons afterward."

"Tell me about Throatlatch."

"Happy little place, with progressive views and an eye for the opportunity. Say, here's where you missed the turn."

He pointed to a dirt road that wound upstream.

"Any work for a foreman?"

"No, you gotta make your own fortune here. It's every man for himself."

"Maybe I'll stick around."

"There's this, though. We're going to have a good future. Progressive types who work hard and prosper. There'll be a spot for anyone who's interested in creating a better world, who can inspire others. Half the people you hire, they vanish into saloons with the first pay envelope."

"Most of them, they don't care about tomorrow," No Name said.

The judge eyed him. "I'd say you have some experience. Come see me."

They reached the outskirts, mostly livestock paddocks.

It was getting brighter.

"I see the express office. Mind if I hop out?"

"They aren't open yet."

"There'll be a wrangler around, unless I miss my guess."

The judge drew up. "The hanging, it's over there, by the river. Take care of your business and we'll have a pile of pancakes at Mrs. Marblehead's. It builds the appetite, a hanging."

"See you there," No Name said. "And thanks. You got me steered right. I didn't get your name."

"Pluribus. As in E Pluribus Unum. My parents were devoted to the national motto."

"Well, thanks Mr. Pluribus."

"Judge Howard."

"Judge Howard. I'll remember you."

No Name slid off the seat onto firm hard ground. The judge lifted his top hat, and steered his black carriage toward the doomsday fields.

Sure enough, a wrangler was haying the horses behind the express office.

"You're up early," No Name said.

"Wouldn't want to miss the party."

"Early for a party."

"They're dropping another. Do it pretty regular. I wouldn't miss it."

"That's what the judge was saying."

"A couple of times ago, they dropped a fat man, and his head yanked clean off. Now that was worth the price."

"Who're they hanging?"

"Horse thief, I hear."

"I've got a bag on the coach east. When is it due?"

"Noon, give or take."

25

"I guess I'll get some breakfast. What's the best place in town?"

"Marblehead. That's the only place."

"They serve a big portion, do they?"

"I can't afford to eat there. She charges four bits."

"Well, you take what you can get. When does the express office open?"

"After the hanging."

"Looks like I'll have to wait."

"What's your name, fella?"

"Whatever you want it to be."

The hostler laughed. "I've known a few like that."

"I guess I'll go watch."

"I've seen a few. Ten or fifteen."

"They hang a lot around here?"

"Now and then." The hostler stabbed his pitchfork into more hay. "They got nothing else to do."

No Name slipped away.

Far ahead he saw a milling crowd. The sun was up. He debated what to do. He knew his shave and haircut wouldn't hide him from the sheriff. Some summer duds would help. He looked for laundry lines and saw nothing. There weren't any women in this burg. The only loose clothing he'd seen hung on a hat rack in the sheriff's office. That decided him.

He headed toward the crowd ahead, noticing the crowd was scattering, not coalescing around

26

the gallows. So word was out: they had no one on hand to string up. He reached the clapboard county building, surveyed its silent confines, and slipped inside, back into darkness. No one was there. He found the hat rack, a makeshift storage for prisoners' duds, and swiftly tried on a rabbit-hair cap, which didn't fit, a straw hat, that did, a flannel shirt, that was long but would do, and a leather waistcoat, which was perfect over the red shirt. In moments he was a new man. He hung his old stuff on the rack, but under several layers of coats and pants. He added a couple of cigars and a corn cob pipe and a few kitchen matches—and some wire-rimmed spectacles that made the distant world blurry but didn't bother him looking at nearby stuff. He left the weapons alone. People had a way of knowing their own arms. Then he slipped into the muddy street, just as a fat boy was trotting by.

"What's happening?"

The kid stopped. "Him they were hanging, he got out. But the sheriff, he's saying they'll find someone else, don't go yet."

"You ain't staying?"

"Pancakes and syrup, that's better than hanging."

The fat kid turned to escape. "They hang me, I'd break the rope," he said.

No Name eyed the milling crowd. A few were abandoning the spectacle. There was nothing

27

to do but drift in. He saw one of the deputies standing nearby, but no one else was armed.

Up on the gallows, the sheriff was laughing. "We got us another," he said. "You want a hanging? You got one."

Some sort of joke.

"Abner, you've had too much to drink," the sheriff said to a doddering old man beside him. "Time to repent."

"I don't repent,' Abner said. "I'll buy the next round."

"Abner, Wellbred County, it's losing its reputation because of you."

The crowd was coalescing again, enjoying the comedy.

No Name spotted the judge, sitting in his buggy, paring a cigar.

"String him up. But he's gotta give me his bottle first," some joker yelled.

The crowd, maybe a hundred, all men, lounged easily in the early light, casting long shadows on the rutted road.

"Say the word, judge," the sheriff yelled. Judge E Pluribus Unum Howard stood, in his rocking buggy.

"What's the worst thing that could happen, Amos?" The grinning victim shook his head.

"Teetotal," the judge said. "You get to be a permanent teetotaler. I sentence you to parch, to desert, to dry, to thirst."

The crowd enjoyed that.

"You got any last words, Amos?" the sheriff asked.

"One more for the road," Amos said.

"Get this show going," someone yelled. The sheriff nodded, slipped the noose over Amos's ragged locks, and tightened it around the old boozer's neck.

No Name stirred. Maybe this wasn't a joke. He quaked.

"Ready, Amos?" the sheriff asked. "Here, you step over here, right in the middle of that trap."

Amos grinned broadly, and did as he was told.

Clyde Clemson waited a dramatic moment, and pulled a lever.

The trap dropped. Amos dropped. He hit the end of the rope with a jolt. His neck cracked like a shotgun. Amos convulsed, and then sagged, and then swung like a pendulum in the quiet dawn of a Throatlatch morning.

The crowd chuckled lightly, then laughed, then whistled. The good citizens of Throatlatch watched Amos twist around and around. The sun was brightening.

No Name forced himself not to puke. It could have been him. It was meant for him. He had spoiled Throatlatch's party, so they held it anyway.

"Number twenty-three," someone yelled.

"You hungry?" a man asked No Name. It was Mitgang Schuster, the barber.

"Not at the moment."

"Don't hang around. Don't go to Marblehead's. You'll be spotted straight off."

"Me? Shaved and clipped?"

"Under your beard, light skin. Not weathered."

No Name rubbed his jaw, suddenly aware of its telltale pale.

"Follow me. I got some hardtack."

They drifted away from the killing fields. The crowd hadn't moved. Amos swung gently.

The barber walked ahead, while No Name kept his distance. At the tonsorial parlor the barber slipped in, returned a moment later with four hardtack biscuits, and gestured.

"Fast," the barber said. "And don't come back."

No Name stuffed the biscuits into his shirt, and drifted away, his entire body shaking so badly he could barely walk.

Throatlatch, he thought. Throatlatch, Wyoming.

CHAPTER FOUR

No Name retreated the way he had arrived, avoiding guarded roads. He walked carelessly, his mind drowning in what he had just seen, unable to shake the image of a harmless old man plunging to his doom to entertain a crowd. What did Roman emperors give to the mobs of Rome? Bread and circuses.

Who was Amos, the old drunk they murdered as a joke? What had he done but fumble through a hapless life? The sound of the man's snapping neck caught in No Name's ears and hung there, refusing to leave. He saw it over and over. The joke, the old man playing along with the humor, the lust for something more in the eager crowd, well-attired men, one a sheriff, one a judge, cheerfully committing murder. Murder that they would get away with. No one with a warrant and shackles would come for either man. They were the law themselves.

A bitter thing soured No Name. The hanging was to be his own. The old man, Amos, would be alive and well but for No Name's own escape. It didn't make him guilty, but it ran a bitter taste through his every thought. Amos might at this moment be sitting quietly in a saloon, sipping his first glass. Instead, Wellbred County would be digging the man's grave, no doubt in a potter's field. An innocent man, probably. If he was killing himself with drink, he didn't need help from Judge E Pluribus Unum Howard.

Scarcely realizing where his feet were taking him, he fled Throatlatch, even as the crowd drifted apart, enjoying the morning's sport. Flee, yes, flee, from Throatlatch and never come back. And yet, as he hurried down the two-rut lane something tugged at him. Something was calling him. He turned, to stare back at the huddle of buildings, feeling the darkness of the place. It was that darkness, that silence in the bright morning sun that caught him. He thought for a moment that he should stay. There was business to be done, justice to be done. As if it was his fate to bring murderers to the blindfolded lady with the scales in her hand. He dismissed the thought swiftly, and told himself to stop thinking crazy thoughts. But he felt the tug, and knew that some powerful obsession had clawed into his mind.

He tried whistling, and couldn't make his lips work. That was strange. He had a future to look to. He needed to find the railroad. He knew how to grade a right-of-way, build trestles, lay crossties, spike down rails, keep men working together. He could find the railhead, find work, find food and a bunk, push the rails ever westward, the rails a part of Manifest Destiny, spanning a continent.

But even if he found the railroad, he would be laying rails that would soon reach Throatlatch. He could not escape that dark place that was tugging him back. Something in him told him he had a job to do though he was no lawman, no lawyer, no reformer, no office holder, and an utter stranger. It was the strangest thing he had ever known.

His hurrying legs took him past the frame house with the barn, its horses lazily slapping flies off each other. Ahead was another country place, the one where the judge lived. He paused. Where was he going? What did he want to do? What were his goals?

He found the answer in his shirt pocket. The red flannel shirt revealed a battered business card, a name and occupation for No Name. J. Arnold Bright, the engraved name read. Mineral Claim Locator and Land Broker.

No Name had a good idea what a mineral claim locator did. Sharpers of that sort had sprung up since the 1872 Mining Law granting access to public lands to anyone locating usable minerals. A locator found such minerals and made fat fees selling claims to people hungry for Uncle Sam's land. It wasn't only about copper or lead or zinc or gold. It was about clay for pottery, gravel for roads, granite for tombstones, limestone for buildings. Those things were everywhere. Anyone could file a claim, dig a hole to prove it up, and take possession of vast terrain across the West. Who else could find a seam of clay and turn it into a bonanza?

J. Arnold Bright. J. A. B. As good a name as any. One thing No Name had learned: lacking a name didn't make him a nobody; it made him an everybody. A name narrowed you down to one brain, one set of eyes, one nose and mouth.

The judge's place lay around the bend. It was a showoff place, a clapboard marvel, country living without grubby livestock. Likely built with prison labor. No Name took it all in, and with one glance came to an appreciation of Judge Pluribus Unum's life. No Name spotted the Mrs. on the front porch, beating the tar out of an oriental carpet. Good. He hiked in, past green fields, while she watched narrowly, her hands probably not far from a shotgun.

"Good morning, madam. I'm looking for Judge Pluribus."

"Howard."

"Whatever you say."

"He's E Pluribus Unum Howard. And you're not local."

"No, madam, I'm a traveling opportunity dealer."

She eyed him from a skeptical long face, somehow melancholic. Her hair needed washing. "What are you peddling?"

"Uncle Sam's land, cheap. I'm out of cards, but have this one left that I'll share with you."

She eyed it quickly. "Oh, Bright. The one they booted out of town two weeks ago. Where'd you find that relic?"

"I'm a land dealer myself, madam, and thought the judge—Howard—might be looking for property. Such as railroad right of ways."

She smiled. "Right-of-way, Bright? The judge is three steps ahead of you. He's in town, hanging a horse thief."

"A horse thief? Whose horse?"

"Mine. More or less. Anyway, Bright, I don't like traveling salesmen and grifters, so you'd better vamoose."

"Did you get your horse back?"

"A stud. He got borrowed for breeding purposes, and returned."

"I guess that's worth a hanging."

He retrieved the card, plucking it from her possessive fingers.

"You're not safe in my sight," she said, gently waving her carpet beater.

He didn't doubt it. "Well, that's putting it on the table, madam. What is your name?"

Somehow, that wrought a smile. "Lydia Langtry Howard."

"You've got Lily Langtry beat. I plan to make Throatlatch my home, and hope to see you in its noble confines."

"Lord love a duck," she said. "You're even literate." She waved the carpet beater. In her thick hands it would be a formidable skin-thrasher.

She stared him down, and he gingerly wheeled around and hastened toward the lane.

"Wait," she said. "You saw the hanging? The horse thief?"

"No, an old drunk. The horse thief got away, they said."

"Old Amos?"

"That's what they called him. I thought it was a joke until it wasn't."

"And the judge—"

"Pronounced the sentence."

She seemed to shrink a size or two.

"You've got no truck. No bags. You had breakfast?"

"The Marblehead's fifteen minutes away."

"And you don't have a nickel."

He turned to go.

"I'll fix you something."

"Thank you, but I'll be going."

"Are you the horse thief?"

"I never stole a horse in my life."

"Where are you going?"

"Don't know. The railroad, maybe."

"Wait here. I'm going to fix you with a picnic basket."

He debated it, and settled to the grass. It hadn't taken her long to figure him out. But there was more to it. Something inside of her had caved in. He wondered what was going on in her mind. It didn't matter, and he'd never know, he thought.

It took her a while, which made him restless. Then she appeared with a wicker basket.

"Ham and stuff. And an oilcloth table cover. For rain. Don't thank me."

"But—Mrs. Howard."

"Don't talk. Not one word."

He hefted the heavy wicker basket.

"One thing. If you return to Throatlatch, let me know."

"I will."

She watched him till he was out of sight.

He wondered what she thought of her husband.

At the lane, he paused to absorb the vast landscape that lay before him. It seemed lonely, eager to nurture settlers, offering itself to whoever might make the best use of its clay and rock and brush and narrow creeks. No Name felt uncomfortable in that giant panorama, but he also felt itchy in cities. Something in between, people living comfortably, with space and elbowroom, seemed ideal. But who was he to choose? The great migration west seemed to follow its own creek beds.

Somewhere east, in the Platte's bed, a branch of the Burlington was pushing its way into the northwest. He would find it. He hiked eastward along the lane until it turned toward the brushy high country, and then he left the lane and headed cross country toward the river road—the road hordes of settlers used to go west into a bright new life. This country was shrouded with sagebrush, each plant apart to commandeer water. He found an occasional cactus, some grasses he couldn't name, and most likely he would encounter a snake or two along the way. The land was mildly inclined and took him toward the wide stream, still swollen with melt-off. The rising sun pummeled his face and hands, drawing color into his flesh.

The river road was muddy in spots, furrowed by wagon wheels, bereft of any grass, and firewood. The few cottonwoods had been hacked to bits for campfires and stoves. For several seasons this boulevard of hope had carried a flood of people, mostly families, toward Throatlatch and beyond. He wondered how many dreams had been shattered in Throatlatch; how many people in need of food or a wagon wheel or canvas had been bilked, or charged with misconduct, and drained of their last cent. No Name realized then that he had formed an opinion of Throatlatch as a den of thieves. And yet there must be some, like the barber, Mitgang Schuster, who lived honorable lives.

He turned east, avoiding mud morasses, sometimes skirting the mucky road, until at last the sun had reached its zenith and the spring day had softened into quiet warmth. He had not encountered a traveler all morning. At a sandstone ledge, he opened his wicker basket, found a slab of sliced ham, some fresh bread, and some cheese. He ate gratefully, thanking the wife of the judge who had sentenced him to die. The woman who somehow had separated herself—a bit, anyway—from the man she had married.

The river ran brown, but he was thirsty and lifted muddy water to his lips with cupped hands.

He hiked eastward, encountering no one. It was too early, the ground was too soft, and few westbound travelers had embarked. So he hiked quietly, alert for trouble that never arrived, and conquered fifty or sixty miles in the next few days. Then from a crown of a hill, he spotted the railhead, a hive of life at the end of silver rails shining their way to the sunrise.

He would find work. The railroad builders rarely had enough hands. No Name didn't know what he would do. Without a name, he could do anything.

He first encountered a handful of timber men, building a small bridge over a creek, cutting and bolting squared, creosoted timbers into a platform for the rails. A mile or so later he found graders at work, plowing and scraping, leveling and filling. They used plow horses and plows and blades. Next came gangs of Cantonese who swarmed over the bed, laying crossties and gravel, leveling out the roadbed, whole armies of mortals carrying wood or wheeling gravel, most of it crushed stone that would lock tight. Behind, an army of Irishmen, many new to the West, was dragging heavy rails into place, bolting them together and spiking them down with sledgehammers, their rhythmic hammering a staccato symphony that rattled No Name's brain.

Ahead a string of flat cars and gondolas stretched along the new rails, followed by a diamond-stacked engine, its boiler barely building steam. A caboose stood ahead of the engine. Behind, some hopper cars supplied coal. A traveling camp supplied food and shelter to the workers. Cooks loaded kettles of stew, much of it buffalo meat along with antelope, coyote, rabbit and prairie dog dragged in by hunters, to feed one gang at a time. Pushing a railroad forward was a huge, brutal task that took its toll in lives lost and bodies ruined. Dead horses went into the stew. In time, this emptying train would back to the nearest siding and another with fresh supplies would steam to the railhead, day by day, mile by mile, an enterprise more complex and costly than anyone could imagine.

No Name found two bosses in the caboose. They looked him over, not recognizing anyone they knew.

"New here?"

"Just walked in."

"You're hired. A dollar a day."

"I'm a right-of-way buyer."

"Little young, aren't you?"

"You're going to have trouble in Throatlatch. They're patenting land along the way, and hope to suck you dry."

The bosses, both burly men with monster gnarled fists, glanced at each other and then No Name.

"Tell us," said one.

"Crookedest town on the continent. County judge and officials bought and sold, everything for sale."

"Who are you?"

"I've had a dozen names. Call me Bright."

The bigger of them grinned. "So, Bright, how are you gonna fix this?"

"Hacksaw the locks on their two-cell jail."

"Bright, start talking, and don't waste our time."

No Name did. A courthouse full of hasty deeds and grants. A hanging judge. A sheriff in striped pants.

"What's going to happen when we get there?"

"I don't know, but it'll cost you."

"And what would you do about it?"

"Whatever it takes."

"What do they want?"

"Once the rails go through, Throatlatch is dead. It's picked pockets on the trail for years, with the

41

only bridge to be found. So they figure they'll get rich before the town tumbles down. They'll pick the Burlington's pocket."

"Look, Bright, our right-of-way runs outside of Throatlatch. It's mostly on public land and we've claimed it. There's a few private parcels where we have an easement, signed and sealed. That was done last year."

"Whose land, sir?"

"Let's see. The judge, Howard. And the sheriff's got a piece. There's more filing on public land next to us. Make a buck. That's fine with us; more freight. I don't know what your game is, Bright, but all this is good, not bad. A railroad needs trade."

"I think they have other plans. Like stopping construction—for what that's worth."

The smaller boss laughed. "You've heard too much saloon gossip, kid."

No Name saw how it would go. "You got a job for me?"

"You bet. Laying ties, hauling gravel. A buck a day."

No Name nodded. It had taken the bosses about two minutes to get rid of him.

CHAPTER FIVE

No Name toiled from dawn to dusk and slept gratefully on hard ground, usually in one of the tents in the moving campground. He hardened, tanned, muscled, and ached. The tent city was a commissary of sorts, where he could get clothing, boots, hot stew, and a shave. The crew lived off the land, fed by hunters ranging wide, and occasional wagonloads of flour hauled from the nearest towns. But not even eight hunters could keep that mob fed.

Some of the stuff was coming from Throatlatch. Each day, the railhead moved closer to the grim little town with its bandit ways. On a good day, the crews laid half a mile of rail, but most days weren't good.

He was always hungry; the stew pots emptied fast, and if you didn't scoop out what you needed, you starved. Men fought over food, bribed cooks, stole sacks of flour. Sometimes No Name wondered what the difference was between these hard-bitten workers and the calculating merchants and officials of Throatlatch. They all schemed to get what they could, however they could. He discovered that a few men knew what roots were edible, especially in the river bottoms, and some moonlit eves it made sense to him to hike toward the river with a knife and dig up roots. But as the railhead approached Throatlatch, the right-of-way drifted north, and plunged into low hills with cast-iron soil.

Then one afternoon, from the crown of a hill, he spotted Throatlatch, and knew that trouble was coming. The next day trouble arrived, a formidable array of armed men, the sheriff, deputies, Judge Howard, and a few merchants. They formed a line squarely across the right-of-way. Both Gus Glory and Majestic Skinner were in that line, with brass badges and black revolvers.

"This is where you stop," Sheriff Clemson announced. He was flanked by badge-wearing men. And businessmen with shotguns.

"What's this?" asked Marcus Penn, foreman of the grading crew.

"Cross this line and you're on private land. Trespassing," the sheriff said.

"This is public land, and we've bought right-of-way," Penn replied. "You want to see the papers?"

Clemson shook his head. "I've seen 'em."

"Then what's the trouble?"

"Sloppy work by the railroad," the sheriff replied. "You should have bought when the buying was good. Now you're stuck."

The judge handed him a sheaf of papers, and

the foremen studied them. A few deputies were grinning. E Pluribus Unum Howard beamed.

Marcus Penn studied one or two. "I've never seen these," he said. "They're new. Wait a minute."

He headed back to the supply train to fetch one of the big bosses. The whole project had ground to a halt. Workers stared. Cooks stirred stew and waited. Some sat down. Others headed for the water pails to quench their raging thirst. Neither the sheriff nor the judge paid any attention to No Name, who was unrecognizable now. He knew what those new papers were. Hasty deeds or claims, probably backdated, duly notarized, signed and sealed. A fraud worthy only of Throat-latch. The very fraud he'd gotten wind of weeks earlier. The trouble he had tried to explain to the bosses.

In time, the railroad's supervisors, Martin McGee and Wallace Parson, appeared, with Penn, looking peeved. "Seems you've reached private land," the sheriff said.

"No, we've proven up every foot of the right-of-way," McGee said.

"Our surveyors staked it," Parson added.

"The owners pulled the stakes. Sorry, gents. This is where it ends. Run your little railroad somewhere else."

"What the hell is this?" McGee asked.

"Just upholding the law and justice," Clemson said, smoothly.

"What do you want?" Parson asked.

"Oh, you show me easements or some new deeds, and you'll get your trains running some day. See you in court. Here's the district judge if you want to say howdy."

E Pluribus smiled. "Got some acres of my own up for sale."

"Then we need another judge."

"No sir, I'm it. Unless you want to sit it out for three, four years."

McGee stared.

"Keep the lawyers and financiers busy, right?" Clemson said.

Parson got steamed up. "What is this? A racket?"

McGee quieted him with a touch of the arm.

"It's my duty to see that justice is done," Clemson said. "Now, if you want to sit down and negotiate, all the landowners are here. You can examine their deeds. They're quite easy to get along with, flexible and solid."

No Name blotted up the whole scene. The railroad was vulnerable. It had spent millions to get here, and was still half a year from running a train, and even farther away from a profit. This was exactly the stage when some ventures collapsed.

"You got a single price for the whole lot?" McGee asked.

"Three hundred thousand."

"Is this a joke?"

"Careful, sir. You wouldn't want to disturb the peace. That's worth a night in the county jail. It stinks in there. Not a suitable place for supervisors."

"That's the game, is it? You'd best get off our right-of-way. Beat it, sheriff."

McGee's giant fists were balled up and ready to flatten the sheriff.

"Guess I have to take you in for disturbing the peace," Clemson said. "Both of you. I'm sure Judge Howard will be pleased to hear your case tomorrow morning."

On some sort of cue, the line of deputies and upright citizens leveled their weapons, until a lot of black bores poked at the railroad men.

No Name was within shotgun range, and didn't like it.

"Come along peaceable or pay the price. There'll be a trial." He turned to the crowd. "This is the line. Private property. If you push through, you and your railroad will pay more than you want."

Clemson left a couple of deputies on the site, and prodded the supervisors toward Throatlatch. The construction crew milled around, watched the county officials head down a road, watched the judge steer his carriage toward town, and stared. No one was in charge. They were scores of miles from a telegraph line.

Marcus Penn was the senior man.

"All right, set up camp here. And keep building right-of-way. We'll stop when we get to this line."

Slowly the crews drifted back to work.

No Name plowed clay the rest of the day, puzzled by himself. He knew he would head for Throatlatch that night. He could not say why. It wasn't his fight. He had already warned those bosses and they had chosen to ignore him. But he felt drawn to head for Throatlatch. It was as if some parent had materialized in him and told him to go. For one sharp moment he wondered about the parents he couldn't remember, the parents who suddenly vanished on the trail, leaving a little boy behind, to be shuttled around by countless others, wondering what to do with the lonely child.

The moment passed. He had no parent. No one watched over him. No one even gave him a name.

The crew toiled at half speed, wondering what would come next. Wondering if they would be paid; if they even had a job. But the sun set, and darkness hid the barren land, and the smell of stew, probably horse meat and antelope, hung in the close air. He ladled a bowl, and slowly drained it into his starving young body.

He didn't know if the sheriff's deputies still guarded the line, if it was a line at all. He could see no one. They would probably head into the village for the night, knowing the crews weren't going to cross that invisible boundary.

So No Name slipped into the dark of a moonless night, carrying nothing, not even the few clothes he had acquired over the weeks of hard work. He headed downslope toward the river, and the trail along the North Platte, and walked quietly into Throatlatch, unchallenged, guided by stars and something else in him that could not be denied.

CHAPTER SIX

No Name studied Throatlatch from a shadowed corner. Darkness shrouded Mitgang Schuster's tonsorial parlor. Across the way, lamplight spilled from the clapboard seat of government in Wellbred County. Several men were visible in the window. The sheriff was ready for trouble. The two railroad bosses were probably in there.

The rest of the town seemed uncommonly dark for this after-supper hour. But dull light tumbled from the JimBob Saloon. Not a soul was on the street. No Name walked quietly toward the saloon, peered through a grimy window and saw a handful of rough-worn men sipping from chipped glassware. He slipped in. The patrons glanced, and returned to their ritual pain relief. The barkeep was bald, with a Vandyke beard. He had a way of leaning on the bar, or the back bar, as if standing were an ordeal, which maybe it was.

"Got a beer?"

The keep nodded, drew a foaming mug, and No Name laid out a quarter. The keep returned a dime.

"Traveling through?" he asked.

"I'm with the railroad crew. I scrape right-of-way. I thought I'd wet my whistle."

They glanced at him now.

"Things quiet out there?"

"Pretty quiet. It's hard work. No one wanted to come in here with me."

"I'm JimBob."

"Call me Tom, Dick or Harry. I got more names than I can use."

"I hear there was a little dust up."

"Right-of-way. Happens all the time. It gets settled."

"I hear they pulled your bosses in."

"Guess so. They'll work it out. Railroad's got its own ways."

No Name slid half a mug of flat beer into himself. No one was talking.

JimBob cut loose from the back bar, and leaned into the bar. "The sheriff brought your bosses in. Disturbing the peace. Judge fined them a hundred apiece, and they're in the lockup until they pay."

"Hundred? What's the usual for disturbing the peace?"

"Two bucks, maybe a night behind bars to cool down."

"That's for disturbing just a little peace," said an onlooker. "A rail boss disturbs a lot of peace, and pays a lot."

51

Someone sounded amused.

"It figures," No Name said. "Railroads, they have money. Except they don't. It takes a lot to build a railroad, and no one sees a dime for a few years after. That's why so many go under. They get new backing and lose that, too. They need freight and there is none."

"That your trade?"

"I've been laying roadbed since I was fifteen. So what's the deal here?"

The hesitation in the saloon told No Name a lot.

"Oh, some officials thought they could throw a couple of snake-eyes."

"Disturbing the peace."

"How about a refill?"

No Name pushed the mug forward and dug another quarter out of his britches. JimBob ran more flat beer into the mug.

"This town has a reputation," he said.

A few smiled.

"I heard you're wanting to build the Wyoming pen here. When they put you in it, you'll be right at home."

"You saying something?" one asked.

"No. I just hear a few things now and then."

"Maybe you should get out of here—while you can."

"I'll do that," No Name said, leaving the full mug listlessly waiting on the bar.

He didn't need a fight. And he didn't have any-thing to prove.

The evening air was bracing. The town seemed to sleep under a midnight anvil.

A gibbous moon was plowing a ridge, throwing orange light on the gallows. No Name knew he'd be visible, but didn't care. He walked over to the gallows, climbed a narrow stair, studied the thick crossbeam above, and stepped gingerly out on the trap. It held him. They built gallows well in Throatlatch. He stood there for a moment, reliving a past that didn't come, thinking of a dozen mortals whose breath caught in their throat when they felt the coarse hemp surrounding their necks.

He was alive, and he didn't know why. He didn't know why he had come to this spot at this hour. He knew where the bodies were buried, last row in the plot near the foothill. He wanted to find Amos. He owed Amos an apology. Amos would be alive, soaked in fumes, cheerful and harmless, but for the twist of fate.

A lamp remained lit in the county seat.

He crossed the manure-laden road, cut down an alley, climbed a soft slope, and found the plot. It was a busy place. Heaps of fresh dirt lay about. There was plenty of death in Throatlatch.

He worked his way to the last row. And there she was, some woman sitting quietly at the foot of a grave.

She stood swiftly, tense.

"If you're an honorable man, you'll leave me alone," she said.

She sure didn't beat around the bush.

"I don't know what I am. But you're safe. I came to apologize to an old man."

"Apologize?"

"I got away so they strung him up, a morning's entertainment."

"Amos," she said.

"It's late," he said.

"It's the safest time for a woman."

She was thin, dressed in dark skirts, her long face barely visible. He thought she had dark hair. He could not guess her age; only that she was young and brimming with some sorrow that was beyond his own experience.

"Who was he?"

"Is it any business of yours?"

"Yes," he said.

She liked that. "We were close."

"Brother? Beau?"

"More."

There were boundaries here he could not trespass.

"He robbed banks. I loved him. They caught him."

His mind swarmed with questions. "I'm glad you love what was good in him and ignore the rest."

"I don't ignore the rest. I talk to him about it every day, every hour, and each night like this."

He wondered how she endured.

She wilted, barely able to stand. "I must go now. I'm sorry to trouble you."

"Where do you live? May I see you again?"

"I have given myself to the dead. That is my entire life."

"But you live here. You must have family."

"You are all the family I may have."

That jolted him.

"I need to see you. I need to know—who . . ."

But she whirled and was gone. He did not even have her name.

He walked back to the rail camp unchallenged except by his strange need to be in Throatlatch, a little town that had attempted to strangle the life out of him. The rail camp was quiet.

Marcus Penn put the crews to work in the morning, but only after a brief announcement.

The construction gangs gathered silently around him, wanting word, any sort of word. But he disappointed them.

"I don't know any more than you do," he said. "I hope you'll work today, finish the line as far as the boundary, or whatever it's called. I'm a foreman, not a boss. I have no authority over you, can't pay you, and can't make any promises. But I've sent the hunters out, and maybe they can keep our stew pots full for a couple of days. May

55

be we'll have word before the day's done. I'm hoping you'll stay, and we can start up fast."

The engine was gone, along with the caboose and hoppers that carried coal and the other straw bosses, who had to head east to connect with the company and get some instructions.

No Name eyed the crews, the Cantonese listening to a translator, the Irishmen enjoying the drama, and assorted tough men gazing at the invisible line that was for the moment, stopping the railroad cold.

The men stayed. Some even seemed cheerful as they set out to grade the final bit of roadbed, lay crossties, and spike rails into place. They worked easily, as if on a vacation, but they made progress as the sun rose, and by sunset they had run the rails as far as they could. And at supper time, the diamond-stacked engine huffed to a stop, and the workmen gathered, wondering if they had jobs.

They didn't.

The two straw bosses, Stan Brandy and Bull Moose, stood at the caboose and dished out the tough news. Moose had started out his life as Bill Moses, but names never stuck in the West. Brandy ran the bridge and trestle crew, and Moose ran the rail spiking bunch.

"We're stuck," Brandy said. "We have no idea how long this will last. We're authorized to issue pay vouchers to those who want to go. Tomorrow, we can take you back as far as Fort Laramie, where you'll be picked up and taken east.

"Some hotshot lawyers are headed here. We're miles from anywhere, and Wellbred County is as isolated as any place on the plains. The judge here is the only law around, and he's, ah, taken sides."

Brandy ended with a request. "We hope you'll stay. This might resolve fast, and you'll be back to work."

"The men have built up to the line, Stan," Penn said. "They'll want pay for today."

Brandy nodded, while workers watched closely.

"Any plan to spring McGee and Parson?" Penn asked.

"I'm taking a blank check into town now," Moose said. "McGee's signature will validate it. Pay the fine. I'm going to get them out of there."

"Heavy fine, I guess."

"Disturbing the peace," Moose said. He shook his head.

"Did you bring food?"

"In there," he said, waving toward the caboose.

Several men from the kitchen crew collected some bags of flour. Pretty skimpy doings.

No Name knew he wasn't going anywhere soon. He had an appointment with Throatlatch, even though Throatlatch had no appointment with him.

CHAPTER SEVEN

No Name arrived in Throatlatch at twilight, finding the town mysteriously bright, as if to celebrate its good fortune. The county building was brightly lit. A lamp burned in the tonsorial parlor, so No Name knocked.

The door swung open abruptly.

"I close at six. Don't you read?" Schuster asked.

"I want another shave."

Schuster thrust the kerosene lamp at No Name, and nodded.

"So," he said. "You again. When there's trouble, there you are."

"Trouble?"

"The railroad man, Moose, he came with a check to pay the fine. They threw him in, too, and took the check. I watched it."

"On what charge?"

"Charge? You think they need a charge? Three hostages, and they got the railroad whipped. It's party time."

Schuster motioned, and No Name settled into the barber chair. Schuster threw a bib over the young man, stirred up some lather in a mug, and brushed it on.

"I was wondering about you, and here you are. A bad penny."

No Name kept quiet. Schuster scraped the young man's face, wiped it clean, and pulled he bib away. No Name handed the barber a quarter.

"So you are working for the railroad," Schuster said. "What do they think?"

"Lawyers are coming. They'll deal."

Schuster shook his head. "Wellbred County might as well be on the moon," he said. "They make their own law. Why are you here? Bad place."

"I don't know."

"Yes you know. Revenge maybe. Justice maybe. Prove something to yourself, maybe."

"More than that. I can't explain it."

"A woman, maybe."

Schuster had struck a nerve.

"I don't know her name. She was at the cemetery. It was dark. The graves aren't marked."

"Old or young?"

"She's a ghost."

Schuster laughed, but kindly. "Fantasies, the ruin of young men."

"I thought I'd wait there. She comes well into the night."

"I don't have any engagement rings or bouquets."

No Name didn't enjoy the banter.

Schuster cleaned up and turned down the wick. The lamp blued out.

"Save oil," he said. "This big man Moose comes in, locates the county office, walks in with his check. I heard some, watched some. There's talk in there. He's going to pay the fine, take your bosses back, but the sheriff, he's got his own ideas, levels a revolver and pitches this Moose into the other cell. No charge, no trial. Now they got three bargaining chips. That's all I know."

"The judge, was he there?"

"He's always there. They do their drama there."

"The judge lets it happen?"

"He's the law. He runs the court."

"No one here objects?"

"Not if they hope to be seen again."

"Who is E Pluribus Unum Howard, then?"

"I ask myself the same question. He's unlike any mortal I've met or read about."

"No conscience?"

"More than that. No sense that he lives among other people."

"Is the sheriff, Clyde Clemson, the same?"

"No, just a lapdog."

"Are those three railroad bosses in danger?"

"The path from those cells to the gallows is well worn. The judge enjoys midnight executions. Here today, gone tomorrow."

"What about the lawyers the railroad is sending? Will they be safe?"

Schuster shrugged.

"If they send another straw boss with another blank check, will he be safe?"

"You know the answer, young man."

"Are you safe?"

"Barbers are always safe. Like priests."

That didn't quite ring true, No Name thought.

"The railroad's in trouble. The bosses tell me things. This is a bad time, when they're building the track but they're two years away from earning much of anything. Every day, every hour counts. The judge must know that."

"Young men get fantasies. You get out and stay out, or they'll try the noose on you."

No Name slid back into his blues. "Thanks for the shave," he said.

He slipped out the door, into full night, except for a low blue strip on the western horizon.

The evening breeze began to dry the sweat under his shirt collar. Across the way, the county building was jammed with loud men, most of them armed. No Name had spent time there. He knew where the sheriff kept the second jail key, but there was little prospect it would still be there. No Name backed away from folly. He had no way to spring the railroad bosses.

He drifted down to the river bottoms, through shadow and moon glow, until he reached the gallows, stretching up toward stars, like a cathedral. Sturdy uprights. Massive crossbar. He could disable the gallows. He could cut rope, wreck the trap. All of which would give someone another five minutes. No more than that. The nearest cottonwood limb would substitute.

"If they want you, they getcha," said someone. The voice rose softly from a thicket. But it jolted No Name.

"You ain't alone here, and I'm not either. There's a few of us thinking what to do. Best to let it rest, who we are. You don't know me; I don't know you."

"You been here long?"

"I ain't talking about me and you ain't talking about you."

"Okay. Why are they holding up the railroad—money?"

"Some."

"Revenge? Like, let the railroad pay for wrecking the town?"

"Some."

"Reputation? Like the biggest hanging judge of all?"

"Some."

"Legend? Like the one in Indian Territory?"

"Some."

"You tell me. I'm out of ideas."

"Fun. They're the P. T. Barnum of Wyoming."

"You're saying this is a show?"

"It's pretty dull around here."

"They hang innocent people for show? Destroy a railroad for show?"

"Sure, and clean out people on the old Oregon Trail, too."

"I got to think about that."

"Do that. I'm at JimBob's Saloon now and then. I was there last night."

No Name heard a faint rustle, and felt certain the man was gone. But he wasn't sure. He waited, trying to make sense of the senseless. The man knew him, but he didn't know the man.

He worked quietly to the burial ground, started a dog yapping, and stumbled on the place which wasn't where he remembered it. She wasn't there. He sat, letting the chill air from the high country eddy past him. Maybe he was early, or maybe late. He waited for the rustle of skirts, but she never showed up, and that sank him. He felt like a hungry boy. He wanted a name. He wanted to see her by candle light. He wanted her to know his name—which was odd. He wanted to be someone, a defined person in her eyes.

He thought about returning to the railhead camp, but Throatlatch was tugging him, tying him with silken thread. He studied the county building, lit by a couple of kerosene lamps. There were several men in there, playing cards, having a good eve. The judge's ebony carriage and trotter were parked in front.

He drifted across wasteland, stirring up something, maybe a snake, and hit the two-rut road, and followed it as it angled toward well-watered pasture—and the judge's comfortable home. He approached cautiously, just to see what he might see. The place was washed in moonlight, but dark. Madam had retired. He didn't know why he was there. He didn't know why he was drifting around Throatlatch.

"I'm alone. Come do your worst," said a woman rather loudly.

He froze.

"I'm on the porch. It's a fine evening."

He didn't respond.

"I thought so," she said. "Did you get to the railroad?"

He didn't reply.

"When you're ready, talk to me. I might be able to help."

He stood quietly, scarcely breathing.

"The judge is celebrating," she said. "He said it's not every day he bags a railroad."

He wanted to reply, to say that most days he's content to bag heads.

She laughed, as if she had heard his thought, and the alarming part was that maybe she had.

"The judge is saying we might build a brick house soon, some place out of the wind, with a few domestics to take care of us. We'll be rich. He's got something cooking, but I don't know what. It's a woman's lot to follow along, whether or not she wants. Chances are, I won't be comfortable at all. It'll be warm enough for me, but I'm not sure they have good domestics in hell. Well, you have a pleasant evening now, young man."

He slipped away, in the general direction of the railhead, trying to make sense of a senseless evening. He reached the camp when the cook-fire ashes were still glowing. The place seemed odd to him, but in the dark he couldn't figure out what had changed.

Marcus Penn was sitting on a wagon tailgate, enjoying a pipe.

"I was over there. They kept Bull Moose."

"So I heard. They sent a deputy back with the blank check. They didn't charge Moose with anything, just took him in and locked him up. They're not looking for a couple of hundred dollars; they want a couple of hundred thousand."

"Wellbred County's a hundred miles from anything. Marcus, what's going on here?"

The straw boss looked around at the quiet camp. "A lot left after supper," he said.

"Left?"

"They loaded a couple of wagons and took a couple of draft horses and said it was a trade for wages."

"Where'd they go?"

"Cheyenne, Casper, Sheridan, Denver. They took the river trail to the bridge, crossed the river, and who knows?"

"How many?"

"A third, half, I don't know."

"Hard to hire more men out here."

"You said a mouth full. The hunters all vanished."

No Name's world was falling apart again. He spread a bedroll outside, after looking for storm clouds, and slid in. He was used to this. The no-name boy was a jobless man. But there was consolation in his hard life: he would find a way to keep on going, working and eating, and find some good in it. If you don't expect much, even the humblest gift is a treasure. His life was full of treasures.

CHAPTER EIGHT

No Name awakened the next chill morning with his future in hand. That often happened to him. He reached his decisions intuitively rather than by reflection. He ascribed that to a rough childhood, where he was a helpless and unwanted little boy, shuffled from one caretaker to another. You don't learn to plan a life or reason out a path when you have utterly no control over your destiny. That separated him from people with a more traditional upbringing.

He would leave. But he would wait out the day, on the off chance that the railroad and Throatlatch would resolve their troubles. He would head for Throatlatch, in spite of the dangers there, for reasons he couldn't grasp. That's where destiny was leading him. He had no reasons.

He looked about him. The work force had thinned out. More had left in the night. The idle flatcars and locomotive still stood at rail's end. Some workers were creating a breakfast stew, mostly of carcass bits and flour.

Marcus Penn, the straw boss, was still around. "You staying?" Penn asked.

"For today."

"You're not alone."

"Nothing makes any sense unless this mess gets settled."

"They're keeping an eye on us," Penn said, gesturing toward a badge-wearing deputy.

It was Gus Glory, one of the sheriff's most trusted men.

But minutes later an engine huffed in, shiny, new, pulling a single coach. It hissed to a stop behind the railhead engine and flatcars. Workmen drifted that way, along with No Name. The coach door opened and two men descended, both spotlessly dressed, bowlers, white shirts, cravats, blacked shoes.

"Anyone in charge here?" one asked.

Penn volunteered that he was the remaining foreman.

"Stonewall Sanders. I'm the company attorney, here to negotiate." He didn't introduce the other man, but No Name was pretty sure the man was a bodyguard. There was a slight bulge in the man's suit coat near the left armpit.

"Fill me in," Sanders said to Penn. The foreman did, noting that Throatlatch officials were holding three railroad bosses hostage.

"Anyone here from Throatlatch?" Sanders asked.

"The deputy over there."

"Bring him."

Moments later Gus Glory stood face to face with Sanders.

"I have a message and you'll deliver it," Sanders said. "First, we're negotiating here, not in town. Second, we won't talk until you release our men and bring them to us. Third, time is money. If this isn't settled within an hour, it won't be settled at all. We'll pull out. Got that?"

Glory nodded, and waited for more, but Sanders had nothing more to say. Uncertainly, the deputy headed away.

"How far are we from Throatlatch?" Sanders asked.

"Ten or fifteen minutes."

"All right, the rest of you gather around. If we can't do a deal immediately, we'll have to let you go. You'll get your pay vouchers, including for today. Time is money. We build track or we shut down."

The men were expecting it.

"Thank you for staying on," Sanders said. "You're good men. We'll help you out. That coach will carry most of you back to Fort Laramie or Cheyenne, and the work train can carry the rest. Meanwhile, figure what we owe you."

"You think this line is done? It just stops here?" someone asked.

"We will reroute it. But that costs hard money and eats time. If we have to do it, we're months away from hiring a railhead crew." He peered into the silent faces. "Any of you sick? Hungry? Head for the coach."

No one did immediately, but No Name knew that a few would welcome a decent meal and maybe a coach seat.

No Name was tempted, but Fate had told him where the future would be, so he waited quietly on naked clay for the rest of the show. He watched Sanders and Penn and the bodyguard climb into the coach.

Well before the hour was up, Judge Howard arrived in his ebony carriage, with Sheriff Clemson and Bull Moose beside him. The judge eyed the camp, and steered his trotter toward the coach, where Sanders greeted him.

"The judge and the sheriff," Sanders said. "And you, sir?"

"Bull Moose, a company foreman, sir."

"Please step here, beside me."

The foreman did.

"You still have two of our men in custody?" Sanders asked Clemson.

"They're our insurance," the judge replied.

"Then there's nothing to negotiate. But before you leave, I will direct your attention to a few things. First, if this comes to litigation, it won't be in your court. It will be in the Territorial capital. Second, we have a nuisance fund, to pay off people like you who slow us down. It's cheaper. Here's an offer. I'm authorized to pay you five

thousand cash if you supply us with the fraudu-
lent deeds, so we can tear them up and return to
building a railroad. You will have an hour to do
that. That's when we pull out. We will extract our
employees by whatever means are available."

The judge smiled, shook his head. "You will
want to consider the future of your employees in
our custody. Additional charges will be filed. As
for the deeds, sir, they are under lock and key, in
proper county custody. The officers of Wellbred
County do not bend with the wind, sir."

"Have it your way, Judge Howard. How did
you acquire your name, E Pluribus?"

"I had whimsical parents, sir. And how did you
acquire your remarkable name, Stonewall?"

"I invented it. My gallows humor."

They stared at each other a moment, and then
the judge flicked the reins. The trotter wheeled
the carriage around, and the sheriff and judge
headed away.

Moose took over. "Fire up the freight engine.
Load loose railroad property onto the flatcars,
and your own if you want to leave with us."

He turned to the translator who was conveying
all this to the remaining Cantonese.

"You want to come?"

"California," the Chinese said.

"I'll see about your pay."

Moose corralled Sanders, pointed to the
Chinese, and Sanders nodded.

No Name had turned invisible again, without meaning to. He collected his few possessions unseen, while watching the remaining crew load heavy tools and iron into the cars. The firemen were building up steam, pouring coal on embers. Some of the workmen hauled their rucksacks into the shining coach.

Marcus Penn handed him a brown envelope. It would contain his last pay, a few one-dollar bills. "You headed somewhere?"

"Nowhere," No Name said. "I think I'll stay."

A half hour later, the engine with the shining coach backed out. Soon after that, the work train, steam up, huffed its way east, dragging a half dozen gondolas and freight cars, plus the caboose.

No Name watched the trains vanish. A fair wind blew fresh air across the empty plain. He should have felt alone, and lonely, but he didn't. Quite the opposite. The door to a new and better life was opening, and he intended to walk through.

CHAPTER NINE

It was amazing. Earlier, this place had been a beehive of human life and ambition. Then the trains and mortals left, and nature reclaimed this befouled place. A few ravens found the kitchen camp and began scavenging. Smoke still drifted from a cook fire. The transformation startled No Name, but whatever was rising within him startled him more. His natural tensions ebbed. He didn't mind being alone. He liked being with people, but a long hard history made him watchful. Here he was sovereign.

He studied the rails that ended abruptly at an imaginary line. What line was this, separating parts of the earth, and how had it torn so many lives and ambitions apart? He remembered that two railroad bosses were caught in the county jail, their lives in peril. It was none of his business—and yet it was.

He rubbed a clean, tanned cheek and knew he would be relatively safe in Throatlatch, even by daylight. Then he dismissed the thought. No mortal was safe in Throatlatch. He looked around. He had a gunnysack with a few possessions, mostly abandoned clothes. He had a few dollars. He hid some in his ancient brogans. He walked down to the river road, feeling his tension mount as he approached the shabby little town.

The judge's black carriage and trotter stood before the county building. Several men smoked outside the door. A good cigar tasted better in a spring breeze. This was a cigar town. Some towns were pipe towns; others were cigarillo towns. No Name saw no women on the street. There wouldn't be many in Throatlatch. He wondered how Martin McGee and Wallace Parson were faring in there, but there was no way to find out.

He wandered toward the JimBob Saloon, found it mostly empty and morose as working men sipped their draft beers. He ordered one from the keep, and settled into a stool, as inconspicuous as he could manage. Someone who came to this tavern was an ally of sorts, but No Name could discover nothing at all.

"I don't like it none," said one to his neighbor.

"Not many do," the other replied.

"It's another show," said the man three stools away.

No Name waited, but it stopped there.

"What's her name?" asked JimBob.

"I think it's Mona. She's a little short-changed."

"Can't count to ten, they say."

"Got funny little eyes."

"Not much use of a person."

"She repaid the old lady by taking the doll."

None of this made much sense to No Name, but he was a patient listener, and the story would crystallize soon enough. He sipped steadily. It was a sour brew that bit his tonsils, and that was fine. His vows of moderation sometimes needed help.

Then Majestic Skinner, the jailer, barged in and ordered a shot of Valley Tan neat.

"Whee—oh," he said, and ordered another.

"You all prepped for the dawn's early light?" JimBob asked.

"She hasn't got a notion. Screw loose, or three," Skinner said.

"What's this for, again?" the keep asked.

"She stole one fancy antique. Collector's item. Porcelain doll, made in Belgium, eyelashes painted on, each one separate, green eyes, Brussels lace. Worth a pretty penny."

"Mona took it?"

"They found her mothering it. She took it plumb away."

"So what was the charge?"

"Grand theft. It got damaged, one arm, so that was added."

"So Mona swings?"

"Dawn tomorrow, and I swear, she's too saddle broke to know it."

A hanging. Of an impaired woman. At dawn. As a show. Mona somebody. The law of Wellbred County was stretching its talons again.

75

No Name had a faint notion that the barkeep was asking questions to put this thing out in the open, so all of those who sat sipping, including himself, would absorb the story.

"Mrs. Lovemore pressed charges?" JimBob asked.

"Naw, the judge decided it. Two-minute trial."

"Any relatives coming for her?"

"None. She's a pretty sorry one."

Majestic Skinner ordered and downed another slug. No Name thought the jailer was uncomfortable.

No Name waited for more, but that was the end of it. The mood of the place had gone gray. A thousand questions swarmed in his mind, things he couldn't ask. Did the Territory have an asylum for impaired people? Was the theft of a porcelain doll a hanging offense? If this Mrs. Lovemore declined to press charges, why did the judge turn it into a criminal case? Who was Mrs. Lovemore?

This was bad. What sort of place was Throatlatch? What could No Name do?

Visions of rescuing the woman swiftly yielded to reality. He could not stop this show.

No Name downed the last of his beer. The saloon had fallen into stony silence, so he nodded to the keep and slid into a pleasant night. He headed toward the livery barn, knowing a cheap way to get a good night's sleep, bargained with the hostler for a bed in the hayloft, laid out two bits, and climbed the ladder.

He didn't sleep. He doubted any other mortal could sleep knowing what would happen at dawn. He wrestled with himself. He did not want to see that legalized murder tomorrow. He could walk away, get out of town. He argued with himself for hours, but in the end he knew that he must go and watch an innocent perish. He wondered why he thought that.

In the gray dawn light, he washed up, combed his sun-streaked hair, avoided all thought of breakfast, and made his feet walk two hundred yards to the gallows. There were fewer people there, and they looked taut and bleak. There wouldn't be much of an audience for this show. He saw no women; only men, with their hat brims tugged low, as if to hide their faces. This place was caught in silence. Even the birds stayed silent.

At the very moment the sun cleared the horizon and began its lofty path, Sheriff Clyde Clemson, along with jailor Majestic Skinner, led the prisoner, a cheerful, smiling little lady, a bit rotund, over naked earth and up the narrow stair to the gallows. A moment later the judge appeared, driving his ebony carriage to his favored perch on the right. E Pluribus Unum smiled, lifted his black hat to acknowledge the deference of the crowd, and watched as Majestic

Skinner tied the lady's wrists behind her. She smiled. She was enjoying this new sport.

Skinner slid the noose over the little lady's neck, and pulled her hair out of the way so the noose would do its majestic duty. He steered her to the exact center of the trap, and smiled at the quiet onlookers.

"Have you any last words?" the judge asked.

"This is fun," she said.

"Very well, then. The sentence imposed by this duly constituted court of the Territory of Wyoming, is death by hanging, for the crimes herein listed in this public notice." He paused, dramatically. He was experienced at this, and knew how to pause when pausing was required.

"Sheriff, you may proceed," he said, and removed his black hat and held it over his chest.

Clemson nodded. Majestic Skinner yanked a lever. She dropped. Her neck snapped with a crack. No Name swore she looked straight at him, and her eyes, at last, brimmed with intelligence.

They let her swing, back and forth, twirling gently, a limp doll.

"Justice always triumphs," Sheriff Clemson said, by way of dismissing the small crowd, which suddenly fled in all directions. A raven flew close to the deceased, a black and clacking omen, and then pumped away in terror.

The sheriff descended the stair, and shook hands with the judge.

"You may proceed," the judge said to the jailer.

No Name did not stay to see the lowering of the criminal to earth, and the stowing of the deceased in a wagon that would take her to the potter's field where she would be buried at county expense unless survivors could be found and billed for the service.

No Name felt rooted to the spot. Everyone vanished except a groundskeeper, who swept the scaffold, shoveled some manure off to a ditch, and collected some fragments of hemp rope that lay about like tapeworms.

CHAPTER TEN

Daylight bore into Throatlatch, scorching the bare earth. Nothing green dared to grow in Throatlatch. No Name walked into the Tonsorial Parlor, discovered a man in the barber chair, with a barbering bib thrown about him, and Mitgang Schuster eyeing No Name dourly.

"I will be with you shortly," the barber growled, his straightedge like an Excalibur and pointing No Name to a seat.

The customer was sheriff deputy Gus Glory.

"Seems I know you," Glory said.

Schuster scraped hard.

"I know you," No Name said. "You're the deputy out at the railhead. I worked with the roadbed crew."

"Yeah, that's it," Glory said. "Whatcha doing here?"

Schuster paused. Conversation and straightedges didn't mix.

"Heading toward some track. I've laid rail since I was fifteen."

"Hard work. I got it easy, just hanging around."

"Yes," No Name said, and cut himself off.

Schuster gestured, drawing his straightedge across his own throat.

No Name clammed up, and the barber finished up the shave. Moments later, Schuster snapped the bib off, took Glory's dime, and nodded at No Name.

Gus Glory vanished into the scalding air.

"At least there's no blood on the floor," Schuster said, as No Name sat down in the warm seat.

The barber's mood hadn't changed, and No Name knew what was upsetting Schuster. The little town smoldered. A couple of stores hadn't opened this morning.

"Barbers know everything. What's happening here? Why is nothing being done about this?"

Schuster slipped the bib over No Name, and began stirring up some lather. "I don't know. No one knows."

"Are they waiting for the railroad to bargain?"

Schuster shook his head. "Who can say?"

"Who am I talking about?"

"Oh, the judge and sheriff. A few merchants. A few lackeys."

"Why do they hang people?"

"I ask that myself, in the middle of the night. I can't say."

"Is the whole town in on it? Expecting to profit?"

"You know the answer. You would not be sitting here."

No Name did know that. The barber brushed lather into No Name's jaw and neck, and then stropped his razor.

"Barbers don't know anything. Just what customers tell them," Schuster said.

"Do you have any theories?"

"Nothing makes sense to my addled mind."

"If the railroad doesn't bargain, will people stay here?"

"Not for long. Not much traffic on the trails now. The Union Pacific takes people west and east. So the bridge here, it means less and less. The officials know that. Now, don't flap your jaw or you'll find out that razors are sharp."

No Name sat quietly, his mind feverish with questions about this mysterious little town. Then at last the barber mopped up with a warm washcloth.

"I went to visit the graves, and found a young woman there at an unmarked grave. She offered no name, and fled."

"Carolina Clemson."

"Sheriff? Sheriff's daughter?"

The barber shook his head. "Ask what is known, and I will say nothing is. Only rumors."

"What rumors?"

"She loved a man the sheriff didn't approve of. How it ended no one knows, but it is the darkest of all the rumors."

"What didn't the sheriff like about him?"

"Sioux. Maybe Cheyenne."

"Was he hanged?"

"Possibly, in the middle of the night."

"Where can I find out?"

The barber sighed. "Let it alone. It is not for people to gossip about."

Another dead end. The barber pulled the bib away. No Name dug out some change and paid.

"You're the only friend I have just now. So I'll tell you. I am drawn here. I don't know why. I don't know what lies in store for me. What I must do. Maybe it's a fantasy. But it's real. It drives me. See? I'm here. Instead of running, I returned. I'm a skeptic, but this isn't like anything else. This is Destiny."

Mitgang Schuster smiled. "Destiny is a beautiful woman," he said.

That reminded No Name of a woman. Not Carolina Clemson, but the uncanny wisdom of the wife of E Pluribus Unum Howard. The woman he had barely seen, but who had seen him, almost as a specter.

No Name stepped into a sleepy street. The judge's carriage was not at the county building. He was a man with no name, no purpose, no plan, no creed, and no attachments. He drifted upslope, toward the foothills, knowing where he was going but not knowing why. Out of town, a breeze freshened the air. From several vantage points he could look back on Throatlatch and see it sleeping in the sun. An illusion made it vanish now and then, a town not worth attention. He found the two-rut lane that led to the judge's ostentatious house, from which the man ruled the nearby town. He did not know what he would do or say. The odd thing about this sense of Destiny was that he was not girded for battle. He walked around the wide curve, and there it was, shimmering in heat. But the shaded porch looked welcoming. The judge's carriage was not in sight.

He turned into the drive, and hiked the final fifty yards.

"I've been expecting you," Lydia Howard said. "Some tea? I have no ice."

"I don't know why I'm here," he said.

"Yes you do," she replied, but did not elaborate.

"Is the judge here?"

"No, he's at the railhead, along with the sheriff, seeing how many miles of rail they can commandeer before the railroad gets wind of it."

"I need to know where you stand, Mrs. Howard."

"A co-conspirator."

He tried to enjoy that, and couldn't.

She smiled. "Not very helpful. Let me pour some tea."

She rose, lithe, athletic, graceful, and vanished within.

The house had been situated for its view. It

might be an empty land, but this house lorded over it all. Nearby was a carriage house. A vegetable garden, hand-watered from a pump. A hayfield rose up the slope. It was elegant and lonely. Its owner barely acknowledged that other mortals shared this vast place. Maybe that was the secret of this estate. Or even Throatlatch.

She returned with a tray, a teapot, two cups and saucers, and condiments.

"Have a seat, won't you?"

He accepted the tea, and settled gingerly on a wicker chaise.

"Are you a prisoner here?" he asked.

"My answer will be a paradox. I am free to leave. And I am a prisoner."

People who talked in riddles weren't worth bothering with, and he prepared to sip the tea and get out.

"I married below my station, and he married below his."

More riddles. She smiled.

"Mortals are not simple," she said. "That's the trouble with it all. I can be above my station on this, below it on that. I can be smarter than he is in one area, and dumb as a stump in some other area. And then there are the genders. Women are smarter than men, but must curb their intelligence."

"What is your relationship to me?"

"We will rescue each other."

"I can't afford it," he said.

Something twinkled in her eyes.

She talked in riddles through two cups of Earl Grey, and then excused herself to prepare dinner. "The judge likes to do everything on the hour," she said. "Eat, hang people, all of that."

He was no further than he had been, but had been treated to a gray-eyed gaze unlike any he had known, and felt himself bereft of even a fig leaf. She was a striking woman, younger than the judge, almost a trophy, someone commandeered as a prize. He saw no signs of children, and wondered if she longed for motherhood.

He started back, all the more mystified, and determined to escape for Denver at dawn, rather than suffer any more mystery and madness. Throatlatch could destroy itself and others without any help from him.

A voice barked.

"You!"

No Name turned, found the sheriff in the two-rut lane.

"What are you doing here?"

"Looking at land."

"I know you from somewhere."

"I worked for the railroad. I was there when you came to stop us."

Clemson squinted, not accepting that. "You got a name?"

No Name dug into his shirt pocket and pulled

out the battered card, once owned by J. Arnold Bright, land and mineral claim broker.

"Read it to me."

That surprised No Name. He read it. "I've built track for railroads since I was fifteen, and between, I buy right-of-way or do land deals."

"This is private land."

"In a way. Is this proven up?"

Clemson stayed quiet.

"Looks like a homestead deal. Seven years to prove up. Who lives down the lane?"

"The judge."

"Judge what?"

Clemson stared.

"This lane's a little high for the right-of-way, but it's the best we can do, with some claims along the laid-out route down there." No Name waved at the flats closer to town. "We deal with this all the time. The railroad's blocked one way, we go another. If this isn't proved up land, we'll go this way . . . That your place?"

No Name waved at the barn he had once slid into during his escape, and the house that lay beyond. Maybe it was the place of tragedy where Carolina Clemson lived. The two places, the sheriff's and judge's, were probably claimed under the homestead laws.

"You're not building any right-of-way here. And the railroad's not gonna know."

"It already knows. Public documents. It's not

ideal, climbs a bit, but it actually shortens our route a couple of hundred yards."

"Maybe you can get the hell out of my county."

"I wouldn't mind, but the railroad would. One way or another, the right-of-way's going through. You'll get used to the trains running through your yard. At first it sounds like they're rolling through your bedroom. They keep you up at night, but then you get used to them."

The sheriff reddened.

"Best thing is to let the railroad run along its staked out right-of-way. The one blocked by some deeds that weren't there when the right-of-way got staked through public land. How did that happen?"

"Listen, punk, you get out of my county, or pay the price."

No Name shrugged. "I hear you. The railroad tells me it'll pay some nuisance money to quiet those claims down there. Take it or get nothing. Or watch them lay rails on this path, right under your feet. You can't fight Cheyenne, or Washington D.C."

"I know you from somewhere," Clyde Clemson said.

"Likely you'll see me again," No Name said.

"I've got plenty of room in my jail," the sheriff said.

"Free meals," No Name replied.

He turned to go, and no rough hand clapped

him. The sheriff watched him amble down the lane.

No Name was cheered. The sheriff had spilled a lot of beans.

CHAPTER ELEVEN

No Name hiked the two-rut lanes that would take him back to Throatlatch, but he felt something strange. The closer he got to town, the farther away he seemed to be. His mind teemed with his two visits, one with a woman who talked in riddles, and one with a powerful man who brimmed with greed.

But greed didn't explain anything. Something sinister curled through Throatlatch, something that tossed human life away, that deemed mortals worthless, that turned hanging into spectacles, that made a joke of public execution. And greed had little to do with it. Getting rich by bilking the railroad had nothing to do with it. Fishing for Territorial money—colleges, asylums, prisons—had nothing to do with it. Something vile and dark had caught Throatlatch, or at least its elite, and No Name hadn't the faintest idea what it could be.

That's why he felt he was pushing against a wall, almost physical, as he closed in upon the shabby little town. Death danced in Throatlatch.

The threads of this mystery stretched to the judge, E Pluribus Unum Howard, who blithely sent people sailing into eternity. What sort of mortal was that? No Name remembered what he could of the motto that had become the judge's proper name. It meant one from many, or all into one. It was employed by the founders to depict the transformation of thirteen colonies into a single nation. And it had expanded to mean the inclusion of all sorts of peoples, from everywhere, into a single new nation. He wondered how the judge had lived with that name, and where it came from, and what it meant to the man, and whether it had anything to do with Throatlatch's sinister habits.

Maybe not even the judge knew. Maybe it was all the fruit of neglect of all the virtues, without reason. Just chaos. But as No Name cleared the outskirts of town, he clearly knew what he must do: draw close to the judge. Rattle his cage.

He didn't know how. He was little more than a drifter, a drifter who asked questions, and loved to read anything he could get his hands on. But Mitgang Schuster was educated, even if he kept it hidden. And Lydia Howard was, even if she couldn't escape her fate. And JimBob, the barkeep, knew more than he let on. And there would be more. The man most likely to have answers was the judge himself, who impressed No Name as a Doctor of Theology. He wondered why he had picked that analogy, and had no answer.

So, then, he would not stalk E Pluribus Unum from afar; he would head directly into that man's nature, and try to make sense of it. No Name stood, lonely, on the main street, whose name he didn't know, staring at the shabby little county building. He wanted to talk to the judge straight off—if he could find the judge.

No Name felt oddly worn, but he had a task to do, and he would do it. He crossed the manure-dotted street, and entered the Wellbred County courthouse, such as it was. Majestic Skinner dozed in a chair. The two prisoners lay in their bunks, looking haggard and dirty. It enraged him that innocent men would be held hostage, bargaining chips with the railroad. The judge wasn't there. No free man in his right mind would linger there. The last time No Name had been there, he was about to be hanged. The memory of it hastened him away. He closed the door, peered down the weary street, and drifted to the restaurant, ordered a bowl of stew, and gratefully spooned it up.

No judge. He patrolled the rest of the street as the afternoon waned, and paused at a small clapboard building at the end of town. The door was open to let the springtime breezes through. The interior was dim, but lit enough to reveal a church. And at the pulpit stood Judge Howard, wearing a simple white stole over his black robe, and addressing a dozen people. The robe was the same one he wore presiding over his Territorial court.

A minister? No Name watched a moment from the muddy street, couldn't hear, and slipped in. A minister? How could that be? And what was this, at six in the eve? Vespers?

Was this really the judge, or someone else? He didn't want to go in; he was not a religious sort. But again he felt that strange compulsion that had drawn him to Throatlatch and wouldn't let him escape. He went in and found a seat in an empty pew made of planks.

The judge eyed him briefly, and returned to his homily.

"The time grows short," he said. "It is just as prophesy says. Do what you must."

And that was it. No Name had caught the last few words.

No Name swiftly surveyed the congregation. It must have included most of the women in town, the ones who would be welcome in a church, at least. It made no sense. The men were nondescript. He could not pigeonhole them as wealthy or poor, leaders, followers, professionals, artisans, laborers.

The raw board-and-batten building had none of the earmarks of a church. No steeple. No insignia. No name. No faith or institution had been inscribed on its walls or front door. .

The judge approached No Name. "You arrived late. We meet on Thursdays at five."

"But what is this?"

"There's a beautiful dawn coming, and we're waiting for the night to pass."

"Are you a church?"

"No, young man, but we do note some telling prophesy in the Bible."

"Are you a reform society?"

"No, not really. Come next Thursday and listen. We await a great burst of daylight. Say, you look familiar."

"I was building roadbed for the railroad."

"Ah, yes. We welcome the railroad; it's part of the dawn. Well, I'm late for supper. The madam puts down the plates at the very hour." He hurried off, still dressed in his judicial robe. The hanging judge feared to be late to his own dining table.

It had been quite a day. And might not be over. No Name headed for JimBob's Saloon, where his questions seemed to find solid answers.

"The usual?" asked the keep.

No Name nodded, wondering how long his railroad pay would keep him afloat here. JimBob drew a mug of sour beer, took some change, and eyed No Name, as if waiting for something.

"What's that board and bat building, raw wood, at the end of the street?"

"Mystery, sort of. The judge built it. End of the worlders, I hear."

"A cult?"

"They talk the opposite. Big Dawn coming, bad old world will fall away. That's what I hear, anyway."

"I was curious. Saw some people in there and the judge looking like a preacher."

JimBob smiled. "Another racket."

No Name sipped, waited for the rest.

"See, it's like this. If the world's ending, what you've got isn't worth spit. So he talks suckers into unloading their houses, lots, livestock— stuff. Bargain prices. When the dawn comes, you won't need your old stuff. He cleans out every sucker in town, and there's plenty of them. Most have sold out to him for peanuts, and beat it."

"So the judge's got property all over here?"

"You'd have to find that out in the county building."

"No one knows?"

JimBob shrugged. "Here, folks watch out for themselves and don't ask questions—like yours."

"I talked to him. He said it's a new dawn coming, but first the old world goes away. He said the railroad's part of the new world."

JimBob grinned. "It is, for him."

No Name thought there might be more, but he doubted he'd find answers here. These were working stiffs sipping beer, downing shots, not looking for utopia. It bothered him. Something was hanging in his mind, something he couldn't reach. Throatlatch was hiding something.

"I was just curious, that's all."

"Curiosity can get you a noose, friend."

"What if it's a real cult? Believers? People who've bought some quack idea? There were some women in there. I hardly see women in this town."

"That's because they're over on B Street."

"Wives. Schoolteachers."

"We haven't got more than six."

No Name watched the keep pour a bourbon neat, and look after others. Where was Carolina Clemson? Where was Lydia Howard? Preparing for the new dawn? Did the sheriff believe that stuff? Not likely.

He drained his drink, stepped outside just in time to see the moon rise between the uprights of the gallows. Bright full moon, that would soon diminish as it rose. The town had pulled into itself, dark except for a few lamp-lit windows. Not far away, the North Platte took the high country water to the Platte, a mile wide and inch deep, and on east and south, to New Orleans. It didn't seem possible. Did the judge's vision of a new dawn stretch that far? Or was this new dawn local? Stupid question.

Spring was in the air. The world smelled young.

He stuck to shadows, peered into the lamp-lit county building, where males sat. He wondered how the two prisoners fared. Disturbing the peace. Endless jail, pawns in some larger game with the railroad. He wished he had some way of freeing them.

The shadows carried him to the cemetery, and there she was, sitting quietly.

"I didn't mean to startle you," he said.

But she was startled and started to flee.

"Your name is Carolina. You lost someone you love. I keep asking, but no one tells me much."

She eyed him, her face lit by pale moon. "It's not your business," she said.

"In a way it is. Only pure good luck kept me from lying here myself."

"For what, may I ask?"

"For nothing. I was passing through."

"They all say that."

He pointed at the grave. "What was his crime?"

"None. I must go now."

"His crime was to be different."

"You've been gossiping."

"I have no name. Or, any name. That means I am not part of one group, one nation, one people or another. Names narrow it down, Carolina. Your name tells me things."

"Such as?"

"Do you believe in a new dawn, a new world, and the old world, evil and dark, falling away suddenly, soon? Maybe a dawn, a day, where everyone is almost alike?"

"Goodbye," she said, and turned away.

"I'll be here tomorrow," he said, watching her hurry into the pale moonlight and ascend a trail that took her toward the foothills.

CHAPTER TWELVE

The shabby structure that Wellbred County called its courthouse exuded malice in the morning sun. No Name dreaded going there, not because he might be recognized as a fugitive, but because the search he intended to conduct might provoke new troubles. Still, it had to be done. He entered the odorous building, with its jail and sheriff office on the left, and the rest on the right. A clerk was the sole official dealing with the public. No Name spotted the two railroad supervisors, desolate in their cell, unkempt, starved, unjustly detained as hostages. It riled him, but he knew of nothing he might do. Majestic Skinner sat over there, picking at his molars.

No Name approached the whiskery and well dressed official, who seemed reluctant to rise from his chair.

"I'm a land broker, dealer," he said. "I want a look at the railroad's right-of-way grants and purchases, and also the deeds that cover the same right-of-way."

"It'd take weeks to get that up," the man said.

"I think you can manage it while I wait."

Most of the county was unsettled. There were not a lot of documents in the place.

"What's your name?" the official asked.

No Name extracted the battered card. "J. Arnold Bright, it says right here."

"Heard that name somewhere," the man said. "I'll check with the supervisors and let you know."

"You'll want to do it now, if you hope to profit from the railroad."

"Peter Dent, county clerk," he said, a certain change of tone in his voice. "Why all this stuff?"

"Profit," No Name said. "I buy and sell. I put deals together. I give comfort to my customers."

Dent yawned, and eyed No Name with a bloodshot eye. "What else do you know?" he asked.

"I defend my clients against fraud."

Dent seemed to exhale sulphur. "Fraud. That's interesting. I'll consult with the sheriff. Come back next week."

A register of taxpayers lay at hand, so No Name took it in hand.

"Hey!" Dent yelled.

But No Name swiftly opened the alphabetized list to the D entries, and found Dent. The C entries listed Clemson on adjoining property. The H entries yielded a whole list of Howard deeds. All three had deeds for half-sections side by side, across the right-of-way.

"That's a public record. You can't look," Dent growled, wanting to snatch it.

The railroad land occupied a special ledger, and most of the paperwork was copied from federal land sales to the company. It would take some digging to get the descriptions and dates he wanted.

"I'll take that," Dent said, this time successfully yanking the register from the counter, and putting it out of reach.

"Looks like you, the sheriff, and the judge have some land squarely in the right-of-way," No Name said.

"Where are you boarding?" Dent asked. "I'll have the sheriff get back to you."

"You belong to the New Dawn society?"

"What? What?"

Dent rounded his counter and headed for the jail to get Skinner.

An armed jailer with cell keys was not someone to trifle with, but jail-keeping was the lowest step on the ladder. So No Name waited, while Dent fetched the muscleman.

"You again," Skinner said. "What now?"

"I'm looking for public records. I want to see who owns the right-of-way that's stirring up trouble around here."

"And why do you want to know?"

"Land broker. Chance to make a bundle, or find a customer who would."

"He's a pest," Dent said. "Pitch him out."

"I've had a quick look. Seems that Dent here owns one parcel, and someone named Clemson owns another, and someone named Howard owns the third, and they've got the railroad tied up in knots. There's money to be made."

"I wish I was in on it," Skinner said.

"You with that New Dawn outfit?" No Name asked. "They're the ones making a bundle."

Skinner went silent, then shook his head. "They don't need to make money. Not with the old world coming to an end."

"What's that about?"

"You better get outa here. You're asking for it."

"How come Mr. Dent here and the others have chunks of land right on the railroad tracks?"

"Railroad messed up," Dent said. "The judge—that's Howard—explained it. Paperwork. Didn't get through the federal land office, so we leaped. The thing is, the road never got the land, and we got it. It's pure gold. They've got to buy us out."

"Show me," No Name said.

Dent did. He opened the tax roster. The railroad owned right-of-way to the point where the railhead stood, and picked up land on the other side of Throatlatch, smooth sailing west after that.

"See here? They missed three half-sections, and that's ours."

"So what if the railroad goes somewhere else?"

Skinner grinned, and jerked a thumb toward the cells. "We've got some leverage."

"Where did the gap come from?"

Dent shrugged. "Clerks. The world has too many dumb clerks."

"What's your price?"

"Some of us will own half the railroad. Seats on the board. Vanderbilt, he'll be a piker."

"So what's the New Dawn society?"

"That comes after. First, the world's gotta end."

"Like judgment day?"

"No one knows. But it's foretold. The Great Seal of the United States. The Pyramid, Novus Ordo Seclorum, the big eye, E Pluribus Unum."

"What do they teach?"

"No one knows. Flood, volcano, plague, strangers."

"Who survives?"

"New Dawn people will know what to do."

"I think I can make a fortune," No Name said. "But that's going to be my private business. For now. When I've got it worked out, I'll sell you a piece of it."

Dent and Skinner stared.

"Look me up. J. Arnold Bright. I'll be around. This town is my pollywog."

Dent's ambition was breathtaking. He and the rest wanted to turn themselves into Vanderbilts? Someone should put some saltpeter into their soup.

No Name stepped into the sordid street. A wind was whipping manure dust into open windows. He had learned a lot, but somehow it didn't matter. The railroad was big and tough and could fight its own war. No Name still didn't know what had driven him back to Throatlatch, but fighting the railroad's battles wasn't part of it.

This place had almost hanged him. That was all that stuck in his mind.

He couldn't understand himself. Why was he lingering in this desolate place, where people enjoyed public spectacles that resulted in death? What kept him there? He had no answer. He didn't even know what to do next.

But even as an unseen hand seemed to steer him, he found himself walking down the main road, which might or not be named, until he arrived at that ugly little structure cobbled of planks so raw they still bled sap. For reasons unknown, he thought that all the dark secrets of Throatlatch lay within.

The structure was low and wide, with a tarpaper roof, no windows, and a door that hung crookedly in its quick-built frame. The door had a small window, so some small light reached within. No sign announced its purpose or ownership. But above the door, charred into wood, was a pyramid. It had a crude eye resting on its tip. He had seen this very image and had once wondered what it meant.

He rattled the door, and to his surprise, found it had no lock. Anyone could walk in or out. It was deliberately a public refuge.

"Come in, young man," a familiar voice said.

No Name peered about, his eyes slowly adjusting, and discovered the judge himself, E Pluribus Unum Howard, sitting in a comfortable chair on what appeared to be a podium.

"Your eyes will help you in a moment. Only the most visionary see in the dark," the judge said.

It was true. No Name's eyes gradually mastered this strange cavern. The judge was alone. He was not in his judicial robe, and wore a simple, dignified suit. The image did not seem to fit the man who had casually sent many people to their doom.

No Name did not know what to say.

"You came here. Curious, perhaps," the judge said. "That's how it always starts. We are curious."

"I just wondered . . ."

"Of course. The structure is makeshift. It will last only a year or two, but that will be time enough. It's not meant to survive. Nothing will survive, except those with the new dawn in their vision."

"You're talking about the real world, the physical world, then. It'll go away?"

The judge smiled. "Ah, that is the usual question of the novice. It's more complex. Evil will go away. Everything we do will be good."

No Name wanted to ask him whether hanging innocent people would be good in this new time, but he refrained.

"I see your skepticism," the judge said. "The New Dawn must be swallowed in small doses. Come Thursday and listen. Little by little, it will change your life."

No Name sensed he was being dismissed. The judge was a canny man, who read people well. "I'm a land dealer. J. Arnold Bright, and if you're looking for the promised land, I'll find a way to deliver it."

The judge arched an eyebrow. "You have much to learn," he said, and slowly rose. He was a head taller than No Name, and a foot wider, and seemed to fill that dark room with some sort of force.

"See no evil," the judge added.

No Name retreated into the bright street, bewildered and angry. He wondered where the anger came from. A harsh wind was whipping the offal into vortexes and unloading it in doorways and alleys. His face was full of it, and he itched for a washtub and a towel.

It was hard enough to understand the actual world, and even harder to grasp whatever the judge was proposing. He wondered if the judge would pass a collection plate at the Thursday eve meeting. He intended to find out, and see who the suckers were that blotted up that stuff.

He'd had enough of New Dawns, and eyed the sour little town that enjoyed hanging people just for the joy of it. He still had no idea why he lingered in a place like Throatlatch, so far from real life that its most prominent people invented an apocalypse.

He headed for the tonsorial parlor. Mitgang Schuster was the only man in the place who had any sense.

The barber nodded, and steered No Name to the chair, and began whipping up some lather in a mug.

"What's the New Dawn?" No Name asked.

"You've been talking to the judge."

"It's a way to turn evil into good, seems like," No Name said. "Is it a local madness?"

"I'm not sure. Most of our upright people belong."

Schuster brushed lather deep into No Name's chin and throat and face, stropped his straight-edge, and began scraping.

No Name didn't respond. Not with the razor scraping his stubble away.

"I'm not someone of any faith. But if I were, young man, I'd call it the anti-Christ."

CHAPTER THIRTEEN

Lydia Howard said she was expecting him. No Name thought she had some sort of sixth sense. "I'm out of tea," she said. "In Throatlatch, you take what you can get."

"It's remote."

"That's why it's perfect for the judge," she said, which startled him.

"I just thought I'd stop by."

"That's naive," she said. "You'll conceal your intentions better as you grow older."

"The judge told me a little about his, whatever it's called. I thought I'd ask . . ."

"I'll save you the effort. You wouldn't know what to ask or how to ask it."

No Name was starting to tumble in upon himself.

"He may well be the cruellest, darkest mortal in the United States," she said. "I'm married to him, I love him, and that poses a modest problem for me."

She was a handsome, vibrant woman, whose gray-eyed gaze seemed to read him. He had no secrets left.

"Pluribus is a gracious man from a gracious

family," she said. "I was flattered by his attentions. My family is comfortable. I had my choice, and I chose him, and have never regretted it. He has charms beyond what any boy might imagine."

He didn't like being called a boy, even obliquely. He wasn't sure he liked her. If she began defending the judge, he'd excuse himself and head down the lane.

"I find reasons to stay on," she said. "The remoteness is a cloak. It hides a town that casually murders people, buries innocents, picks on the weak, robs travelers, and considers it all harmless fun, but something to hide. My husband fostered it, sent many people to the gallows so the town could hear their necks snap. Here's the thing. It is all fostered in the name of a cult, a vision of a sublime new world. It is done to shatter the old, imperfect world. He not only embraced that, he teaches it, he collects supporters one by one. He corresponds with others who share his vision. He is proud of his growing graveyard. And of course you are wondering why I don't report it. In fact, I have, with anyone who stops in this remote place and asks questions. But in fact, nothing I say matters. That's a woman's lot. Worse, I've come to bear it, to leave it alone, to comfort him and enjoy him, to feed him and delight him if I can. I suppose that makes me a part of it, a contributor to unspeakable darkness. I suppose I am. I have no answers, or any insights about myself. I wish you could see him here, enjoying the prospect, a panorama of the good world, a place where his soul is serene." She gazed at him. "You're blotting it up, horrified, wondering what sort of madness affects me. But I am all here, not hidden. What you've heard here is me, undiluted. I'm not your ally. A word from me to him would cost you your life."

"No, you haven't even started to reveal yourself," he said.

For once, she retreated a bit.

"Maybe you are two or three selves," he said.

"If I had tea to serve, I'd pick up your cup and saucer and thank you for stopping by."

He stood. In one sense he was closer to understanding Throatlatch, but actually he was farther from his goal than ever. She stood, watching him collect himself. He nodded, and walked away, along a two-rut lane, back to the darkest place in the Territory. He followed the track, the innocent earth under his feet, and mystery of good and evil a lump in his brain.

He wondered how she could love the judge; how she could fully understand the enormity of his offenses, and yet continue to love him. Was she guilty? Of course, but his mind kept tugging him to question that.

There was an open threat in what she said. A word from her, and a noose would tighten around his neck. Maybe the most criminal of all people were the smooth-talking, cultivated, civilized elite, who could rationalize any conduct.

"Stop or you're dead."

The sheriff was standing behind him, an enormous blued revolver aimed at No Name's middle.

"You again. I'm taking you in."

"Is it illegal to walk down a country lane?"

"If I say so. What's your name again?"

"Here's my card. I'm a land dealer, looking for land."

"Maybe," the sheriff said, glancing at the card. "You're not looking for land. Tell me what you're looking for."

"A New Dawn."

That stumped Clyde Clemson. He motioned with his revolver. "The jail," he said.

That's how it went for ten minutes, until they reached the main street and what served as a courthouse for Wellbred County. The sheriff opened, steered No Name in, and pushed him into the empty cell next to the railroad supervisors.

"What am I charged with?" No Name asked.

"I'll think of something."

The barred door slammed shut, a lock rotated, and once again No Name was caught in a stinking cage with a hard bunk, no blanket, and a pail.

"I wish to plead my case."

"Next year," Clemson said.

No Name watched the sheriff pull the big brass key, return it to a key ring, and smile.

"May I have some water?"

"No."

"How about a meal?"

"It comes out of my budget, and my budget is all for me."

"Is there a lawyer in town?"

"The judge himself has some law."

"Then I'd like to hire him. New Dawn, and all that. A New Dawn, get it?"

The sheriff stared uncertainly, and muttered something.

No Name knew he had turned the right key.

The sheriff whirled away. No Name stared at the iron bars, feeling that old claustrophobia overwhelm him. Helpless again. He was dependent on others for life, water, food, breath, warmth, and even hope. It was all he could manage to stay quiet. The other two, in the next cage, kept their silence, no doubt for some reason. They were both unkempt, down to bones, and filthy. No Name thought that they would not survive much longer, and wondered why the railroad hadn't long since bailed them out, for whatever it cost.

"I know you," No Name said to them.

Martin McGee nodded. "Later," he said.

That seemed unduly cautious in an empty cell room. But an open door leading into the sheriff's cubicle invited eavesdropping. After a long while, the sheriff left his office and vanished from the building.

"You are?" Wallace Parson asked.

"One of your roadbed crew."

"He's the one with no name," McGee said.

"Why doesn't the railroad come get us?" Parson asked.

"They've tried."

"That's the worst news."

"Can you explain this?" McGee asked.

"Not yet. I'm looking. I don't know why, but I am."

No Name didn't know where to start, and gave up. They would think he was crazy. "I got out of here once," he said. "I had a date with the noose."

"They won't need a noose for us if this keeps up."

"You got water?"

McGee filled a tin cup and passed it through. No Name drank gratefully and returned the cup.

"You said something to the sheriff. New Dawn. You said it twice, and he backed off a bit. What is it?"

"I'm trying to find out. It's a cult. The judge is one. He's recruiting others. I don't know what it means, but I've got this much: it's a vision of a new world, a perfect world, but it won't come until this evil one falls away. It makes no sense. I tried talking to the judge, and he said I'd know in time. And just what it means to me—and you, too—I don't know. It's all nonsense."

112

"Except that the sheriff suddenly paused. We watched. You said the words, and he quit pushing you around."

No Name wanted to give the man hope. "Try it. Try it on Majestic Skinner. Tell him whatever you feel, but use those two words. It'll get back to the judge fast."

"It's like a church confirmation," McGee said.

"Words. Say the right words and doors open or close," Parson said.

No Name told them about the meeting hall, the judge preaching, the aura of religion even though he said it wasn't one. They listened now, listened hard. It was the first glimmer of a way out that they'd had for days.

The two railroad supervisors sank into their benches, their thoughts riding in their faces. No Name simply felt despair again, the helplessness of a caged mortal, utterly at the mercy of others who had designs.

Then the judge walked in, this time garbed in his judicial robe. The prisoners leapt up, clenching the bars. Behind the judge, Skinner kept his own brutal presence.

"This court's in session," the judge said to No Name. "Stand up. You too," he said to the supervisors. "You going to confess?"

"I haven't been charged."

"I don't mean that. I mean acknowledge the bloom inside of you."

Skinner smirked. The deputy didn't believe in anything but a pay envelope.

"What am I supposed to say?"

"Tell the court."

No Name had a headache. "New Dawn," he said.

"You confess? You'll take direction?"

"New Dawn." He wasn't going to take direction from anyone or confess anything.

"You're free," the hanging judge said.

Skinner unlocked the cell.

No Name stepped back into the world.

"Your honor, we respectfully ask to confess. We're both New Dawn," McGee said.

"You're pulling wool over my eyes."

"We want to learn," McGee said, an edge to his voice.

"Too late. You're a part of the dark."

No Name saw McGee's white knuckles clamp the bars.

The rail men slumped, as nighttime stole the light from their cell. The look on McGee's face was one No Name knew he would never forget.

"Thursday at the meeting house. No backsliding," Judge Howard said, fixing No Name with a clear cold eye. "Don't thank me. It's not my doing."

No Name walked into a late afternoon liberty, celebrating the sun and the stars.

CHAPTER FOURTEEN

No Name stood in the grubby street, suddenly free. Throatlatch had twice thrown him in prison, once tried to kill him, and now intended to recruit him in something he didn't understand. Strangely, his need to stay in town spiked him down like a rail on a crosstie. Throatlatch harbored something like a religion.

The judge had evolved from a casual murderer of innocents for entertainment, into some sort of gospel-giver. Somehow, the sheriff and deputies and other officials stumbled along with the judge. The only thing that made any sense to No Name was Mitgang Schuster's dour conclusion that E Pluribus Unum Howard was an anti-Christ.

He had to get a job.

Then he realized he had one. He was J. Arnold Bright, Land Broker, according to the crumpled business card in his pocket, and any records kept by the sheriff.

Land Broker. That was as good as any. If he was going to broker land, buy, sell, rent, lease, trade—he'd better look at the land. The town stretched along a main road from the bridge toward the foothills, and the main drag and a few branches that were lined with houses or empty lots. He couldn't imagine why anyone would live in such a forsaken place—unless someone was hiding from the law. There wasn't another town within fifty miles. This one slumped wearily in the dry air, a place that lacked amenities. For a view they had some foothills and the river. This country, like most of Wyoming, was barren and harsh. Who would buy any sort of real estate here—and why?

He started with the main street, fronted by clapboard or board and batten structures, roofed with tar-paper. Not a shingle in sight. Few of these stores even had much glass. You had to take some light with you when you wandered in. A few had hitching posts. One had a bench. One had a shaded gallery with a few chairs. Few were painted, but some where whitewashed. Most had outhouses to the rear, and on some hot days they let themselves be known. Trash, mostly broken bottles, lay between the structures. The whole street radiated despair. Not a single place had any decor or ornamentation. No one could afford paint.

He spotted a CLOSED sign in one, and a FOR SALE sign in another, and that started him looking. Eight or ten of these businesses were closed or for sale—and looked like they had been abandoned for years. No Name began patrolling the side streets, and found that they mirrored the main drag. Shabby, decrepit houses were empty, with FOR SALE signs in their windows. Empty lots were heaped with tumbleweeds. Some of the side streets were better, with enclaves of bright, manicured houses with wicker furniture on front porches, and tiny gardens. Some had shallow wells with hand pumps that could be jacked into filling a pail. They probably tapped the river aquifer. There were FOR SALE signs in the windows of these places, too. Much of Throatlatch was for sale, which No Name assumed was pure common sense. This was a get-out-as-fast-as-you-can-place.

He guessed the town once had a thousand, and now had maybe seven hundred. But that was only a guess. It was plain that Throatlatch was a hardscrabble town, and things were getting worse. It had relied on the river trail for its income, and now the railroad was outmoding all foot and wagon travel. He wondered why people had settled there in the first place. But if there had been a few moist springs and summers, and the river bottoms looked green, maybe a few optimists thought that it might turn into a paradise.

Not much of a place to set up as a real estate broker.

He eyed the cemetery, where the rear row was populated with unmarked graves—the final insult to those who had been hanged. But now No Name eyed the rest of it, and found only a handful of marked graves. No one stayed in Throatlatch long enough to die. But that only deepened the mystery. It was a county seat. Some people liked it.

It was the middle of the day, but he ventured into JimBob's and found the keep alone, washing glasses. Wordlessly, JimBob filled a mug.

"On me," he said. "You escaped the noose, I hear."

That was worth drinking to.

"I've been touring town and have some questions, if you're not busy."

"I like questions."

"A lot of this town's for sale. Stores, houses, lots . . ."

"I'm for sale. Want a saloon?"

"And falling apart. Empty buildings, dark, some with broken windows, and old FOR SALE signs everywhere. Why's that? The land's worth something."

"Naw, it's not deeded land. No one owns it."

"Okay, how did that happen?"

JimBob shrugged. He had a knowing look, the eyes of someone who'd seen the best and worst of people. "Hardly a town in the West has owned land under it, at first anyway. What happens is, something draws people to a place. Big gold discovery, or something, and people rush in. They need a town fast, and the government's real slow about transferring land. People can't wait. Some sharpers with a tape measure and all, they lay out the town, measure up the roads and streets, stake out lots, and start selling them. It don't matter none that it's not deeded. That's how it always goes. The government, it eventually recognizes the property and those who got homes and buildings sitting on it get a deed under them. But that come a year or two or three later, after streets are lined with houses, and big stores with false fronts stick up on the main street. That's how it mostly is out here. Hardly a new town in the whole West got real property under it."

"So, that's true here?"

"Here it's worse. If it looks like a town's about to die, the federal land office doesn't bother deeding the land, parceling it out. Some people hang on, and file claims, and usually they get their lot if they pay for a survey, but a lot of little places in Wyoming, Colorado, and so on, they're checkerboards, bits here and there, federal or state in between. Sometimes, it's company land in between. The mining company gets a bunch of land, and parcels it out so they can have a town for their miners."

"And here?"

"All public land, plus a few homestead claims that could be proven up."

"Any deeds in the courthouse?"

"Nope, but a few claims."

"So the judge, he and his friends got some claims on the right-of-way. Do they stand to make anything if Throatlatch blows away?"

"I ain't that smart," JimBob said.

"Let's say people quit, pull out, and it's a ghost town here. Does the judge make a dime from it?"

"He could. Once people quit these lots, they lose any claim they might have. The judge and all of them, they could pick up every lot they wanted, for nothing. Abandoned property, ready for the Federal Land Office to deed wholesale, one big chunk. A whole town, ready to become a railroad place, serving the whole country around here, putting that old wood bridge to use, maybe freight yards, round house, engine shop, cattle pens and stockyards."

"Is that what they're doing?"

"Old world, falling apart. New Dawn's coming."

"Why'd they hang people?"

"Faster that way. If it's falling away, give it a kick."

"But I mean, commit hanging, death, just to pick up land and lots? The West's full of empty land, and most of it better than this."

"It's called a cult, Bright. It's a cult. They've got their own world, and it has nothing to do with buying and selling and trading and plowing and mining. It has to do with Paradise, and plenty of people would murder to get into Paradise—if they're believers."

"Thanks, JimBob."

"Are you a believer, Bright?" There was a hardness in the keep's face.

"No, not ever. Not even if it got me out of jail yesterday."

"Then you're welcome here," JimBob said. "Ever since they hanged my brother, I've been particular."

"What was his name?"

"George Little Moccasin."

CHAPTER FIFTEEN

A sharp whistle caught No Name's attention. He discovered a man across the road waving at him. It turned out to be Marcus Penn, railroad foreman.

"I've been looking for you," he said. "You're still here."

"Don't ask me why," No Name said.

"You want a job? I got one. In a few days we'll start building railroad again. We need all the help we can hire. You, and anyone else in town that wants a job."

"Laying track? What happened?"

Penn smiled wryly. "Railroads don't like to be messed with. The big cheeses went straight to the Federal Land Office, found the clerical mistake that stopped right-of-way purchases, and got it fixed."

"Fixed how?"

"Error corrected. Right-of-way restored; the homestead filings here, by the judge, Howard, the sheriff, Clemson, and the clerk, Dent, they've been voided. It won't end up in court. It can't be litigated. It's an error that is now corrected. Anyway, they're putting together a new railhead crew. Most of the previous one's gone, so it's slow going. They're collecting some off the boats, looking for any sort they can train. This time you get to be foreman of the grading crew—like my job."

A flood of worries crowded into No Name's head. "Have you talked to the judge and those people?"

"I will. That's next. I got a Land Office notarized fair copy to give them, a letter telling them not to interfere, and a little muscle too. The government's sending a U.S. marshal along to make sure there's no trouble. He'll be here for as long as it takes."

"There might be a few here willing to work," No Name said. "Town's half empty and fading. It's a puzzle."

"What's puzzling?"

"I can't put words to it."

Penn stared. "When you can, I want you to tell me. Can you at least give me some idea?"

"It's a way of believing, with the judge in charge. A new age is coming, and an old age, bad to the core, is fading away—with a lot of help from the elected."

"You been drinking?"

"Marcus, I've spent days here trying to figure it out. Something bad's eating this place up. I tell you what. Go talk to JimBob, the keep at the saloon. He's better with ideas than I am."

"You got me curious." His gaze settled on No Name.

"I'm known here as J. Arnold Bright, okay?"

"We've got some talking to do, as soon as you can do it."

"Ask the keep why the town hung a harmless little woman a few marbles short, just for entertainment."

Penn stared. "Meet me this eve. I'll spend the afternoon making the case to the 'homesteaders' that their claims are worthless, and they've been thrown out."

"I guess I'll take that job. I'm down to my last buck. I'll be at the saloon looking for you."

Marcus Penn nodded. He didn't look as confident as he had minutes earlier. "One thing," he said. "Where's Martin McGee and Wallace Parson?"

"There, in that poor excuse of a county building. They're getting sicker and starving."

"We'll bust them out."

"Alive, I hope," No Name said.

Penn stared. "Is there anything else I should know?"

"Yes. The judge, sheriff and county clerk plan to own the railroad, or most of it."

"Am I deaf or something?"

"You heard me right. And keep this in mind. That barber there, he's a friend."

"All right. And here's what you need to know.

The railhead crew and equipment will be here in a few days. It takes time to get it all together. And there's nothing going to stop them."

"Be careful. They were planning on stealing the rails."

"I'll pass that along. We may have to run a handcar ahead."

Penn lifted his billed cap and settled it again, a modest homage to No Name. And then he arched his shoulders and headed for the county building. No Name watched him enter, and watched the door close behind him, sealing him from the sunny street.

He studied the silent courthouse, and knew it would keep its secrets. He headed for JimBob's Saloon, and found the place empty. That's how it was in Throatlatch. It was good to get out of the heavy sunlight. He found a bar stool and waited. JimBob didn't show.

But the longer he waited, the itchier he got. That restlessness that had stalked him in Throatlatch poured through him. He couldn't define it but he could feel it, and it was making him crazy. He slipped into the intense light. The town, always quiet, now seemed morbid. He spotted no one on the streets. He edged along a sidewalk, seeing something even stranger. Shops had thrown their doors shut, closed tight midday. A dog walked stiff-legged, careful-footed, across the road. No Name edged toward that meeting hall, that hollow shell where the judge rattled souls, but it was silent and empty.

But at the county building two deputies, Gus Glory and Majestic Skinner, stood at the door, both of them holding shotguns and wearing side arms. He ducked into shadow. Something was happening. He edged into the judge's meeting house, which seemed the safest place in Throatlatch, and was glad he did. The courthouse doors swung open, an armed procession emerged, the judge in his black robe leading, followed by the sheriff and a couple of armed men, followed by Marcus Penn, whose hands were tightly bound behind his back, and followed by half a dozen males No Name could not identify. And in one horrible moment, he knew where this procession was headed, and it made him crazy. Then it got worse. Behind Marcus Penn was the barber, Mitgang Schuster, whose skilled hands were also tied behind his back.

The parade moved leisurely, as if it existed for the entertainment of this whole city. No Name stared at windows, and saw a shade roll down. The parade meandered toward the riverfront area, an afternoon picnic in the park. It stopped at the gallows.

The judge, E Pluribus Unum Howard, turned toward the crowd behind him. He seemed cheerful, a smile building along his lips.

"Mr. Skinner, do the honors," he said.

The deputy climbed the narrow steps, swung a coil of hemp rope over the crossbar, built a fine, professional noose, and tightened it all down with experienced hands. Then he cheerfully lowered the noose over Penn's neck and tightened it until it was just right, turning it enough to snap the neck sideways, the approved and most humane method.

Marcus Penn did not play the hero. Tears rose in his eyes, and wet his cheeks. He stared at the sky, as if the sky alone held promise.

"Mr. Penn, the court of Wellbred County sentences you to death almighty," the judge said, oddly. "Let justice be done."

Skinner hustled the railroad's messenger onto the exact center of the trap, and then pulled the lever.

Marcus Penn died instantly. His eyes saw nothing, and then slowly closed, pushing a last tear along.

He spasmed once or twice, and spun loose. Skinner let him swing.

The judge smiled. "And you, Mitgang Schuster, we have nothing to hold against you. But you don't belong in this place. I will spare you, but you must pack and leave before sunset, or you will meet the same fate."

No Name trembled.

They cut the barber's hands loose. The short, balding man trembled, his face a mask.

"You could thank me," the judge said.

Mitgang Schuster simply stared. And then they let him walk free. The barber put one foot in front of the other, stumbled, fell, rose, stepped ahead, one leg at a time, down the empty street, walking, walking, walking.

No Name waited for the joke to end, but it wasn't a joke. The righteous judge had let the barber go.

CHAPTER SIXTEEN

That old loneliness he knew so well, engulfed No Name. All his life, it had pounced on him at odd moments, reminding him of how alone he was in a large world. Yet, as he stood there watching the drama, Mitgang Schuster stumbled toward the old wooden bridge, not even bothering to collect his possessions in his barber shop, just driven by some terrible force to stumble free.

No Name quietly watched the small crowd dissipate and then the street was all harsh sunlight again, the only darkness at the gallows where a man's body rocked slowly in the breeze. No Name, suddenly aware, slipped swiftly through back lots and alleys and caught up with Schuster just before the barber started out on the bridge.

"Come with me, sir," he said.

Schuster continued to stagger away from town.

"Please come with me. I am your friend."

The barber stared, his eyes large and sad. No Name gently took him by the elbow and steered him back, through alleys, until they reached JimBob's Saloon. No Name led him inside. Schuster peered about, plainly lost, and No Name realized the man had never been in this place.

JimBob was standing quietly at the bar. "I'll close the place," he said.

"But we need to talk."

"That's why I'm closing it. The rest of the town's shut down too."

The keep bolted the door and flipped a CLOSED sign in its window.

"Sarsaparilla?" he asked the barber.

Schuster shook his head. But JimBob filled a glass of cool water and handed it to the man, and then steered them all to a rear table, where it was dark and quiet.

"You don't need to say a word," the keep said. He turned to No Name. "What'll happen now? Does the railroad know?"

"I don't know. Penn came alone, as a messenger."

"We're a long way from wire, at Fort Laramie."

"Then it may take a couple of days," No Name said.

"What happened in the courthouse?"

No Name told JimBob what he knew. Schuster was listening closely now.

"There'll be a militia showing up here, or maybe some soldiers."

"Railroad may have a work train here any time now. But the judge and his bunch know it."

They hashed it out for a few minutes, neither JimBob nor No Name knowing what to do.

But one thing was urgent. They needed to keep Schuster safe and help him recover his wits. The barber listened intently, as if swallowing every word, but said nothing. No Name had a faint feeling of optimism. The three of them were together, and they could work out something. But what?

"What do you need from your shop, sir? We can get it. I think they'll ransack it as soon as it's dark enough," JimBob said.

"I can't think," Schuster said.

"Clothing? Family things, records, barber tools?"

"All, all," Schuster said.

"We could lock it, but that won't stop them," No Name said. "I'll go over there and get what I can. A couple of burlap bags—"

"No. They'll be watching, and string you up."

That was likely.

Schuster seemed to grow granite around his eyes. "Yes, there are things I'd like. But nothing is worth a life. I can find new clothes. New barbering tools. Yes, there are some things— family things, things that connect me, those will be lost. But they are always in my memory. No object, no material thing is worth your life, my life. Let it all go."

His voice was so firm, his decision so plain, that neither JimBob nor No Name raised any objections.

"I've some shirts, a coat, other stuff. People leave stuff here all the time. It's yours."

Schuster nodded.

In time, they worked out a plan. When night cloaked them, they would help Schuster out, not across the bridge, but down the road to the railhead. With luck, he would find safety in the railroad work train. They would equip him with food and clothing and a greenback or two. He would be the one taking bad news to the railroad, most likely, and all the more protected because of that. No Name would escort him as far as the railhead, and once he reached the rails he would know where to go. Fort Laramie lay down those bands of steel.

Someone rattled the saloon door, gave up, and vanished. No Name and JimBob put a kit together, pretzels, lucifers, gloves, a thin blanket, cap, a jackknife. Enough to keep a man going through a late spring week.

Full dark settled, and it was time to go. JimBob stared at No Name.

"Come back," he said.

"Sometimes you don't. Life takes you in some other direction."

The bar keep had read him well. No Name nodded, hoisted Schuster's burlap bag, and the two eased into the night.

It took some getting used to. Throatlatch had never been so black. No lamp lit any window, and if anyone was on the street, they were prowling. No Name didn't have to tell Schuster to stay quiet.

They passed the barber shop, and starlight revealed it had already been ransacked. A door swung on its hinges.

Schuster muttered something, but stayed quiet. It was all No Name could do to find the river trail, the one that would take them down the North Platte to a place where the railhead silently waited. They saw no one. No Name knew they didn't have a chance against a gang, or even three or four. But the night remained shrouded in silence. By some good calculation, No Name found the cutoff, a foot trail that wound across flats to the railroad. He touched Schuster's shoulder, and the two left the river and quietly stumbled across open fields.

The railhead loomed up suddenly, lit now by starlight poking through a break in the black ceiling. And there, barely visible, was a Sheffield handcar. No Name swiftly realized it had carried Marcus Penn here—to his doom—and was intended to take him back. The tough foreman knew how to put miles under the wheels.

Maybe it was an opportunity.

"Sit, while I look," he said.

Schuster settled on the car, his bag beside him, while No Name circled the area, looking for whatever there was to see. He saw nothing. The empty site sat in the dark, abandoned. He sat down on the car, beside the barber.

"This changes things. I need to figure it out."

"I wouldn't know how . . ."

"I might go with you. Take you to Fort Laramie, the telegraph. This was Marcus Penn's way out."

"God in heaven."

"I would take some bad news with me. With us."

"On this thing?"

"The walking beam works up, down, turning the wheels. We could be in Fort Laramie before dawn."

"I'm not much good at this business."

"I'll do most of it. You can spell me now and then. It's heavy work, especially on grades, but we get a break on slopes."

"So then, what happens if a train is coming, eh?"

"Two men can usually tip this off the rails."

"So the train comes around a bend and hits us?"

"It would be the work train, flat cars in front of the engine, flagman in the first car, ready to signal. And maybe ten miles an hour, if that."

No Name studied the car, the wooden brake handle, and it all looked fine. Schuster was worried about this sort of travel, but he would get used to it. But what might happen in Fort Laramie was anyone's guess—including the possibility that no one would believe them.

"Let's go, Mr. Schuster. Watch me, and learn."

It was not going to be comfortable. He helped the barber settle, and then took hold of the beam, and began pumping. The car groaned, squeaked, and settled into an uncomfortable rattle. It was a hard-used device. Still, as No Name pumped, the handcar gained some speed, until it was rolling about eight miles an hour.

Schuster watched, studied the rising moon, and after a bit stood, and volunteered a spell at the rocker. No Name let him. Schuster would soon feel better about this strange flight from terror. The man did well, and lasted a mile before he began to wheeze. But they gained a mile, and another, and climbed a grade, and coasted down the other side, and the moon rose, giving them more light. It would be a long trip.

A sort of rhythm caught No Name, and made his labor easier.

"What happened in the courthouse?"

"Curiosity, I should know better. I saw the man arrive, and walk in, and he had a black case, or portfolio, and I knew that the time had come, so I went to have a look. There they were. He was showing them the official letter, explaining it all, and how he'd been sent by the Railroad, and also the Land Office. The judge, the sheriff, and Dent the clerk, they read this thing, and asked a few questions. And then it all happened so fast. Hardly time for a bolt of lightning to strike the earth, and they landed on your friend the foreman, and then they saw me, and I was witnessing what they didn't want anyone to see." He shrugged. "Simple enough. It is easy to catch a barber."

No Name could picture it. No imagination was needed. It had all lasted for a minute or two, and that settled Marcus Penn's fate.

"It was a sad thing. Mr. Penn, he knew his fate, and he fought hard, and the look on his face, sir, I'll never forget. He knew all about these men and their plans, and how he was the messenger from the railroad, and they grabbed me, the barber who had seen this, and I feared for my fate."

No Name pumped the handcar up another slight grade, and let it roll down the far side, while he let his weary body rest. At that point they were near the river. He let the car wind down and it creaked to a stop.

"What is this?"

"We'll take a break. I want to wash in the river, maybe eat some of JimBob's hard-boiled eggs and pretzels."

They headed for the silvery flow, scared up a deer, and washed in the chill snow-melt water. They would reach the telegraph in a few hours, and then hell would break loose.

CHAPTER SEVENTEEN

They rounded the bend and saw Fort Laramie ahead, softly lit in early light. A work train occupied the rails ahead, a string of loaded flatcars followed by an engine. Another train rested behind, that one simply an engine with two elegant, enameled private cars.

No Name was worn down. Pumping a handcar was harder than he knew, and the barber wasn't much help. He stopped ahead of the lead flatcar, which was laden with rails. A faint breakfast smell lowered over the busy site. He saw few people. Mitgang Schuster clambered down, stretched, and gathered his burlap bag with its remnants of his life.

"You hiring on?" a man asked.

"No, we need to talk to the bosses."

The man thumbed them toward the two shining passenger cars to the rear. No Name walked slowly, hurting from a long night forcing the heavy handcar forward. It had taken longer than he had expected.

There didn't seem to be many workers around; far fewer than the old crew, now dissipated. The stool was down and the parlor car steps open. No Name smelled bacon.

He knocked. A lumpy man who had jammed himself into a yielding business suit appeared above, and eyed them.

"Hiring at the front car," he said.

"Not that. I have some bad news, from Throat-latch."

"Yeah, what?"

"Your man, Marcus Penn, is dead."

"Say that over."

"This is the town's barber, Mr. Schuster. I worked with the railhead crew and hung on in Throatlatch. We came on the handcar, all night, to talk about this."

"Penn and the marshal were due here this morning. So what's the story?"

Somehow, No Name and the barber coughed out the events that had driven them here, which the boss listened, a growing smile on his face.

"Dead, eh? That takes the cake," he said. "What's your game?"

"Your messenger's dead, hanged, and your company faces more trouble."

The lumpy boss yelled to someone. "Hey, Junior, hear this."

Another boss, rail thin, with patent leather black shoes shining brightly, appeared with a fork in hand, chewing some breakfast.

"Okay, try it again," lumpy said.

Somehow, Schuster found the voice to tell about Penn's arrival, the meeting in the Wellbred County building, his curiosity, and then watching it all fall apart, in horror. "And they took me, too. And almost strung me up, sir."

"Yeah, and who else was there?"

"In the cell. Your supervisors, McGee and Parson, looking bad, sirs, very bad."

Lumpy shook his head. "Is this a racket of yours?"

"Who am I talking to, sirs?" No Name asked.

"Sharp, that's me, and Hollister, whose old man owns the outfit."

"We came all night to tell you this."

"Where's the marshal? Penn and the federal marshal went together. Handcars, it takes two to Tango, right?"

"There was no marshal there that I saw, sirs," Schuster said.

Hollister smiled. "We'll hire anyone who can walk and talk. Report down at the work train. They're pulling out after they get steam up and should be at the railhead around noon."

"I'm trying hard to tell you something, sir," No Name said.

"So am I, pal," the big gun replied.

"My scrambled eggs are getting cold," said Sharp, who then vanished into the lacquered interior.

No Name watched the pair vanish, and then

turned to the barber. Tears were collecting in Schuster's eyes.

No Name felt more worn than he could remember. He steered the barber toward the front of the train, past a handful of Fort Laramie soldiers policing the grounds, and past the first engine, a Baldwin two-eight, where firemen were building steam. Then they passed car after car laden with ties, rails, tools, kitchen camp stuff, and tents.

"I'm hiring on. I hope you will too," he said.

"What is left for me, eh?"

They found a team leader. No Name would work on the grading crew, Schuster would work in the kitchen. They had led Throatlatch, and now they were going back. No Name thought that it was the story of his life.

Twenty or thirty laborers made themselves comfortable on rails and ties and kegs, and then the work train whistled, and chuffed slowly west, covering familiar ground.

"So where's the handcar?" Schuster asked.

"On a flatcar. It took six big men to lift it."

The other train, with the big shots and their purple cars, didn't follow.

No Name fought his melancholia a while, and then stretched out on some crossties, and tried to rest, which the clattering old cars pushed upriver. His life had been nothing but dead ends, and futile efforts that led nowhere. Schuster pulled into himself, no doubt wondering why he was on his way back to the town that had nearly hanged him.

With the sun at its zenith, the train edged up to the railhead, and the flagmen signaled a halt. No one greeted the train. No armed men wearing badges opposed the crew. He saw no single man waiting, someone who might be a United States marshal.

"We should be all right here, Mitgang, but not in town," he said. The barber had turned pale.

Schuster shook his head. The new straw bosses didn't waste a minute. One summoned the kitchen crew to start hauling boxes and rolling barrels. Another put No Name to work dragging shovels and picks and wheelbarrows and sledges forward. Still others began carrying the heavy ties, one by one, and unloading them along the right-of-way. The big men in the rail crew wrestled bolts and plates and spikes into place. It was hot hard toil.

Then one of the new supervisors, Mick Malone, approached No Name. "Where's Penn? He's supposed to be here. Junior Hollister, he told me you had a crazy story."

"What did he say?"

"That you two are nuttier than fruitcakes."

"Then let's leave it that way."

"Lissen, Bright, don't mess with me."

No Name sighed. "Dead. Hanged by the big-wigs in town."

Malone laughed. "Tell me again tomorrow."

All that afternoon the crews pulled and tugged equipment into place. Tomorrow they would start building a railroad again. It would go slowly; there weren't many workers on hand.

Late in the afternoon, a gray-haired man on horse rode in, leading a mule with a doe tied onto it. There would be venison. No Name had never seen this hunter before. He was clean-shaven, wearing Levi Straus jeans, ranchers' boots, and a wide-brimmed hat. The hunter helped to hang the carcass from a cottonwood branch, surveyed the new camp with care, and then rode away. The man was utterly unlike the buck-skinned straggle-toothed hunters the railroad had employed before.

No Name kept an eye on the barber, who seemed to do his work well enough. That night, in spite of being exhausted because of a hard trip, he quietly laced his boots and slipped away into the deep gloom of a moon-sliver light. The trail to town was silent. He didn't know what he would do. He slid silently along shadowed streets. Not even the county building had a burning lamp in it. The gallows were empty. The ugly cross-bar blocked a bit of starlit sky, and made him shudder. That led him to hike up a side street to the growing cemetery, and look for a new grave.

The fresh grave of a man who shed tears as they manhandled him into place on the trap. The grave was there, all right, at the end of the row, raw dirt heaped up in a hurry.

Marcus Penn's eternal resting place.

He wanted to talk to Marcus, but didn't know what to say. But it felt right just to sit there and pay his respects to a good man, the victim of greed and some sort of cult.

"Marcus was a fine man," a male voice said nearby.

That startled No Name, and he flattened himself.

"No need for that. I know who you are. I came with Marcus on the handcar. That's a job and a half to move."

"The federal marshal."

"Just now, the railroad's hunter."

No Name processed that, not getting all the jigsaw pieces in place.

"We'll talk about it later. I want to know everything you can tell me about the judge, and the rest, and the cult, the New Dawn group."

Now there was a man present, a few yards away, but No Name didn't trust him. "What did you bring to the railhead on the mule?" he asked.

"A doe. I helped string her up to the cotton-wood."

"I don't know much. But I've a lot to tell you about this place. If you're who I hope you are."

"I'm going to show you my badge. Here's a lucifer. Scratch it when you're ready."

No Name did. The match flared. The badge glowed brassy, and faded.

"They almost hanged your friend Schuster, too. Why did they let him go?"

"You'd need to ask the judge that. He's the strangest man I've met. As bad as they come, but there's more to him than that. His wife won't leave him."

"That's a cult for you," the marshal said.

"Why weren't you with Penn yesterday?"

"My employers, the Justice Department, has larger concerns, and I was renting some horses to begin having a look. What name shall I call you?"

"What name do you know me as?"

"No Name. Ever since you were orphaned and handed around. Or would you prefer J. Arnold Bright?" He chuckled. "A barber listens to his customers."

"I don't know who I am. But maybe I'll know, and have a name. I'd like one."

"What does it feel like?"

"Like I'm no one and everyone. But I want to be someone."

"I'm Tor," he said. "And between us, we have some work to do here."

CHAPTER EIGHTEEN

Nothing happened. No Name waited for the sheriff with a line of deputies to block the way again, but they didn't show up. The sun rose on an empty prairie, serene under misty skies. They would build rail this day, and enter the ground claimed by the judge and his bunch.

As the sun climbed, the other train showed up, dragging its purple private cars, and the two bigwigs clattered down steel stairs to the humble ground. Art Sharp and Junior Hollister strode forward, past the work train, only to find an empty field. No Name thought they looked disappointed, a pair of hotshots who were going to put the lawmen in their place. They prowled the railhead, stalked into the disputed turf, peered at horizons looking for the enemy, and finally gave up.

Then Art Sharp spotted No Name.

"You again. So where is Marcus Penn?"

"I told you yesterday."

"That's rich. When he shows, tell him we're looking for him. We want the rundown."

No Name chose not to reply. Art Sharp eyed him, looking for an excuse to deck him, but subsided. The muscles in his shoulders rippled his suit and threatened to split the seams. The man probably needed a full-time seamstress to mend his damaged suits.

"We're rolling out of here. There's no problem here. We've got things to do," Sharp said.

No Name nodded.

The pair eyed the work train, the workmen, the breakfast fires, and then retreated. No Name had the cheery idea that Sheriff Clemson would have lifted Sharp by the heels, shaken loose change out of his pockets, and sent him packing, while Junior stood by, giggling.

But that delectable fantasy faded as the pair boarded their purple parlor palaces, and their train began backing its way to Fort Laramie. Some people went through life rear-end first.

Mick Malone began his quiet command, and soon the thinned ranks of workers were grading and graveling roadbed, laying down ties, and hauling heavy rails into place. Ahead, a survey crew was pushing into the disputed land, and driving stakes.

About ten, the first rails were spiked down and the shining steel penetrated the disputed land. There still was no sign of the judge or sheriff. That's how the sweaty day proceeded, and No Name wondered whether the Wellbred County officials even knew that the railroad was building line again.

But they had to know. They were given the Federal Land Bureau's letter and supporting documents and findings. Maybe they were simply caving in, but No Name didn't believe that. Something was afoot.

It was Thursday, and that meant that the judge would preside over his usual meeting of the New Dawn group. No Name intended to go if he could slip out a little early.

He found Mitgang Schuster scrubbing tin serving plates.

"You surviving?"

"They found out I could use a blade, so they had me gut the doe. I didn't take any pride in it."

"I'm going to Throatlatch. I want to hear what the judge is saying to his New Dawn bunch."

Schuster drew a line across his neck. "I think I will stick to the kettles and stews."

"I'll see what's left of your shop. And if they left the barber tools, I'll collect them and bring them."

Schuster gazed solemnly. "Not always do I have such friends."

"There's a man called Tor I talked to. I could hardly see him. But he's a friend."

"I know him."

"If he comes in with more meat, tell him I went to town, and why."

Schuster nodded.

He found Mick Malone.

"Tell me when it's twenty to five. I'm going into town. I have good reasons."

The team leader stared. "I knew it. I knew it. I read people pretty well. When you can, tell me about this."

At the appointed time, Malone waved at No Name, who abandoned his pickaxe and washed up.

The trip to Throatlatch was uneventful, even though No Name was on his guard. He walked along the slumbering main street, feeling that the town was somehow disjointed, cockeyed, like a big scab over a bad wound.

People were congregating at the odd structure ahead; well-dressed people, even some women, and cologne was in the air. He wore shabby clothes, and intended to sit in a workman's place, rear row. Instead of the dozen or so he had seen previously, this Thursday meeting had drawn fifty. The judge eyed him briefly, and adjusted the white stole over his billowing judicial robe. If this wasn't a church of some sort, it sure seemed like one.

Clyde Clemson arrived, with Carolina on his arm. The sight of her melted No Name. She wore a stern gray summer suit, with a jabot at her throat. Her gaze caught his, and held, as she did the mental arithmetic of what might bring him to this meeting, or put him for or against her.

She seemed puzzled. No Name nodded, and she

smiled warily, almost ready to switch to a frown on demand. But a galvanic current, something he had never experienced, coursed through him like a spark. Some sort of invisible telegraph ran between them, and his head was jammed with Morse Code.

But she was not the only woman to catch No Name's eye. There, in a front row, sat Lydia Howard, wife of E Pluribus Unum Howard. She had seen him first, and gazed directly at him, her gray eyes absorbing his work-torn clothing. He wondered if she could explain her presence to him, or whether he could explain himself to her. She was as gentle and mysterious there, in that rundown hall, as she had been in the judge's parlor. She also was an island of serenity in that sea-tossed hall.

The judge withdrew a gold turnip watch, eyed it, and stepped to his lectern. The New Dawn was prompt. A lavish bouquet of ruby roses stood in front of the lectern. They were shocking in a raw town like Throatlatch.

He welcomed them all to what he described as the greatest event of their lives.

"The beginning of everything," is how he put it.

"Right now, this moment, is the start of everything," he said. "The old will fall away, the darkness of mankind, the wickedness, the empty quest for possessions, along with its greed and theft. And that will usher in the very thing we've all pined for, yearned for, ached for, as far back as we can remember. The New Dawn. A world without hurt, without dark memories, with the scent of sweetness blanketing the land."

That was a heap of change, No Name thought. But the people around him were eager for it, aching to hear about it, their gazes focused on the judge.

"Property will vanish," he said, "vanish, and the very idea of ownership will slip into the cesspools of history."

He paused, amiably, letting it soak in. "Today, the railroad is pushing its way into our communal land, but it doesn't matter. It will soon find itself communally operated, by the New Dawn."

That seemed a bit beyond No Name's reasoning, but he was there to absorb what he could, and to find out how this glimpse of paradise was connected to the gallows and graves that made Throatlatch like no other place.

"When no one owns anything, everyone owns everything," the judge said. "You own each other, but so do others own you. Each loving wife will enjoy a hundred husbands, and each loving husband will enjoy a hundred wives."

He let that sink in. No Name wondered whether any of the women present wished to own a hundred husbands. He wished he could read Carolina's mind, and Lydia's mind, but they both sat in granitic composure, their private thoughts beyond reach.

"They have come with their railroad, and have taken the land, but they will find, come the New Dawn, that all of us own it, and it owns all of us. We will all own ranches with their herds, and flocks with their sheep, and ranchers and sheepherders will own our doctors and dentists and merchants. We will all own each other, and nothing at all."

No Name wondered whether he would own a name when the New Dawn came. Probably not. No one would need a name, because no one was a private person in this new world. But somehow none of this was helping him. What he wanted to know was how the New Dawn could deprive innocent people of their lives, like that poor lady they hanged because she lacked something or other.

Why were these people devouring all this? Did they lack critical sense? He stared about him, studied rapt faces, watched the women who would soon have a hundred husbands, watched their spouses eye other women with a fresh curiosity in their gazes. He couldn't say, but he knew that having no name now gave him some perspective. The whole business was horse apples.

That telegraph he was imagining was clicking in his head now, and he somehow conjured up the message. Help me. Take me away. Save me.

151

I don't want a hundred husbands. I don't know you, but I know you are the one who can help me.

I will, he thought. I will. He glanced at Carolina just as she glanced at him, and the whole message was sent and received in that moment. She smiled, ever so slightly, and he nodded.

"In the New Dawn," the judge was saying, "all work, all hardships and burdens, will be shared and fall so lightly that no one is burdened. The New Dawn may not eliminate the need to launder sheets and mangle them, or clean vaults, or hoe the cabbage patch, but there will be a hundred workers for every task, and harmony will prevail."

No Name wondered where a hundred women would volunteer to launder hotel sheets, or where a hundred men would volunteer to empty outhouse vaults. Or, for that matter, how the New Dawn would make human life better than the struggle people endured now. And what of the woman who just didn't want a hundred husbands or a hundred children?

As bad as all this was, nothing here answered the question that badgered him: what did the New Dawn have to do with this town's murderous ways, with its casual hangings, with its grand theft, with its lack of pity?

"And how will the New Dawn improve the fate of the ill, the injured, the crippled, the blind and deaf, those whose bodies are eaten up by consumption or malaria? The New Dawn has an answer. We all own tragedies. We all will suffer the wounds life brings to human bodies. And no one escapes, which means all disease and disaster is shared during the new dawn, and the help given to the needful shall be multiplied for every sick person shall enjoy a hundred nurses.

"And now, treasured colleagues, let us turn to the dark present, when the world seems to cling to property as if it were more important than joy. The New Dawn has started right here, but it will swiftly spread, layer upon layers, mile upon mile, into wider circles. Providence has chosen this little place, Wellbred County, to transform the whole world. Watch it happen. Watch it overturn the proud, the evil, the demonic."

No Name wanted to ask how, but he held his peace. At least the judge was connecting the ugly present to the idyllic future.

"It requires perfect unity, a flawless agreement of those of us now present, to bring it to light. It requires us all to surrender our property, our savings, our real estate, our homes, our companies, our livestock, our very lives, to the New Age, and do it all voluntarily, with a big heart and absolute certitude."

So that was it, or part of it, No Name thought. Turn it all over to the judge and his cohorts. Empty your purses, pass along your wives, hand it over. But what about the hangings?

"Everything has a price," the judge intoned. "There cannot be a New Dawn without a sunset. What lies in the path must be set aside until the road to the sublime is unimpeded."

Some of the audience stirred. Lydia was looking at No Name.

"Dear friends," the judge said, "there sits in this very sanctuary one whose heart is not in accord with the rest of our hearts. It is time for that person to make himself known, so we all may see who disturbs our dreams. I invite that person to stand, and leave unharmed."

People craned to look at one another. No Name thought he heard a clock ticking. He knew, too, that some depended on him. Maybe two people did. So he stood, faced them all.

The judge, the sheriff, a couple of deputies stared at the land broker.

Then Carolina Clemson stood up proudly. "I am not one of you," she said. "I will leave now."

She began to make her way out, but the sheriff grabbed her hard, and yanked her back, half undoing her gray skirt until it threatened to drop. He slammed her down. She shrank, clutching herself.

"I believe she's allowed to leave unharmed," No Name said.

"She's not leaving," the sheriff said. "Unharmed or harmed."

CHAPTER NINETEEN

So much for Paradise. No Name stood in the grimy street, watching dust devils spin dirt and layer it over the town. He wasn't sure whether the New Dawn intended to lock everyone in or kick everyone out. He thought of Carolina, yanked hard into a life she wanted to flee. He thought of the look in her eyes that said she was close. They didn't know each other, and yet they did.

He drifted to JimBob's Saloon. The proprietor eyed him and drew some suds.

"I hear the railroad's building," he said.

"It is, and no one's trying to stop it."

"Maybe that's because of the marshal." JimBob knew a lot more than he was saying.

No Name described the meeting and his ejection, and the sheriff's grasping hands.

"They want property now? Donations? Looks like it's all coming to a head."

"If you can figure it out, you're smarter than I am."

JimBob eyed him, sensing an edge in his words, and headed elsewhere with a bar towel in hand. The bar was nearly empty. The regulars weren't there. He wondered about that. Maybe the town was emptying out—more free property for the New Dawn crowd.

"Where are your friends?" No Name asked.

The barkeep shook his head. "Wish I knew."

"Any talk of building a railroad station, now that the track is coming?"

"Not a word."

"You hoping to stick around?"

"It's funny. I like it here, but my cash drawer doesn't."

"I hope you'll be open next time I come to town."

"So do I."

JimBob didn't know what tomorrow would bring. No one knew. No Name didn't know either.

"I'll be here, working with the railroad. I don't know why I'm here; only that I'm compelled by some need. I'm crazy, I guess."

"The deepest needs have no name," JimBob said. "But you're here, a marshal is here, the barber's with us, I'm here, and there's more. There's a darkness here, men and women have been murdered for no reason. There's us, and maybe we can shine some light on it."

He offered a hand, and No Name shook it, and slipped into twilight.

No Name thought of one more errand before he hiked to the railhead. He walked to the Wellbred County building in twilight, saw a lit lamp within, and entered. Majestic Skinner was there. But the two prisoners weren't.

"You causing more trouble?" Skinner asked.

"Bright. J Arnold Bright. Me. Where's the two railroad men who've been in your tender care?"

"Gone. The sheriff cut them loose."

"Who?"

"With Gus Glory."

"Where are they?"

"Like they're gonna tell me?"

No Name scouted the building. McGee and Parson weren't there.

"Did the sheriff say anything?"

"Good times are coming, he said."

"Where's he?"

"At that meeting."

No Name nodded and hurried into the night, a dread building in him. He raced toward the gallows on some crazy impulse, but the gallows were silent and empty. Good times weren't coming, not as long as the scaffold stood there. He felt some ghostly sensation that prickled the hair on his neck, but the gallows kept their secrets.

The nearby meeting hall, mysterious and makeshift, stood dark and empty. The meeting had broken up long before. He stood there, the mystery of Throatlatch before him, a strange cult's hall and the gallows only a few yards apart.

He called softly toward the river bottoms, and got no response.

"They're gone," said the judge.

No Name whirled. The judge stood behind him, in his usual business suit.

"Good times are coming. Too bad you wouldn't believe it. Now you're trapped in the fallen world. You're curious, of course. We let the railroad foremen go; we simply needed them to make sure there was good faith on the part of the railroad and the government. But that's history. We welcome the right-of-way, and the beginning of a new world here. Now, have I satisfied your curiosity?"

"Well, no. What are your plans? Your society."

"You'll see."

"What about these gallows?"

"They'll be the first to fall. There'll be no gallows in New Dawn. No court or jail, either. Those are for the fallen. Such as yourself."

"New Dawn?"

"Throatlatch is no more. This is New Dawn, temporarily of Wyoming Territory, but that is only a first stage. New Dawn, North America. New Dawn, World."

"What will you do with the fallen?"

"You'll see."

Some instinct drove No Name to leave. The world was starting to choke him. "One last thing, sir. You've worked out something with the railroad. Why did you resist it?"

"You'll see," the judge said. And oddly, the

judge whirled away, even before No Name surrendered to his own impulses.

It was only then that he spotted Mrs. Howard, Lydia, standing in deep shadow.

He hastened away, and no one impeded him. He couldn't unscramble this, but maybe the rail men who had been imprisoned and starved and brutalized for days, might do it better. Or the marshal he had barely met. His fevered thoughts gave him no clue.

Back at the camp at the railhead, he found Mitgang Schuster, enjoying a pipe.

"I was starting to worry about you," the barber said.

"What's happened? Where are they?"

Schuster stared. "Who? No one has come."

It took No Name a while because he couldn't make sense of it, but he finally conveyed it all to Schuster, who puffed calmly.

"I think this isn't the beginning of the New Dawn, but the triumph of the old dark world, but I don't know why I think that," Mitgang Schuster said.

No Name was tired of all that. Whatever was happening could wait until morning. He thanked his friend, washed, and headed for his tent, which was stuffy in the warm night. He was exhausted, but unable to sleep, not with the moon sliding into a new orbit, and the world turned upside down. But his body soon defeated his misgivings, and he slumbered restlessly, his dreams gone back to the moment his parents had vanished when he was a child, barely old enough to know they were gone. Would he ever escape that fear? He told himself that the world had actually been kind. Strangers had fed him, handed him to others, kept the nameless boy alive. They had even comforted him when he cried. There was good among people, at least some of the time.

He was awakened at first light by shouts. Running feet. He pulled on his boots, stretched, and pushed open the canvas. Dawn lay down the rails to the east. The west still lay in night. Several workers were congregating at the railhead, the very place where the rails ended. He headed that way, wondering what new sensation was disturbing the peace. He soon found out.

The bodies of Martin McGee and Wallace Parson lay there, their throats cut.

Mick Malone showed up, took stock, and found No Name.

"Who?" he asked.

"The foremen. McGee and Parson. The ones in the Throatlatch jail."

"Why?"

"No one knows."

Malone had two men carry the bodies to a flatcar and cover them. He stood beside these two foremen, caught in someone's web, used and abused, their young lives over all too soon. Malone's face was granite.

"We'll go find out," he said.

CHAPTER TWENTY

Along the trail, No Name instructed the supervisor.

"The sheriff and his daughter, and the judge and his wife, live in big homes out of town. I'd suggest we go there, first, Sir."

"Lead the way."

By the time they reached Judge Howard's home, the foreman had a solid understanding of what had happened in Throatlatch, what had remained a mystery, and what role the judge and sheriff had played.

"I don't get it," he said. "They killed the railroad's messenger, along with the offer? Who did this?"

"Penn was hanged suddenly. That should tell you."

"We'll find out."

Mick Malone was a big man, not one to trifle with.

"We may face armed men, Sir."

"I'm a pacifist."

They were greeted by Lydia. "Why is it that I knew you were coming?" she asked. She waved them toward her porch, while Mick Malone assessed her and the place.

"The judge is off saving the world," she said. "But I have some Earl Grey; some came to town and I bought the lot. May I serve you some?"

She vanished without waiting for an answer, while No Name and the foreman settled into wicker porch chairs. Neither spoke. The view was majestic. It opened upon an anonymous land that reached infinity some hundred miles distant. It wasn't aesthetic; it wasn't purple mountain majesties, but it spoke of dominion. To live here was to own a large piece of the planet.

She returned with a tray, and engaged in her ritual.

"I'm sure you have questions," she said. "Maybe I can help. I'm a guilty bystander."

Something about that wrought a smile in Malone.

"It's explanations I need. For paradoxes."

"Sugar wrecks Earl Grey, but you're welcome to it."

"One day your husband and his colleagues, mostly county officials, stop the railroad cold. Armed men shut down the track-laying. The railroad's effort to solve the problem is met by hanging the messenger. But the next day, more or less, these people welcome the railroad, kill two innocent employees, and want to change the town from Throatlatch to New Dawn. You tell me why, please."

"Males are crazy. Women wouldn't have done it that way."

"Done what?"

"Started up heaven on earth."

"Is this a get-rich scheme?"

"It certainly is. E Pluribus would like to make Mr. Rockefeller look like a piker."

"Is that why he's asked followers to give him their property, and had driven out town people so he can pick up abandoned property?"

"I think he wants to own the railroad, too."

"Does Judge Howard think of the lives he's taken? Innocents choked for some reason, such as the town's amusement?"

"That was Throatlatch. Now it's New Dawn. He will build a railroad station down there, where pilgrims can step into his new world."

"Would he hang us now, just for his amusement?"

No Name thought that was a powerful question.

"No, not a chance. That was Throatlatch. Now it's New Dawn."

"Was Throatlatch named for the strap under a horse's neck that holds the bridle in place?"

"Absolutely. All those people were throat-latched with a bit of hemp."

She was being all too clever about murder, No Name thought. One moment, this place was all darkness, and now it's all sunlight, and the change is all in the minds of the judge and his confederates. He knew little about religion of any type, but thought he was experiencing something like it.

Mick Malone was phrasing his questions thoughtfully. He didn't sound like a prosecutor but more like a confessor.

"If you knew your husband was doing things that hurt others, did you do anything about it?"

"You're using delicate language for random murder. No, I didn't. Who should I go to, the sheriff, his colleague in all this? I wish to remind you: a woman is confined to her station. This is one of the most isolated corners of this nation, which is why the judge wishes to turn it into Utopia."

She emptied the teapot into her cup. She was the only one sipping her tea. No Name's tea simply grew cold. He couldn't explain why he rather enjoyed this woman.

She eyed Malone. "Your railroad will soon have its rails. It will soon have passenger trade as pilgrims come here. Are we done?" she asked, rising.

Malone wasn't, but he nodded, and they soon found themselves heading to the homestead next along the lane, where Carolina Clemson was being held against her will. No Name wanted to talk with her, and pushed aside romantic thoughts of rescuing her.

They strolled along the lane to the neighboring

house, admiring the view, that stretched to eternity, and offered a sense of possessing land as large as a state. To their surprise, the sheriff was present, and welcomed them heartily on his veranda. He was unarmed. There was no good reason to wear a heavy revolver in one's own quiet home.

No Name saw no sign of Carolina, and itched to see her. He wondered whether she had been hastily sent away.

"You're the railroad people, I imagine," Clemson said.

"Mick Malone. I'm running rail. And you've met my assistant. We've some questions. We're trying to lay track. One day we're rebuffed; the next day we're welcomed. Where do we stand?"

That struck No Name as a pretty discreet way of saying it.

"There's no more barrier to finishing your line. In fact, the county welcomes it," the sheriff said. "We regret the confusion. It had to do with property claims. But the federal land office straightened us out on that—some paperwork problems—and now we're ready to roll. We're even changing the town's name to New Dawn, and that's going to bring you some traffic."

"Well, fine, sir, but why did Throatlatch resist us?"

"Fear," Clemson said. "When you live in a small place, and a big, powerful corporation threatens to tear your town apart, why, sir, people worry. And as a lawman, it's my job to protect our people and make sure that the company's abiding by all our laws."

That was smooth, No Name thought, and nicely dodged realities.

Malone listened closely. He was never in a hurry. "Well, sir, what decided you and other officials to leave Throatlatch behind and, shall we say, turn over a new leaf?"

"The vision of our judge, a man with a name so unusual it rings bells. E Pluribus Unum Howard. Have you ever met a man with a name like that?"

"One made out of all," Malone said. "This change is all the judge's idea?"

"His vision, sir. He saw the future. He invited us to form a new order, to surrender all we have. This very house and land, sir, will go into the new order—when I prove it up according to the homestead laws. In a year or two, I suppose."

Malone gently shifted the topic. "Throatlatch is a tough town. Watch your step there, that's what people said."

"Yes it was. This town sits on the trail west. People come in here, and steal. They're desperadoes, half of them, looking for ways to cheat, to rob, to swipe. We didn't sit still for that. We never will."

"You got a reputation."

"Yes. Watch out around here. You'll stick your neck in the hemp."

"You applied for the Territorial Prison."

"Yes we did. But it didn't happen. And now we're New Dawn."

"And no people here ever molested a traveler?"

"I can't say that as a fact. I just had that impression. But we didn't have any crime around here."

No Name wanted to challenge that, but stayed quiet. His life had almost ended here in an isolated corner of Wyoming Territory.

"But that's all changed, Sheriff? You'll be welcoming pilgrims to New Dawn? You'll meet the trains coming in, and greet the passengers, and meet them in that meeting house the judge built? And then steer them to your nice city lots?"

"Cut that out, Malone; nothing's ever perfect. There's always a few roaches in the corners. That's why I'm here. Someone's gotta protect the pilgrims."

"And who owns this new place, New Dawn?"

"The outfit. That's what the judge is doing. He's taking possession of every piece of land we can find—abandoned, on behalf of a certain outfit. People are quitting town by the dozen."

"And you?"

"I'll keep the peace, like always."

"Who thought this up?"

"The judge. He's a reader. He went to college . . . You done now?"

168

No Name had a question. "If people don't like New Dawn, can they leave?"

"What's to stop them?"

"They could go to the train station, buy a ticket, and go?"

"They won't want to."

The sheriff rose, and Malone followed suit. The sheriff was looking itchy, and was clamming up. Clemson had a short fuse, and it was spitting sparks.

The day had turned hot. Malone decided not to go into Throatlatch for now. He had track to lay and a schedule to keep.

"What do you make of it?" No Name asked.

"It's either a fraud or a racket, or both. A church or a jail, or both."

"Do you think travelers bled Throatlatch, or the tough little town bled the people heading west?"

"I'm not ready to say. I don't know whether New Dawn is another version of Throatlatch, either. But one thing I'm sure of. When we run the rails through, and people buy a ticket to New Dawn, hoping for a new life out here away from everything, they ain't gonna find it."

"Are you going to report all this to the big bosses?"

"Yeah, I have to. They want to know. We're putting up wire, you know. Poles going up from Fort Laramie. They're not going to get trapped by silence. Within days, this'll be connected to the rest of the world, and the railroad will know everything as fast as it happens."

"The New Dawn outfit won't like that at all."

"That's one good reason to do it," the railroad man said. "It'll make 'em behave."

They hiked back to the railhead, lost in silence. Mick Malone was trying to make sense of it and running into all the contradictions. No Name could sense the way the man was wrestling with himself. He'd never run into a Utopia before.

The crews were working hard. The surveyors had more stakes in the ground. The grading outfit had leveled another hundred yards. The track layers were settling crossties and pouring gravel. But there was something new. A dozen or so abandoned dogs were sniffing and whining, starving to death as residents fled.

CHAPTER TWENTY-ONE

No Name worked hard at the railhead, glad to have some cash coming in. Nothing impeded the crew as it pushed the track ahead through the long spring days. It seemed almost too quiet. One day the supply train backed its way to the nearest resupply depot, and returned with a change in the plans. There would be a siding installed at Throatlatch. The supply train brought the switch points, frogs, guard rails, and switch levers. That made sense. The siding would allow two trains to bring supplies. But No Name wondered why the siding was being built next to a dying town.

With some pay in hand, he headed for Throatlatch one eve, only to discover that the shabby little town was almost deserted. Breezes gusted dust into storefronts. JimBob's was closed and silent. He peered into the dusky interior, and found no bottles on the shelves, nothing but a hollow shell of a business. He wondered what had happened to the barkeep, his friend and ally. He wandered to the grocery, and found it open but almost bare. Tillotson, the proprietor was there.

"I'm selling out. Can't run a store with nothing coming in," he said.

"How will people feed themselves?"

"What people?" the grocer replied.

No one was in the Wellbred County building either, but county records lay on the counter, available to anyone. It was too dark to read much, but someone had been recording real estate transfers, and in every case, abandoned or tax-delinquent land was being claimed by some entity called the New Dawn. So the judge and his cohorts were sweeping up the remains. The jail cell doors swung open, but No Name found no key to them. He slipped into the street, somehow troubled and desolated. Throatlatch had been an ugly, jerry-built town, but it had breathed life and hope once, but now a great sorrow seemed to haunt it, and the dry air of Wyoming was slicing it away, bit by bit.

He started to leave, but noticed the gallows. They still stood, unharmed, malevolent, disturbing, and swept clean of dust . . . by what appeared to be a broom.

"Just in case," said Sheriff Clemson, in the shadows.

The sheriff, who was growing a belly, emerged. He was unarmed, which startled No Name.

"Town's gone," No Name said.

"New Dawn's just getting going," the sheriff said. "The railroad's going to build a siding so we can get folks in here. A couple of weeks from now, after the track and siding are finished, we'll start inviting people in, and then this place—it'll be the beginning of a new world."

"Invite them in?"

"We'll do a little advertising. You know, little classified ads in the papers back east. Full of hope and promise."

"What'll you charge?"

"They've got to travel on their own dime. But we'll get them rolling here. Just wait a few months—what's your name again?"

"Bright."

"Yeah, Bright, you just wait. Maybe you'll want to join us."

"I'm building the railroad, Sir."

"Well, that's good." He dug around in his shirt, and pulled out a rectangular slip of paper, colored blue. It looked like a greenback, but wasn't. "Keep it. It's an invitation to begin your new life here," the sheriff said. "It's a New Dawn promissory note, that'll be worth a dollar when the time comes."

"It'll buy stuff?"

"That's the miracle of it. One New Dawn note will be worth more than scores of greenbacks. We don't know how much, but plenty. So give it some thought."

Clemson tipped his straw hat and drifted away

through the hollow cathedral of New Dawn, empty streets and dusty buildings.

No Name marveled. This deadly man sounded so soft and quiet and earnest that it was some sort of transformation, like he had switched souls. It seemed real. Somehow the sheriff who strung up living, innocent mortals for the town's amusement had turned himself into a St. Francis, or maybe a Buddha.

No Name abandoned the town, but was not at ease. What had become of JimBob, and what had happened to the United States marshal he knew only as Tor? Why was there no one in the county office, which was a Territorial entity? He decided to return some afternoon when he had some daylight, and look at that tax and real estate record. Maybe it would explain things. There were more questions than ever crowding his mind. The siding was a mystery. Why was the railroad putting it there, in the middle of Throatlatch? Who had been talking to whom?

Well, enough. A gentle night carried him to the railhead, which was now just outside of town, a few minutes away.

"Would you like company?"

Another voice in the gloom. The barber.

"I came to see," Schuster said. "Got a little time off. Look at this."

He was carrying a cloth sack, and showed No

174

Name a collection of costly German barbering tools.

"Maybe I am in business again. Maybe not."

"I think your building's been taken from you."

"They'll give me another. They'll want a barber. Why did they not take these? Worth good money."

"I just talked to the sheriff. He was unarmed. It was like seeing the sun rise in the west."

"What was he doing?"

"Someone had just swept the dust off the gallows."

Schuster processed that a while. "Maybe it is time to move to Denver."

"What do you know about these groups? I've heard of them. Cults."

"I shave hair, not the mind."

No Name dug into his pocket, found the note, and handed it to the barber.

"It's blue, and it's called a New Dawn promissory note, and the sheriff himself gave it to me. He said it'll be worth a lot more than greenbacks some day."

The barber fingered it. "Too dark. Show it to me tomorrow. But this tells me something. Some cults just want to carve out an enclave that will let them do what they want without having to deal with outsiders. Like the Mormons. They mostly want to be left alone. Or have their own state, Deseret, the beehive. That's their emblem, the beehive. But not here. New money means a new nation. Or some sort of walled world."

"That's more than I can cope with. You must have a college degree."

Schuster sighed. "A barber listens, and that turns into a college degree sometimes. But no one's ever talked to me about this. Carving out a new place."

"Who's at the center of this do you think?"

Schuster sighed. "I am not a prophet, young man. Don't look to me. But I would say the judge. No, not him. His wife, Lydia. The judge bends with the wind."

Somehow, that ran a jolt through No Name. Not Lydia.

It troubled him so much he had nothing more to say, at least for the moment. They slipped into a darkened camp. The pleasant spring night added cheer to the railroad builders, and most of them watched the last light of day blue out in the northwest.

Mick Malone found him. "What did you see in there?"

"Town's dead, empty houses. The grocer's selling his stock and leaving. The sheriff was around, keeping the gallows clean."

Malone grinned. "He needs something to do."

"They've got big dreams there."

"We all do."

"They're counting on the railroad to bring in the pilgrims."

"And the railroad's counting on them to earn some cash."

No Name headed for the kitchen tent, and found what he needed: a kerosene lamp. He scratched a match and soon had a light within the neglected chimney.

He put the New Dawn money on the table, and flattened it. Then he began to blot it up. This was a New Dawn dollar. Legal tender. The corners had a numerical one, and under it was the word, Unum. An oval portrait displayed the image of a woman, but he could not identify her. She was not dressed in classic, or Grecian robes, but in current clothing. He raced through the images he had seen in Harper's or Leslie's and other magazines, but could not connect. She was not named. She was alone, without a man standing behind her. She wore her hair in braids that were coiled on top of her head to form a sort of crown. No doubt it meant something, but it was beyond No Name's grasp.

Along the base of the blue bill were familiar words: E Pluribus Unum. One formed from all. The reverse side was even stranger, and seemed to be not currency but a contract, with two blank lines that could be employed to designate the donor and recipient. Apparently, to transfer a Unum, the donor signed his own name, and the

177

name of the recipient. That struck No Name as a costly way to do business. And it wasn't really money.

He stuffed the Unum note in his pocket, and turned down the lamp.

When he stepped into starlight, an idea came to him. He knew why the United States marshal was hanging around here, and why he was so shadowy.

CHAPTER TWENTY-TWO

Carolina was standing beside the right-of-way, looking for No Name. She had a wicker basket in hand. He recognized her, and set down his shovel.

"Well, hello," she said. "I brought you a little lunch."

She smiled warily. It all seemed odd, but pleasant. She was dressed in starch this noon. Her white shirtwaist was stiff, and so was her gray skirt. He nodded, welcoming the break, and left his crew. Ahead a ways, a new railroad station sat, hastily thrown up by Throatlatch's remaining people. It had been finished even before the railroad siding was complete.

She led him to it, and he found a ticket counter within, and some pews, gotten from somewhere far away. God wasn't within five hundred miles of Throatlatch. It was good to escape the sun and wind.

"There now. Some sandwiches. I hope this is all right."

"It's a treat. May I call you Carolina?"

"You may."

She handed him a beef sandwich, fresh bread.

He had no way to wash his hands, but took it gamely, even as she bit into a daintier one of her own.

"I haven't seen you since—that evening."

"I'm so embarrassed. I had it coming."

The beef was good, tender and lightly salted. He eyed her again. Something had changed.

"Isn't it wonderful? This new town rising from the old. I'm so glad to be a part of it."

"Is this a change of heart?"

"Yes. I was so blind. There was beauty in the world, before my eyes, but I didn't see it. The New Dawn changes everything. You'll see."

"You're planning on staying?"

"I was being a child."

Those gentle eyes softly studied him. He, in turn, found a different person. He hadn't known the earlier Carolina well; a few fleeting encounters, but had thought she was desperate, feeling oppressed, and aching to go away, anywhere. But this was no rebel.

She sensed his confusion, and smiled.

"I was thinking of myself, and things. That was the old world that's fallen away, and not the new one. I hope, when you've finished building your railroad, you'll come here. It'll be the sweetest, kindest thing that ever happened to you."

"I don't know that I'd want to spend my days in Throatlatch."

"Not Throatlatch. New Dawn. It's more than

the Territory. It's more than the country. It's the beginning of everything a mortal can be, when all hurt and hunger fall away."

"And your father will still be sheriff?"

"Well, ah, not exactly. We're ending Wellbred County and starting New Dawn. He'll watch over us, but mostly to protect us from people who haven't seen the light. The judge, too. He won't be a judge any more; he'll be our higher friend, our counselor and advisor. Not even New Dawn will be perfect, you see. A good counselor will help all of us, especially those who stray."

"And this is what you've discussed with your father?"

"Yes, and others. I'm ready. And it's my heart's desire that you will find your way here, and join us."

The sandwich was good. He could have devoured another. She smiled, and folded her linens into her basket.

"Is anyone left in Throatlatch?"

"You shouldn't call it that name. It has a new name, filled with hope and joy. There's no one there. The last one—who turned out to be the very image of the serpent in Eden, was, well, sent on his way."

No Name didn't like that. "Who was he?"

"Oh, you don't need to know. His evil place of business is closed, and he lies quietly in the old Throatlatch cemetery, which is where he deserved to be."

No Name felt a jolt run through him. "Sent on his way?"

"Yes, one last cleansing, in the dark of a midnight, with my, ah, father doing what was necessary. We'll let that platform stand as a monument and reminder, because human nature is not perfect, and there is always the chance that someone may despise Eden."

"Did this person have a brother?"

"A half-brother, and a bad influence on me. I am fortunate to have an observant father, who kept me from peril."

If Carolina had been an inviting stranger once, now she was something beyond his experience. He knew little about women, because that is how life tossed its bones his way, but here was beautiful Carolina, smiling gently.

"Do you know Lydia Howard?" he asked.

"She's like a mother to me. She's so knowing. She seems to know everything."

"Do you have a mother?"

"She died of consumption when I was a girl."

"What's going to happen next?"

"Well, they tell me as soon as the siding is built and the railroad is ready, people—pilgrims, really—will step off the train cars right here, at this little station, and we will greet them and give them a parcel of land. There's no ownership in New Dawn, but each person or family will be given the use of something belonging to the whole of us, and enjoy life the way it was meant to be."

"Will they work?"

"Who wants to work? No, they will be free to sing songs, paint portraits, compose poems, and walk with nature at our shoulder."

"I can imagine," No Name said.

She looked hurt.

"Someone has to grow food, herd animals, build shelters, scrape roads, sell tickets, drive wells, butcher meat . . ."

"I worry about that too," she said. "It seems a little idealistic. But we must have ironclad confidence, and then it will all work out."

"Somebody has to work."

"They say that the Indians were put on the reservations for that." She smiled softly, as if resolving everything in single thought.

"Will the Indians have any say about it?"

"We'll see," she said.

It was past time when he was due to return to his crew. He rose abruptly, nodded curtly, thanked her, and left her to shake the crumbs out of her white linen. There was one task that was burning in him. He hiked into Throatlatch, which now lay adjacent to the railroad, and headed for the cemetery. A new, unmarked grave completed a long, thin line. Another sunset.

"JimBob," he said, torn apart.

He stormed to the empty Wellbred courthouse, found the register of deeds, and noted a transfer of real estate to the New Dawn Society. The last holding in Throatlatch had vanished.

No Name felt alone. More alone than ever, more alone than when he was abandoned as a child. And no one to turn to. Well, yes, there was one: Mitgang Schuster, whose kindness, virtue, faith and courage make him a man of steel. And he needed to talk to Mick Malone.

No Name toiled through a hot afternoon, feeling detached from the world. When at last the supper gong sounded, he washed up and headed for the caboose that served as a rolling office. Mick Malone was there, totting up workdays for the paymaster.

"Have a seat, whoever you're calling yourself."

No Name sat, and told him what he had learned, and what lay in the little Throatlatch cemetery. Malone listened intently.

"You know, don't you, that the railroad's up to its eyeballs in all this?"

"I figured. Suddenly the bosses were cutting deals."

"It's a quick bonanza. Traffic to the New Dawn, along with tons of supplies, money coming in even before they get the track laid into Montana Territory. But it's temporary. And this outfit is going to have to do a lot better than printing

184

up its fake currency and passing it to suckers. Its blue money will light a few cigars, but isn't good for anything else. We're going to be paid in dollars or gold or there won't be anything going into New Dawn. No one in the railroad thinks New Dawn will last more than a few months. It simply serves the larger purpose of the company, to open up a lot of land in the Northwest. It's not really a blot on the railroad."

No Name wasn't so sure. "I just wanted you to know. And that's a friend of mine down there in that grave. And Throatlatch had one last hanging after all, a midnight murder."

The head man stared out the caboose window. "I'm glad you told me. I'll be thinking it over. There may be a few steps we can take. I'm not making any promises. I've got supervisors looking over my shoulder. But damn . . ." he shook his head. "I'm with you, and I'll do what I can. It's odd, isn't it? I mean, how close heaven and hell are. Sometimes you can't even tell them apart."

CHAPTER TWENTY-THREE

The railhead crew didn't get far that afternoon. They'd hit a shallow drainage, and debated what to do with it. Mick Malone finally settled the matter.

"Timber it," he said.

"That'll cost us a day," a young, new straw boss said. "Do it," Malone said. "And the next time you ride these rails after a week of rain, be glad you've got rails under you."

That was Malone. No Name watched the foreman vanish toward his caboose, even as workers headed for the flatcar with timbers on it, and others started to work out the postholes. No Name spent those hours hauling posts, drilling bolt holes, creating a small, tough platform of creosoted wood that would carry a train safely over a flood. It felt odd, building that bridge over a bone-dry yellow clay crease in the Wyoming high country. Wyoming was a vast Territory that swallowed up mountains and deserts and turned toiling men into ants. It dwarfed mortals, and at the same time inspired dreams without boundaries. Where in the Territory could anyone draw a line or survey a border?

He wondered where the marshal had gone. Tor, who had hunted for a day or two, mostly as a pretense for whatever he was doing. Tor, the marshal without a last name. But that badge looked real in the light of a kitchen match. Tor, who had bought a packhorse, a saddle horse, a saddle and tack, and then had vanished into a land so large it hurt the mind to think of it. The man was gone. Like JimBob. Like Marcus Penn, like Martin McGee, and like Wallace Parson. And maybe a few more, soldiering in a cause that never reached daylight or newsprint.

The supper gong rang, and weary men abandoned their picks and shovels, pulled slivers of creosoted wood out of their battered hands, threw some water over their faces, and filled their tin mess bowls with stew made from anything on hand, all of it brought in with the work train. No Name spooned anonymous stew into him, fueling his body to toil and sweat the next day, and he dropped the empty bowl into a sloppy tub, a graveyard of a meal.

Schuster eyed him. "Yes, let's talk. A few minutes, eh?"

Mitgang Schuster had filled a corncob pipe each eve, and shared the day's news with No Name even as full dark crept out of the east and rolled over last light in the west. They always settled into the hot earth facing west, so they could watch the blue light sliver down to nothing.

"So, you saw the girl," he said.

"Woman."

Schuster grinned.

"Sheriff's daughter Carolina. She was a girl at that New Dawn meeting a few Thursdays ago. The one who wanted to bust out of there, who wanted me to drag her away from her pa. Now she's a woman, clothing starched stiff as a board, nothing soft about her."

He described the lunch in the pew in the new station, a couple hundred yards away.

"Now she's an apostle, or maybe just a fish-hook."

"I've been thinking," Schuster said, knocking ash into the clay.

"That's what gets you into jackpots."

"Bright, I want to say something big, something very big, and I want you to pay attention. Listen to me. Listen to me like you were in the barber chair."

Something in his voice subdued No Name.

"You're in trouble and don't know it. You're next."

"You find a bottle somewhere?"

Schuster did something strange. He clasped No Name's shoulder and dug in with his fingers. The ghost of humor vanished from No Name's face.

"Now in the dead of the night they string up JimBob, our friend, and cut him down and plant him and hope no one ever knows. That means you're next."

No Name suppressed his objections and stared.

"Witnesses, witnesses," the barber said. "You're the last one. They don't know about me. They think I'm far away."

"I'll hire you to give me a shave tomorrow."

Schuster glared. "It's not like you think. Why'd they hang the foremen, the railroad men? They wanted the railroad to come through here. That was the big deal. The railroad would come, and then New Dawn would come. So why did they string a noose over McGee, and Parson, and Penn, the man the railroad sent to deal with them? Why, eh? Witnesses. They saw, and they could tell, and so they had to be strung up as criminals."

The man was on a rant, but No Name couldn't help but listen.

"And now the saloon man, who listened and learned, and knew too much."

"Mitgang, mind if I call you that? Mitgang, they tried to hang me. I was no witness. I was someone who wandered into Throatlatch. And a few weeks ago they did hang that poor little lady who could barely count. She wasn't a witness. No, they're simply cruel people."

"I think maybe you're next. Because you are a witness. You left their meeting. You pointed a finger at yourself. Yes, you."

"I'll want a shave tomorrow, before work, all right?"

The barber shook his head. He rose in the soft night, and wandered off, done with all talk. Maybe done with friendship. No Name watched the man contain his anger and wander away. The barber had a stubborn streak. The night had gone sour. This whole job had gone sour. Maybe he would take his pay and drift again.

Witness? Schuster didn't make sense. Everyone in Throatlatch was a witness. If they meant to silence witnesses, why didn't they string up half the town?

He thought of the two foremen, McGee and Parson, rotting in that cell for weeks, hearing everything in that miserable county building, released and murdered. And Marcus Penn, who met his fate there.

The sheriff's deputies were still around. Gus Glory, Majestic Skinner, they didn't wear a badge now, but they were around, lounging at the New Dawn railroad station, watching the railhead crew stretch the rails.

No Name found his cot, settled into it, not wanting a blanket on a warm night, and stared at the smelly canvas above him, wondering when a knife would cut through it. He didn't sleep. He didn't rest. Schuster made him mad.

It was a long night, even though the sun broke

early. He pulled on his pants, found Schuster in the kitchen, and asked for the shave.

"No. Let your beard grow. Maybe when it's grown they'll remember you, the one that got away."

That ticked off No Name, and he headed for the coffee, but it hadn't boiled yet, and he'd have to wait and wait. He rubbed the stubble on his cheek, remembering how Schuster's shave and haircut had saved his life not long ago. He watched the barber build up the cook fire, and then scoop rolled oats into a giant kettle, add water, toss in some salt, and stir the meal a little.

He headed out to the railhead. The drainage had been timbered, ties bolted across the beams, and work had started on the roadbed beyond. They had only half the crew they had earlier, but they were advancing.

He saw a familiar man watching him from the station. Gus Glory, lounging there before full dawn. No Name headed that way, while the former deputy chewed a toothpick.

"You want a job? We're hiring."

"That's hard work."

"It pays well enough."

The deputy had grown a big belly, and looked soft. "We get New Dawn up and running, and we'll have plenty of cheap help."

"Off the reservation."

"Yeah, and the newcomers and all."

No Name heard the breakfast gong. When the gong sounded, you showed up fast or you didn't eat. He nodded at Glory, and headed into camp where sleepy men, some half dressed, lined up with their all-purpose tin bowls. This restaurant was not endorsed by Diamond Jim Brady but gave a man all the gruel he needed to survive a hard day.

The next days were tough. These untrained workmen had to put in a switch, which was exacting work. The switch connected a half mile of siding running through Throatlatch. Getting the frog and points right, and the lever that would throw the switch in place, was so exacting that Mick Malone himself supervised. But when it was done, they were a step closer to being able to support the rail-building with two work trains. When they got another half mile of track down, they would be able to shuffle trains.

Throatlatch sat glumly beside the right-of-way, drawing curious workers to stroll its empty precincts, peer into dead stores and sagging houses. It made the whole work crew uneasy. It was a graveyard of dreams. What troubled them even more was the gallows, for some reason swept clean of grime, its heavy crossbar and cruel trap a monument to a fading frontier. Every time No Name gazed at it, well aware of how close he had come to being one of its victims, a jolt of fear ran through him.

The railhead camp had moved beyond the dead town, and Throatlatch diminished day by day in the summer heat. Yet it still called to No Name, the same beckoning he had felt for months now, a sense of unfinished business there.

He found Schuster who was scrubbing pots.

"You want to look around the town again?"

"You're crazy."

"I guess I am," No Name said.

He hiked easily into Throatlatch, enjoying a cool breeze out of the east, and headed purposefully toward that one jerry-built structure he had avoided, the New Dawn meeting hall. It was never locked. He opened, and discovered something new. Instead of a lectern, there now stood seven plush wingback chairs, their wood gilded gold to match their gold fabric. The one at the center was higher. These chairs had come by wagon some great distance. He wondered where and how. They appeared to be the thrones of a council of elders, the lords who would rule New Dawn in the near future.

On a polished table was a green leather ledger. It was too dark for him to read the contents closely, but it appeared to be a list of properties deeded to the New Dawn Society, all neatly recorded in the same hand. Some of the listings surprised him: they were not lots, but large landholdings, stretching out ten, twenty miles from Throatlatch, or New Dawn. The society seemed to embrace not just an abandoned town but a vast hinterland, the size of a Wyoming county; probably more land than in a small eastern state. New Dawn was no small enclave; it might be the beginnings of a nation. He saw nothing else of interest in the failing light, but it was a sign of what would come.

He turned to leave, but found his way blocked by Majestic Skinner and Gus Glory. Skinner was clinking his jail keys in his hand. Both were smiling broadly. No Name knew instantly that if these two jailed him, no one else would ever see him again.

"Inspiring start to your new society," he said, amiably. "You'll build a paradise?"

"Your paradise is about ten feet by ten," Skinner said, rattling the keys.

Gus Glory laughed.

No Name sprang for the door, but they caught him, hands clawed at him, boots connected with his shins.

"Hey, Bright, just come along peaceful," Skinner said.

But No Name was not at all peaceful. He had spent a life avoiding brawls; his safety had always been his invisibility. Never his prowess. He didn't know a sucker punch from a knee in the groin. But he discovered something else.

194

His weeks of brutal labor had molded his body into a powerful machine, and his tough arms and big hands were taking their toll, and the blows raining on him by Skinner and Glory seemed to bounce off of him.

It went faster than he knew. He wrapped his massive arms around the necks of his tormentors, an iron grip that caught their throats in the crook of his elbows, and suddenly both were gasping, frenzied, failing to land a kick. They were out of breath, burdened with flab, and the victims of their own leisure.

"You're choking me," Glory gasped.

"Sounds familiar," No Name said, but he eased his grip a little, and both men gulped air.

"I guess you know all about that," No Name added. "Skinner, drop the keys."

Skinner did. The brass jail keys clattered on the floor.

"Go sit in those chairs up there," No Name said. "And don't move."

He let them go. They didn't resist, but staggered to the podium and sat in chairs to either side of the center one, which remained empty.

The judge's chair, No Name thought.

He picked up the jail keys and pocketed them. Then he backed to the door.

"I'm going to close this door. If I hear it open, I'll come at you again."

They said nothing.

"And maybe I'll have a talk with some of those people who are going to run this show. They should know you're out of shape."

He quietly closed the door, and listened a moment. He heard no movement. He quietly hiked to the river and tossed the jail keys into it, and then to the right-of-way and followed the rails out to the camp. He found Mick Malone in his caboose, and told him exactly what had happened.

Malone nodded, and offered no comment at all. But neither did the boss fire him.

CHAPTER TWENTY-FOUR

No Name found Judge and Lydia Howard enjoying the cool of their veranda. Both were dressed to the nines. He wore a suit and cravat with a gold watch fob spread across his middle. She was in a summery dress with bouffant shoulders that made her look like she was ready to fly away.

"What is your name again, sir?" the judge asked.

"My card says J. Arnold Bright."

"That's an odd way of putting it."

"A peculiarity of mine, sir. I've come to let you know that the railroad is almost ready for you to promote your village."

"Oh, it's more than that. It's a new life. And you're with the railroad?"

"I'm with the grading crew. We've completed the siding and are stretching track ahead, and when there's enough laid, you'll be able to bring in your newcomers without disturbing our progress."

"Ah, yes, and why did you bring this news to us?"

"I thought you'd like to know. The railroad's connecting us by telegraph, but that's still a while away. I'm simply reporting that you now can draw your members."

"Members. Not the right word. Adherents, perhaps. Pilgrims perhaps." The judge eyed No Name. "I gather you've visited our temple."

"I'm a curious man. And the door is always open."

"And what did you discover?"

"Seven upholstered chairs, and the middle one higher. Will you be in it?"

"Not I, sir. Mrs. Howard and I are awaiting the one who will sit there. The time has come. We dress each eve. It could be anyone. It could be you. But we honor him by readying ourselves."

"Who will that be?"

Mrs. Howard smiled. "That's the mystery. We don't know. It could be you."

That struck No Name as so far afield he had to stop and put the world back together. Then he smiled. "No such fate awaits me, madam."

"What did you discover in our registry?" the judge asked.

"That your claims go far beyond Throatlatch, and embrace a large part of Wyoming. Will you be a new county? A new state? An enclave?"

"I surely don't know, Mr. Bright."

"You bought out all the neighboring ranches?"

"Ah, they donated these lands. We haven't money to buy them."

"You have a blue currency."

"No, just promissory notes that must be executed."

"They look like dollars."

The judge rose. "Thank you for telling us about the progress. We'll ask the management if the time has come for New Dawn to be born."

"Sure. When the telegraph's hooked up, I'll let you know."

"We don't consider it a blessing, Mr. Bright. We chose this place because it's far from the worldly world."

Lydia nodded.

There was no explaining these people.

Out on the lane he paused a moment. The sheriff's house and barn were nearby. Sheriff Clemson had been a walking arsenal, but things had changed. Maybe. No Name hiked that direction in the pleasant June evening, enjoying the late light. He turned in, passed the barn, and reached the house. No lamp burned.

"Who is it?" The voice rose from the porch.

"Oh, you," she added, answering her question.

"Ah, I was looking for the sheriff, Carolina."

"He's not here. Ah, what is your name, again?"

"J. Arnold Bright."

She stared. "That doesn't fit you. Forgive me."

"I have no name. I was orphaned. I use any name that's handy."

Carolina was sitting in a wicker chair on the broad porch. She was wearing soft clothing this eve, a loose summer cotton, and not the starchy clothing she wore at the station.

"I like that better," she said. "That fits you."

"I'll leave a message for your father. The railroad's almost ready to bring your customers here, your group."

"We call them pilgrims."

"Well, tell him that. I just told the judge and Mrs. Howard."

She nodded, uninterested, so he turned to leave.

"Have a seat," she said, gesturing toward the other chair. He sat, gingerly. "I'm curious about you. My, ah, father is, too. He paid no attention to you until that day, at the meeting, when you stood—and I followed. Now you're on his mind."

"I can imagine,"

"Your tongue is a little tart, No Name."

"What would you like to call me? Any name is fine."

"No Name. That's you."

"That's fine. My life goes better without a name."

"Why is he so interested in you? He had me seek you out and take you to lunch at the station."

"That was his idea? Maybe he wants to correct my impressions. From when he was sheriff of Throatlatch."

"Yes, exactly."

"The town had a reputation."

"Yes, it did. Anyone will tell you. We grew tired

of travelers showing up and stealing from us. He cracked down, hard. I could tell you stories."

"Travelers have told me the opposite story— that they were in mortal trouble here, and lost every cent."

"I prefer my family's version," she said, closing the topic.

"But when I stood up, when the judge said someone was there at the meeting who wasn't welcome, and I stood, and you started to follow— and your father sat you down hard. What about that?"

She smiled. Her smile was sweet in the dusky light. "A daughter can make a mistake."

"And he corrected you."

"Yes. It took him an hour. But I listened."

"So I'm on the wrong side."

She shook her head. "You aren't on any side, and won't be until you take a name."

"And you won't give me one."

"Only you can name yourself. But let me know, all right?"

"Who was the person you were visiting at the grave? When we first met?"

She stiffened. "I think I'll head inside. It's chilly, Mr. No Name."

"It's warm," he said, rising. "I'm glad we talked."

She stood there, mute, disturbed. He hastened out the long drive, and into the lane, and across open fields toward the railroad tracks and town. This place was still Throatlatch. And she didn't know who she was, just as he didn't know who he was.

He counted it a valuable evening, but it was not over. When he reached his railhead camp, a stranger accosted him.

"I've been looking for you, sir. Would you join me for a few minutes at the caboose?"

The man wore a summer suit, was graying, and had rimless wire glasses.

No Name climbed into the caboose, and the man followed. Mick Malone was nowhere in sight.

"I'm Tor," the stranger said. "And you're a man who has no name."

"But you're not the one I met at the graveyard."

He smiled. "For our purposes, we're all anonymous."

He withdrew a breast pocket wallet, and showed No Name the bronze badge. "I'll clear up some mysteries straight off. We're investigating what may be a major breach of good order. A Territorial county has vanished. Because Wyoming is not yet a state, it is a federal matter. The officers of Wellbred County are, at the least, guilty of dereliction of duty. A large portion of the Territory is without governance. You cannot transfer a deed, get married, pay a tax, summon a sheriff here. Above all, crime is rampant and there is no system of law enforcement here. Everyone here lives at his own peril, and there is reason to believe the officers of Wellbred County are part of a criminal conspiracy. What complicates matters is the existence of a cult, which may or may not be legal. The country's full of them. There's one in Oneida, New York, that promotes free love." He smiled. "I've thought of joining it. Most are communal in nature, in which there is no property and all work is to be shared. But they last a few months and die off because no one wants to work. They are usually legal, but just stupid. At any rate, we've had our eye on you, and wish to let you know that, and ask you to help us. One of our tasks is to sort out innocent people caught in foolish beliefs from the criminals promoting the cult for their own purposes.

"Why me?"

"You're a witness. And something draws you here, probably a wish to see justice done after your narrow escape."

"Uh, narrow escape?"

"You were tried in about ten minutes on a horse thief charge and sentenced to hang. You weren't even allowed to plead, much less to defend yourself. It was a mockery of much that this nation believes in and stands for. Your own courage gave you a chance to escape during a gin rummy game."

"You've been talking to a certain person."

"Yes, Mr. Schuster is one of our most valued observers here. From him we learned that you are an orphan, handed around, and have no name. You've come to live with that, and even find safety in it. That's your choice, but I personally would like to be known as someone. Especially to my wife, in St. Louis."

No Name choked back a powerful feeling that seemed almost to take him over. Tor watched intently.

"We've work to do, and are running out of time. The railroad will soon be bringing desperate people, dreaming of paradise."

"Does the railroad know?"

"We've told Mick Malone why we're here, without sharing any details, because the railroad itself may be a party to some of this. He's given us the use of this caboose."

"Two of you?"

"The other marshal, the drover, has been out looking at the perimeter. He's nearly done. If New Dawn intends to declare its independence from the United States, it needs boundaries of some sort, and these are known to us only by horseback examination. So far, we've found nothing at all. For all we know, New Dawn intends to claim all of North America—which would be more than it can swallow."

No Name found himself enjoying this man. "Independence, sir? Like the Confederacy?"

"That's a good enough analogy. Your acquaintance, the judge, is from a border state. He may be involved in sedition, treason, inciting rebellion, and certainly madness."

"He seems a civil man, a gentleman."

"So were many of the Southern generals who betrayed their oath to defend the United States."

No Name realized that this marshal seemed to be waiting for something, wanting an answer to an unasked question.

"I'll do whatever I can, sir."

Tor relaxed, then. "I have a request. I'd like you to focus on the sheriff and the two deputies, Gus Glory and Majestic Skinner. Learn what you can about their backgrounds. The judge may have conducted sham trials to give the hangings a veneer of respectability, but it was the sheriff and Skinner who built the nooses, slid them over necks of prisoners whose hands were tied behind their backs, who forced them to stand on the center of the trap, and who pulled the lever and murdered man and woman alike."

"There's nothing I'd rather do."

"Including any evidence of a crime done by Carolina Clemson?"

That hit No Name hard. "I can't do that, sir. I . . . care for her."

CHAPTER TWENTY-FIVE

Nothing much happened during the hot summer days. The telegraph crew completed its line to New Dawn, but no one knew how to operate a key. Mick Malone knew Morse, and taught himself to transcribe and receive and send, but he barely succeeded. Word from the outside would have to wait.

The New Dawn Society started to run classified ads around the country. The railroad promised twice-a-week service to New Dawn; a baggage car and coach. But no one bought tickets and the runs were cancelled. A few pilgrims arrived by horse and wagon one day, looked around at the sun-bitten town, and left.

The U.S. marshal confiscated the few records remaining in the Wellbred County building, and began a close study of who bought and sold what. He was growing impatient.

"It's hard to make a case without witnesses," he said. "They fled when Throatlatch collapsed. "You're a witness, but not a valuable one because you weren't here until the last, when they tried to hang you. The barber is the only witness who saw most of it, and I've warned him to be careful.

The New Dawn people don't know he's serving railroad meals, and he's not advertising it. My best chance for conviction is to get one of the New Dawn people to rat on the others. I'd like to get Gus Glory or Majestic Skinner to spill a lot of beans. Another candidate for that is Lydia Howard, but testimony from a spouse rarely cuts the mustard. And for some reason, she likes her judge."

"You think this all is falling apart? They'll walk away?"

"No, I don't. But it's not as easy as it looks."

That's how it went, through summer showers and a long drought. One day a diamond-stacked engine pulled in with a baggage car and coach, and about fifteen pilgrims emerged, warmly greeted by the judge and sheriff. They got the grand tour, a good dinner, and some bunks in the abandoned houses. The next day the entire lot boarded the coach and headed back to Fort Laramie. New Dawn was becoming midmorning dawn and then noon dawn.

Mick Malone didn't like it. "I thought this outfit was going to earn us some quick profit," he said. He had pushed his new track six miles beyond town, and his work crew was moving farther and farther away. For the marshal's sake he left the caboose parked on the siding, with enough provisions for the marshal to take care of himself.

But No Name never failed to visit, sometimes using a handcar to get back to town.

"The judge and the missus invited me to dinner at their place," the marshal said. "They asked me what I was doing, and I said I'm a federal inspector, which is true, and that I am gathering the records of Wellbred County, which is also true. They served good beef, and offered a great view. I could see the town below, and the station, and my yellow caboose on the siding. They and their neighbor have got this whole country under glass."

"Did they talk about the New Dawn society?"

"Not a word. But something's up."

That proved to be an understatement. The next day a train with two baggage cars and two coaches arrived, unloaded about a hundred fashionable people and a mountain of baggage, including steamer trunks. The sheriff, his deputies, and the judge met the crowd, but Carolina and Lydia did not.

The marshal watched all that, and presumed that the New Dawn pilgrims had arrived at last. And so far, at least, Tor saw nothing that violated federal law.

"So here they are, at last," the marshal told No Name. "I have a task for you. Find out who they are, what they believe, and anything else you can. The locals know me as a federal inspector and keep their distance, but you're innocent of any association with government."

The idea appealed to No Name. The town of Throatlatch still tugged at him, for reasons he couldn't explain. And the farther away the railhead moved, the more he felt that tug.

"I've already consulted with Malone," the marshal said. "He accepts it. The railroad's in a hurry, but less so now that it's reached here and has some business. By the way, my full name is Torvold Gran."

"You already know mine. Any will do."

"Here's what I can tell you," Tor said. "These people belong to a radical order called the World Anarchist Union. They don't believe in government, which is why they've gathered here. They intend to create an ungoverned enclave."

"No government? They'll soon be at war."

"Well, it's more complex than that. I've talked to some. They believe in self-government. Every man a king. That means that each member governs himself. Conscience rules, rather than kings or congresses. That's not so different than a dozen other fellowships in the country, such as the Oneida Colony in New York."

"So no one leads them?"

"Oh, yes, they have a leader. An Alsace professor named Hannibal Rottweiler. Don't laugh. He says his family developed the breed, and a dozen of them will patrol the borders here."

"So they have some policing after all."

"Mostly to defend against outsiders," Tor said.

"They do everything possible not to police themselves. Professor Rottweiler has two doctoral degrees and is a student of human nature. I'll introduce you. Now, like all these utopias, they're starved for labor, and they'll pile their blue currency on you if you work for them. They've already started to fix up these tumbledown shacks."

"I don't know. Blue money?"

"It'll buy anything their stores offer, but isn't worth a plugged nickel out of town. You couldn't buy a coach ticket with it."

"Are they communal? No private property?"

"I don't know."

"How do they treat the judge and sheriff?"

"Founding fathers. Revered."

"Where do you stand?"

Tor frowned. "Right now, I don't stand. They've usurped federal land and blotted out public law and government. Those are federal crimes. But most of these groups vanish in a few months, and that's how the government looks at them. So I'm here to keep an eye on them, but not to make decisions at the moment."

"You're alone?"

"Now I am. Which is one reason I need you urgently."

No Name peered out the caboose window, and saw something he never imagined he would ever see there. A lady in fashionable attire, with a vast ostrich-feather hat, and white gloves, was walking a powerful-looking black dog with brown face—her black Rottweiler.

"I'll do it," No Name said.

"I'll let Mick Malone know. And he's privy to what's happening here now. The railroad itches to make money from this place, but it depends on federal bureaus for right-of-way. There's always politics. I'll take you over to the professor, but one last word. Most of these people are educated, moneyed, idealistic. But there's an under-class here, people who think of anarchy, lack of government, as a chance to plunder. You'll spot them fast, and those are the ones who worry me the most."

"I feel as though I belong here," No Name said.

Tor stared.

"These anarchists almost hung me for the fun of it."

Tor smiled wryly.

"Evil is at its worst when it looks like good-ness."

Gus Glory was walking two leashed Rott-weilers. Majestic Skinner was walking a third.

Torvold Gran took No Name for a tour. A grocery had opened. The saloon had opened. A dry goods and hardware outfit was stocking up. Houses were being whitewashed, there being no paint. The old Wellbred County building was being turned into a meeting place. Professor

Rottweiler had a desk there. For anarchists, that was as close to government as they would come.

The professor was an amiable dumpling of a man, with cherub cheeks, rosy forehead, and long clean fingers. He barely fit in a pinstriped black suit. A simple sky-blue banner hung behind his desk, with sans serif lettering that said, World Anarchist Union.

"Aha! Help at last!" the man said, forgoing introductions. Some European accent softened all his consonants. He and the marshal had plainly been talking.

"This young man will answer to any name you choose to give him," the marshal said.

"Perfect! We would never dream of imposing a name on another mortal. A cruel fate, sir, to be named."

"Uh, why?" No Name asked.

"We don't have the authority," the professor explained. "A name is for you to decide when you are sovereign and ready to do so. That lies at the root of things."

"I'm here to work, sir. I gather workers are in demand just now."

"Yes, certainly, but wages must be deferred for the time being, until we put the exchange of goods and services into traction. We all function on good faith."

"I've been working for the railroad, with the railhead crew. We get a weekly pay envelope."

"Just what we're looking for. Handy at everything. We've roofs that need tar paper, clapboard that's fallen loose, broken glass in some windows. Are you up to it?"

Judge Howard materialized from his old chambers.

"He's not one of us, Hannibal."

"Of course not. I saw that at once. He wants money."

"I would advise, sir, that sometimes Utopian dreams can be damaged by a bedbug."

The professor paused, eyed No Name. "I tell you what. Come this eve to our meeting, and listen to my nightly lecture. In no time at all, you'll see things differently, and would be eager to build a new dawn, a new civilization, first in North America, and then the world."

No Name shook his head.

"Young man, wages are a source of contention, and one of the worms that can infect the world we are building. Come this evening, and let me change your mind. I have a vision to share with all my guests."

Torvold Gran looked unhappy.

"All right, I'll come listen."

"We'll be meeting in the chamber erected by Judge Howard, which will do until we finish our bell tower."

"Bell tower?"

"A carillon. It summons us. It will have a chime

that will summon us each eve. But of course no one is required to come. Every man a king, sir."

"Every woman a queen, then?"

"Well, Mother Nature gave them their own status and responsibilities, and above all, we honor what is natural and probative."

"It'll be over my head, Professor."

"Of course it will. But we all have to start somewhere. That first step, out upon thin ice, is the most important you'll ever take."

The marshal nudged No Name. "He'll be there," Gran said.

He steered No Name into the busy street, now occupied by hurrying people in summer clothes. One sweet lady even had a tasseled parasol.

"I think I know how you feel," the marshal said.

"I thought anarchists built bombs and threw them at tycoons and czars."

"No Name, that's why we're here. I'll see about putting you on a salary from the Justice Department. This is turning into one of the major challenges faced by the government. Beyond these ladies with parasols, and pro-fessors dreaming of bright-colored revolutions, are bomb-throwers, people who would happily snuff out what we call civilization. I can't offer you a motto on a sky-blue banner, but I can offer you something else: the belief I hold that we are doing the most important work, pursuing the most important investigation, of our lives."

CHAPTER TWENTY-SIX

JimBob's old saloon served food too, so No Name ordered a bowl of stew. Then he remembered he had no blue money, and explained it to the new owner, a man with enormous muttonchops.

"I'm a stranger here," No Name said. "I've got some greenbacks and change."

The owner scanned the crowd, leaned over and said, "two-bits, and slide it quietly. And if you return, do it that way next time."

No Name slid a quarter to the proprietor, who pocketed it swiftly. It was time for the big meeting. He slipped outside, and found the streets almost as empty as before. Throatlatch had once housed almost a thousand. The newcomers, barely a hundred, scarcely made a difference. The small group that gathered at the judge's old meeting house was certainly a novel sight. These were the affluent types, the ones with the gaudy hats and billowing summer skirts and soft white shirts with long collars. No Name saw none of the other sort, the rough customers who wore untrimmed beards, slouch hats, grimy boots, and sour smiles that revealed missing incisors. That was a relief. If he was to associate with anarchists, he would prefer the scholarly variety. An oral argument was an improvement over a knife blade.

Exactly on the hour Hannibal Rottweiler appeared, and settled himself in the center chair, the one higher than the others. Next to him were people No Name didn't know, but also Judge and Mrs. Howard, and Sheriff Clemson and Carolina.

Rottweiler clapped his pocket watch shut with a snap.

"Promptness is an improvement on godliness," he said, with a faint European accent No Name couldn't identify.

The little hall, with its uncomfortable benches, was not half full.

"Well, then, we're here. Let us rejoice!"

Polite applause rippled. "I believe in short seminars. First, welcome to any strangers who have stopped in to learn about anarchism, the hope of the world. Second, my central message is that anarchy is not what you have heard it is. It isn't about the lack of government or lack of good order. It's about moving the seat of government to its proper spot, in our bosom. Every man a king. Every man rules himself. If he fails, he is invited to leave our good company.

"Now all that's more troublesome than it sounds, because we are all different, and come from everywhere. So we're here to agree on common principles, to wit: the triumph of virtue.

216

When we're virtuous, the need for government withers away because we have ample government within to guide and prosper us. That's all I'm going to say this glorious summer eve, but some have questions, and my colleagues and I are here to help."

That was fast, but it got the message across again. No Name eyed the eager crowd.

A gray-bearded man with calloused hands rose.

"Sirs, I'm concerned about money. Blue Dawns might purchase my supplies here, but it won't buy me railroad fare if I need to visit relatives. How are we going to fix this?"

"Why, no trouble at all," said Rottweiler, hurrying into the fray. "Newcomers are arriving almost daily, and purchasing shares, and exchanging their greenbacks for our New Dawns. All you need do to pay for a railroad ticket is exchange your blue New Dawns for some greenbacks and you'll be on your way."

That would work for a while, as long as the society drew people, No Name thought.

A lady dressed in lavender tulle and lavender cologne rose quietly, and stood until the professor nodded.

"Honored sirs, I am from a civilized town in Massachusetts, and this is my first venture west of the Erie Canal. I didn't expect the raw west to be filled with ivy-covered red brick buildings, but neither did I expect to find a great, sinister gallows rising perversely at the end of town that should be a glorious riverside park. It would do me much good to see that relic removed. It is a reminder of the world we all wish to escape. I understand that. But that's why I'm here. To escape jails and gallows and everything connected to government."

The professor eyed Judge Howard, who nodded, adjusted his cravat, and smiled before he spoke.

"Welcome to New Dawn," he said. "We have a few relics of the past, when this was a rough frontier town, but the past is past, and in due time we will celebrate the end of the gallows with a triumphal parade and feast."

"Yes, but why is it here? What happened here before we came?"

"Yes, of course, it needs to be answered. I was given a unique name by my learned parents, E Pluribus Unum Howard, and it was that very name that led me to become a charter member of the World Anarchist Union. Now in those dark days, before we gathered here, this was a town that catered to travelers heading west, and as it turned out, the town fathers had to defend the town from road agents and others of that sort, who sought to rampage and pillage this peaceful place. It was only when the town's fathers built that edifice that the troubles ceased. Some government was needed at that point to protect our peaceful citizens from barbarians. But the railroad has just about eliminated foot and horse travel, and the old town withered, giving us the perfect opportunity to create a new world, entirely among those who voluntarily join us and abide by our basic ethical and moral ideals. Does that help you?"

"Well, sort of. But how many mortals were— I mean, how many human beings, well you know."

"A perfect question, and one that cannot be answered, madam. No one really knows. Relatives took the remains of many with them."

"Of many?"

"Here, madam, let me lend you my handkerchief."

"People died there?"

"Oh, I confess, some did not walk away."

"And who did this?"

"The territorial county of Wellbred no longer exists, madam."

"Are any of those people still here? I cannot hope to sleep at night if even one soul from Throatlatch is present among us."

"Let me put it to you this way, madam. Anarchy's a transformation that reaches into the very soul. If any people here date back to those dark days, they wouldn't even recognize themselves. That's the miracle of New Dawn."

No Name needed to escape the bad air.

As soon as the meeting broke up, he slid into the clean air, and sucked it in, exhaling the sour air he had absorbed in there. He wondered why he was so starved for air. The crowd dispersed, scarcely noticing the gallows that stood darkly at the foot of town. He was sure they would think about those gallows soon enough.

"Good evening, Mr. Bright," Lydia Howard said. "Kindly walk me home."

"I'd be pleased to."

"The bats are out, and it's bedtime." She collected his arm, and he began escorting her.

"Where's the judge, madam?"

"Groveling at the feet of the professor, Mr. Bright. By the way, you're not Bright. I know it. Who are you?"

"I have no name, madam."

"Then I'll call you No Name. The judge is derelict in his duties, and I must get whatever help is available. I'm legally married but I keep forgetting it. What did you think of the professor?"

"He has some good ideas, madam."

"Rubbish. There's no such human being who can live without governing. This crowd that rolled in here, it's harmless enough. Mostly academics and their kept women who want to find free love in a free world."

They reached the rails and the little station, and the caboose.

"Are you in that caboose?" she asked.

"No, an inspector is. He's examining the collapse of the Wyoming county."

"His eyes bore into me, those rimless glasses of his."

The caboose was dark, and No Name wondered where Gran was. No Name's few possessions were in there.

"You can stay in our hired man's room. The carriage house, you know."

"I'd better stay in town, madam."

"This lot of anarchists is probably safe enough, but the next few won't be. They're a nasty lot. Some are criminals, looking to avoid sheriffs and judges. Some are laboring men who think bosses should be beheaded. Others are socialists, who think that mutual ownership combines perfectly with anarchy. But the worst are madmen who won't govern themselves and won't submit to government by anyone. So here we have a little stewpot of nasty sorts."

"Are you an anarchist, madam?"

"I think I told you I'm a guilty bystander."

"You stay with your man."

"We all have our follies. What did you think of the judge's response to the woman in lavender?"

"We're at your gate. I think I'd better head down the hill."

"Aren't you the diplomat. It was rubbish. We've been preying on travelers for years, not the other way around. Look at the nice shoes I wear, and this diamond ring." She paused at the gate. "All right, then. You're a good boy."

He didn't respond.

"We'll see if you're a man," she added, and left him there in the dusk.

He didn't know what to make of her. He eased back onto the lane, and followed it into Throatlatch. During the entire walk, she had been educating him. She wanted him to know a lot of things. Terrible things. There was something else: in spite of her bravado, she was afraid and was asking for help without saying so. Maybe she would sit down with the United States marshal and resolve a few mysteries.

He collected his sack of clothing from the dark caboose, gulped down another bowl of stew at the saloon, and then hunted for a place to spend the night. There were empty houses, but he shied from them. In the full dark, he drifted toward the river, and came upon the gallows looming upward into a black sky. The only sleep the place offered was the eternal variety. And yet it offered safety. No one lurked around the gallows. There was plenty of room under the floor, and he found a place where he could stretch out and get through the night.

He drifted off into a light sleep, but was awakened some while later by a struggle and low voices on the platform above him, and someone gasping and begging. He heard hoarse commands. Stand there, dammit. Don't move. Don't, don't, don't, don't, don't! He heard men wrestling with things, and then he heard someone pull the lever. The trap swung down, and a pair of legs and boots dropped, thudded, and turned slowly in the night air.

"Don't," cried a strangled voice.

No Name ached to get out of there but he made himself wait and wait.

Then he beelined for the caboose, racing through midnight, and rapped steadily until a window slid open.

"Can it wait?"

"No."

Gran sighed. In a minute he let himself out, carrying a bull's eye lantern, unlit.

"Tell me."

No Name did, leading the marshal through a quiet town to the gallows. A body lit by starlight swung in the breeze.

Gran scratched a lucifer and lit the bull's eye lantern and held it up. The dead man was Majestic Skinner, and he had been hanged with a lariat that had gradually choked the life out of him.

"Not a good way to die," Gran said. "You know him?"

"Majestic Skinner, one of the deputies. Also the hangman. He or the sheriff did the honors, usually in front of half the citizens of Throat-latch."

"What's your theory?"

"He kept saying don't, don't, to someone he knew. Don't, that was his only word."

"That's helpful. Who's on your list?"

"Sheriff, judge, Dent the county clerk, Gus Glory, anyone associated with them, or someone related to one of Skinner's victims."

"I think we'll wait and see. Meanwhile, not a word, right?"

"Not a word, sir."

"Even a hangman shouldn't die at the end of a lariat," Gran said.

No Name found himself agreeing. Skinner was the very man who would have pulled the lever that dawn, but slow strangling to death was worse than anything Skinner did—except hang the innocent.

"If you want, come to the caboose. I doubt that either of us will be sleeping the rest of this night."

No Name gratefully followed, and entered the dark caboose. He marveled that such a hard-seat interior could offer so much comfort. This caboose had a cupola where a brakeman could sit. Some cabooses had narrow side windows that afforded a view forward. A small stove added comfort and a kitchen of sorts.

"Don't say a word if you don't feel like it. If you do, tell me anything else you know."

"Skinner was the jailer. He tormented the railroad foremen tossed in there for no reason."

"Vengeance? Trouble in the county staff?"

"Skinner and Gus Glory got along. So did the sheriff. I don't think Judge Howard knew Skinner or cared."

"Someone trying to wipe out the last witnesses?"

"I don't know who those are, sir."

"Maybe we will when we see who shows up and how they handle this. It's going to upset all these newcomers."

An understatement, No Name thought. That was Gran, understating everything. Tomorrow a hundred anarchists would see a hanged man and want to get the next train out. But there was no next train.

CHAPTER TWENTY-SEVEN

Dawn brought muffled cries, excited whispers, people gathering into little knots that soon shattered, and finally a silent crowd of staring people. No Name and the marshal watched quietly. Someone would approach the gallows, study the swaying body, and stop well short as if halted by an invisible wall, and then back off. No one ventured close. The invisible wall kept them all distant.

"Are we safe?" a man asked.

The judge and sheriff watched blandly, but said nothing. No Name watched them. They knew who was hanging there. They had to know. So did Gus Glory, who joined them.

"Who's taking care of this?" someone asked, loudly, but no one responded.

Then, as daylight rose, the professor, Hannibal Rottweiler, appeared, nattily dressed, and took upon himself the task of bringing order to an anarchist community.

"Every man a king," he said. "If anyone is responsible for this, his own conscience should inform him that he must act. He must first accept the blame, and then depart at once. Now then, will the party or parties please come forward?"

No one did. No Name noticed that the town's few women seemed braver than the men, and approached the gallows far enough to make out who had perished.

"This is a model community that is self-governed," the professor said. "We must each do what our own virtue demands. The criminals must depart. But we also need faithful workers, ones to restore order here. Are there volunteers?"

Far from volunteering, many of the anarchists quietly turned away and retreated to their new homes. A sullen silence descended. Larger issues arose. The fate of the New Dawn hung in balance. The town would empty out whenever the railroad sent a train.

"Anarchy requires brave hearts and minds," the professor cried. "Where are the good and faithful workers, who serve others?" he asked.

No Name studied the judge and sheriff, not finding the slightest sign of guilt or innocence. No one else seemed to care. A criminal had been hanged in the night, but who knew he was a criminal who had sent dozens of innocents to their death?

No Name stepped forward.

"Who are you, sir?" the professor asked.

"It doesn't matter. I'm am not a member of your group."

All alone, he approached the scaffold, climbed

its narrow stairs, studied the awful, twisted face of Majestic Skinner, and began the grim work. The lariat had been thrown over the crossbeam and tied to an upright. He untied the lariat, and eased the body down slowly until it vanished under the platform. A groan lifted from the distant crowd.

No Name approached the red-hued face of Skinner, and with some trouble slid the loop of the lariat away, and lifted it from the body. Skinner's open eyes stared. No Name coiled the rope, climbed back, and set the rope on the platform. Just releasing the body seemed to change everything. A man with a wheelbarrow arrived, and another with a spade. There were good men among the anarchists, and now they came forward. They eased Skinner into the wheelbarrow.

"Is he known?" one asked.

"Yes," No Name said. "He was a sheriff's deputy of Wellbred County, named Majestic Skinner."

The professor, who had edged close, nodded.

"You can find out more by talking to the sheriff, and Judge Howard, over there."

"How do you know that, sir?"

"I worked for the railroad."

No Name led them to the little graveyard, where the volunteers swiftly dug a grave and lowered the deputy into it. Various volunteers took turns shoveling the clay over the strangled man until he was well and deeply gone from sight, and maybe memory after a bit.

The professor swiftly assumed command. "Let us go forward now. This is an incident out of the past, from a town that is gone, not our New Dawn. It draws us together, and makes us strong."

"When does the next train come?" a man asked.

"You are free to follow your own virtues. Every man a king. But we've only just begun to build the most beautiful community in the history of mankind."

It was barely sunrise in New Dawn.

The professor approached No Name. "Thank you, sir. I'm hoping you will join our new world."

"I'm not a joiner."

"We need workers, young man. If there's any weakness to anarchy, it's that self-governing people don't wish to do hard work."

That was quite a concession, coming from the very voice of the World Anarchy Union.

No Name made his way to the caboose, passing through a town that had quieted down. He found Tor Gran breakfasting on oat gruel, warmed up by the little stove. All that had happened this terrible day had played out before breakfast.

Gran nodded at the pot. "Have some," he said. "And tell me what you make of it."

"Are you staying here?" No Name asked.

"As a federal marshal, I'm empowered to look into any irregularity in any territory, as well as federal crimes. I'm free to work undercover if I choose. For the moment, I'd like to find out more about this cult without showing my badge. I can get more done using proxies, people like you. And there are unsolved crimes to deal with, some from Throatlatch, and now New Dawn. You're now a federal employee. You're my eyes and ears. I'll be relying on you. Have you ever done any investigating?"

"No, but I like to ask questions."

"Then do that, and keep me posted. And we'll have help soon. Your friend Mitgang Schuster."

"I could use a shave."

Tor laughed. He rubbed his well-shaved jaw.

"I think Skinner was murdered by someone he knew. And that means the ones who were here before," No Name said.

"All right. Find out who."

No Name wondered why he had agreed to such a crazy task. He headed into the morning heat, toward the old Wellbred County building. New Dawn was deserted this grim morning but the ramshackle building was occupied. Clyde Clemson was there, wearing his badge, and so was Gus Glory.

"A little law and order after all," No Name said.

"Why are you here?" the sheriff asked.

"I'm working for the federal inspector. He

wants to wrap up the Wellborn County file. The government wants to know what happened here."

"There's nothing to tell him. The county collapsed."

"I'll have a last look, then, and tell him so."

"Suit yourself. We'll be out patrolling. This place needs some steadying down."

They left. Walking the town was probably a good idea. Even anarchists could welcome a badge.

The shambles of the old county building discouraged No Name. But there was a place to start—the sheriff's desk.

He found nothing. Not even a scrap of paper. He examined every drawer, every closet, every cranny of the whole building. Someone had carefully removed whatever was there.

He should have known, instead of wasting his time. He left the subdued town and walked up the slope to the sheriff's house. He hoped the sheriff was still patrolling. The handsome house didn't belong there next to a hardscrabble western town. The house was meant to last, and to lord over the panorama below. Here the grass was still green; below, the town was baked brown and its foliage had surrendered to the heat.

He knocked. Carolina answered with a tentative smile. She wore a summery white frock.

"Why, what surprise, Mr. ah, um, so early."

"Any name will do," he said.

"My father's not here. He said there was trouble."

"This isn't about that. I work now for the inspector, the Washington man who's looking into the county government—what happened to Wellbred County. He needs records, and there are none at the county building, so I thought I'd come here and see if you have them."

She was hesitant. "Yes, he brought them. They're here. But I'd need to ask him about giving them to you."

"They're public records."

"Yes, of course. Would you like some coffee? It's so early."

"Some other time I'd enjoy that more than I can say."

She smiled. "I would, too. I think I know where they are."

"More than you can carry?"

"No, an armful. The county was only getting started, you know."

She vanished into the sunny interior, while he waited on the spacious porch. It seemed to take forever, but eventually she brought the armful, maybe six or seven ledgers and some loose papers in a folder.

She looked worried. "I hope I'm doing the right thing. I'll tell my ah . . ."

"Yes, of course. They're public. And also federal, because this is a Territory."

"I know, but I don't feel right about it."

He smiled. "I'll get them back to you as soon as I can. I don't suppose the inspector will need more than a few hours."

She sighed. "I'll just wait to hear from you. But do let me know, as soon as you can."

He took the records, which indeed were slender ledgers.

"When you're in town, look me up," he said. "Just stop at the caboose and ask for me."

She smiled, but there were little worry creases around her eyes.

He hastened down the lane, hoping not to encounter the sheriff, and when he reached the caboose he entered swiftly. Tor Gran peered up, saw the ledgers, and nodded.

One thing was absorbing No Name. His own record. He found one labeled district court, and discovered that there were only brief notations. The court had no clerk, apparently. The notations were in a single hand, probably the judge's. No Name plowed through the notes until he found what he was looking for.

Unidentified young man, est. age twenty-seven, charged with horse thievery. My two trotters, recovered by sheriff, who arrested the horse thief. Tried immediately, found guilty by jury, and sentenced to the gallows at dawn.

There was no notice of his escape. A bare sentence that contained the most explosive

233

moment of his life. The record, like the hasty trial, was a mockery.

He shoved the ledger toward the marshal. "That's me, my life taken from me in a few words."

The marshal read it. "Are the jurors named? Who selected them?"

"The judge or sheriff, I suppose. I think the same jurors sent all the rest to their doom."

"Then we have some business ahead of us," the marshal said. "There appear to be more criminal acts recorded here than I can summon to mind at a moment's notice. But here's a task for you. Who were in the jury? And were they always the same men?"

CHAPTER TWENTY-EIGHT

That meant a visit with the judge. No Name hiked up the familiar lane, into the foothills above Throatlatch or whatever it once was, and turned into the judge's drive. The great, comfortable, imperial house lay just ahead. It was not yet noon of a bloody day.

Mrs. Howard greeted him. "Well, it's you," she said.

"I've come to see the judge, ma'am. Is he available?"

"He's too available," she said. "I wish he'd settle down in a saloon like other males I know. I'll fetch him."

In a moment, the judge appeared, this time in shirtsleeves.

"Yes, young man?"

"The federal inspector looking into the county asked me to interview you. He's puzzled about a few things."

"Oh, I'll stop by and talk to him directly."

"I'm employed by the federal government now, sir. I'm an investigator. You're free to share what you know with me."

"You are, are you? Well, we're busy. Now that we have rail service we've decided on a trip.

You can't imagine how it is to live so far from civilization. The railroad offers us a dream come true. Namely, a year of travel. Paris in particular. My wife, educated woman, is starved for a little French gossip and wine and fashion."

"It'll only take a little time, sir. We can visit on these porch chairs."

"I'll keep on packing," Lydia Howard said.

"Your memories would be helpful, ma'am."

"Aren't you the polite one. You must have been raised well."

"Oh, all right. Five minutes then," the judge said.

They settled in those chairs on a veranda that looked out upon a vast slice of the continent.

"The inspector has the county records, sir, and is puzzled by the court entries."

"Oh, those. We didn't even have a clerk of court, that's how cash-starved we were. I kept some bare records as best I could, of course, to comply with Territorial law."

"Those are what puzzle him. The names of the jurors aren't listed in any proceedings. He thought you might remember them."

The judge blinked, and blinked. "Well, of course, it's impossible to remember that far back. I do know we couldn't manage a dozen jurors and alternates. Not in Wellbred County. So we always had a jury of six. That sufficed to satisfy the law."

"Good. The same jurors?"

"Well, it was hard to get the right people. You know, judicious people. I'm sure there was some overlap."

"Always the same?"

"Pretty much the same. Mostly people I could trust. That saved time and got results."

"I'm curious, sir. What did you do before you were a judge here?"

"Oh, let's not get into that or you'll have me rambling all morning. I was an independent scholar."

"At a college?"

"He wouldn't go near a college," Lydia said, "and they wouldn't let him set foot on a campus. My, that was fun."

"Uh, your honor, what was your field?"

"Don't your-honor me. I'm not a judge. My field is too complex for addled minds, and I don't have time to explain it now."

"Everyone's addled, including you," Lydia said. "And your company."

"Is there a name for it?"

"I call it eugenics. Now are we done?"

"What's that, sir?"

"Over your head. Wasn't that a disaster this morning? I'm still shaken by it. Here we began a new town, brimming with hope, new people, and then this."

"That's another thing that interests the

inspector, sir. The dead man was a former deputy and jailer, we understand."

"I don't remember, young man."

"He was a rotter," Lydia said. "No wonder someone strung him up."

"You knew him?"

"Everyone in Throatlatch knew him. He stayed on, looking for new people to string up, and paid for it," she said.

The judge fussed. "Well, that's not how I remember him. A good man with a deputy badge. Now, sir, are we done?"

"To string up, ma'am?"

"A figure of speech. That's my educated wife for you."

"Yes, strung up. He was the executioner in Throatlatch. He's the one who put the noose on, steered the poor wretch to the trap, waited for the crowd to grow quiet, and then pulled the lever."

"Lydia, we have a lot of packing to do. Empty steamer trunks."

"Did the jury sentence, or did you, sir?"

"I wouldn't remember. We were overworked. The Territory was no help."

"Are any of the jurors still here?"

"I wouldn't know, young man. They did their job, brought order to a frontier town, and went on to better things."

"Well, I'll rely on others' memories, sir. I'm anxious to talk to the sheriff."

"You won't get anything from him. He keeps all his knowledge in his head. I don't think he could even write a coherent sentence."

"Good. Then he'll be able to help us."

The judge rose abruptly. "The next train's tomorrow, and we've much to do."

No Name nodded. He started down the long drive, feeling four eyes boring into his back.

Who would know those jurors? What did the jurors do for a living? Were there any innocent verdicts? Did any mortal brought to that court escape a guilty verdict? No Name's mind prickled with questions, but the chances of finding answers were slimmer than ever. He could number on his fingers those who might know.

He headed for the old Wellbred building, hollow and full of ghosts, and waited for the one person who might talk even a little bit. Gus Glory was something of a mystery, hanging around but not at the center of anything. Glory wasn't there, so No Name hunted for him and found him in what had been JimBob's Saloon.

"Gus, how did your patrol go?"

"This is one scared town."

"Do you go for this anarchy stuff?"

"I go for peace and quiet and a night stick for bad boys and mean dogs."

"Mind if I have some java?"

No Name didn't wait, but settled next to the former deputy.

"The inspector in the caboose, he's looking for information about the jury system here, when Throatlatch was going and the county was still here. You know anything about that?"

"That was a strange deal, but I don't want to talk about it."

"I'm paid now as an investigator. He hired me. He wants to shut down his work here and get back to civilization."

"What's he gonna do?"

"Give the government a report on how a Territorial county collapsed."

"No money coming in. That's all. We hardly got paid. The judge didn't even have a court recorder. Lousiest job I ever had. But now that you mention it, yeah, those jurors were an odd lot. Well dressed, like from a big city."

"Just six, usually, I hear."

"Same six. I wondered if they were friends of the judge. They got a dollar a day for jury duty."

"Were they businessmen?"

"Naw, not here. They came and went."

"How could they go in and out of here so far from a railroad?"

"Beats me. Well, time for my nap. I wore my boots out, hiking around here with the sheriff, showing the badge. No one paid me, either. Call it public service."

Gus Glory rose suddenly, eager to escape.

No Name watched him go, wondering what

else he could have squeezed out of the man. The mystery had only deepened. Where did that jury come from if it wasn't local people? Maybe across the bridge somewhere. No Name admitted he knew nothing about that country on the other side of the North Platte. That was a huge chunk of Wyoming Territory and a blank spot on the map. The Territory had vast bowls separated by ridges of mountain, and more privacy than all the other part of the country combined. He'd go have a look sometime.

He headed back to the caboose to report. Cran was a listener. He seemed to blot up and weigh everything that No Name said.

"They want to leave tomorrow? For Paris?"

"Bit of a hurry if you ask me. Can you stop them?"

"How? I have no charges to bring. And there's no court anywhere nearby. No, I can't. Now what about the jury?"

"Six well-dressed men. The judge knew them slightly. They thought alike. His wife didn't exactly approve of them. I like her. She's got her own mind—and her own will."

"What about this business before he came here, independent scholar?"

"I guess he's not appreciated by academics. They both made that clear."

"Did he have a name for this discipline?"

"Eugenics."

"Never heard of it."

"He said it wasn't for addled minds like mine."

Gran grinned. "That's what I like about scholars."

"I talked to the deputy, Gus Glory. He added a little. Yes, the court used the same jury, six men, all neatly dressed. But he didn't know where they came from. They weren't even local as far as he could tell. But there they were, handing down guilty verdicts."

"And filling up the graveyard?"

"That seems to be the story."

"You've done well, No Name."

"I'm just getting started."

He headed into the empty street of New Dawn. The day had started cruelly, and had continued to wear him out. But he liked the investigating. It was like putting a jigsaw puzzle together except that a lot of pieces were missing and would never be found.

CHAPTER TWENTY-NINE

No Name spotted the sheriff hurrying toward him, and knew more trouble was brewing. He paused, waiting for the lawman.

"You," the sheriff shouted. "What were you doing at my house?"

"Collecting Wellbred County records."

"Where are they?"

"The inspector has them. The one sent by Washington."

"Him?"

"In the caboose. He hired me as an investigator. The inspector general looks at things."

"Tor somebody. I met him."

"Torvold Gran, actually. Things fell apart here. He's looking into the crime rate and why the judge didn't keep records, and why no taxes were collected, and a lot of stuff."

"And you went to my house without my permission."

"I asked your daughter for the records, and she got them. There isn't much in those ledgers. Like the whole county was someone's secret."

"Don't you ever never walk into my place. And leave my daughter out of it, understand?"

No Name nodded. "I work for the government and do what I'm asked. I've been asking the judge some things. Like the jury. That six-man jury sure interests the inspector. So I asked what was happening, and he said he was busy. He and his wife are leaving for Paris on the next train."

"Paris? You mean Paris, like in France?"

"That's the usual one, yes. They're loading up steamer trunks. Going for a year. He's complaining because there's no help around here. Good anarchists don't want to work."

The sheriff digested all that. "What else did he say?"

"That jury, they were acquaintances of his. And that he's a scholar. And he and colleges don't get along. Mrs. Howard sure agreed with that."

Clemson thought that through. "He's not going anywhere. I'll tell him to unpack."

"How can you do that? He's a free man, and this is an anarchy place without government."

Clemson stuck a finger at his own chest. "I'm the government for now. That's me, and the judge isn't going ten feet, much less across an ocean."

"I guess you'd better tell him that. I think he is counting on you to get his steamer trunks to the station."

"That tub of butter's not going anywhere. What else are you looking for?"

"You'll want to talk to the inspector, Mr. Clemson. He's getting a long list together. It

244

seems things were sort of irregular around here."

"What's he saying about last night?"

"The gallows? The deputy? It's on his New Dawn list. The main list is Throatlatch."

"If he's smart he'll tear up those lists and get out on the next train. Some gray-haired guy with big glasses comes in here and talks like he owns the place."

"Well, in a way he does. He's the federal inspector. He's the government's man here. And I'm helping him."

"If you're smart, you'll get onto that train, too. When is it? Tomorrow?"

"Tomorrow, yes. A baggage car and a coach. It'll let off passengers here. Mostly New Dawn people, and then go on to the railhead, up a few miles, and let off new workers and pick up the injured ones. Building track is no picnic. They'll lay off some food from the baggage car, come here, maybe use the siding to shift the engine around, pick up the judge and Mrs. Howard, and head east. That's what I've heard."

"It's not going to happen that way. And when the train leaves here, it'll carry you, Gran, and railroad people. If you want to stay healthy."

"You'd better tell that to Gran."

"You can tell him. I got things to do."

"Who's left around here from Throatlatch? You and Glory and the Howards. Is that county clerk, Peter Dent, still around?"

"What are you, some detective?"

"I guess that's a good enough word. That's what I'm paid for. I get green money, not blue. And I work for the Justice Department."

The sheriff grabbed No Name by the shirt and drew him tight enough to spill bad breath over the young man. "You're all gonna be on that train, get it?"

"Can't make it. I'm taking your daughter to lunch tomorrow."

Clemson yanked No Name's shirt so hard he ripped it half off, then stalked away.

No Name waited, and then headed for the caboose. There were things to tell his employer, including the likelihood that the clerk, Peter Dent, was around here somewhere. He was the invisible one who had a homestead claim on the right-of-way that got tossed out. The one who kept the county books. The one who could answer a lot of questions for Torvold Gran. Maybe he could tell the inspector who hanged Majestic Skinner. The one who never stopped hiding.

Gran's face lit up. "You told him you were taking his daughter to lunch tomorrow?"

"I had to say something."

"I'd give you a raise on your first day, if I had the power."

"I'm worn out."

"I would certainly think so. But you've made more progress in one day than I have from poking around here. Clemson's got the judge tied down?"

"That's what he says."

"What do you make of it?"

"The sheriff ran Wellbred County."

"We didn't know that until today."

"I woke up with two legs dropping through the trap at the gallows, and it's been downhill from there."

"Why are you here?"

"There's something I can't explain, but it draws me here. It's not revenge, it's not justice. It's not a vision of a good land. But here I am. I like to read. Maybe I just want to see how the story ends."

Gran eyed him as if No Name was an orangutan.

"You're alone. You've no father or mother, no brothers or sisters, no kin. Does that explain it?"

"No, nothing does."

"You're well read. For a person with little schooling, you speak well. Tell me about that."

"When you have no family, you have books. I love books. They're not as good as a father or mother, but they do well when there's nothing else. And they give me something—possibility. You don't have choices if you don't know what you might choose."

"You want to settle down here? Maybe become an anarchist?"

"No, I just want to see how this story ends, and then keep on going."

"To where?"

"Back to the Oregon Trail, right where my parents vanished, or people found me."

"And then?"

"Start over. A little boy. With a name, with kin, with someone with a name inside of me."

Gran eyed the young man gravely. "I'd help you if I could. But the only one who can do that is yourself."

No Name nodded. "I guess I'll take a walk before some supper. I want to cross the old wooden bridge and see what's there."

"That bridge will take you into another county. With a government, with order, with responsible people, with families. There's none of that here. There never was. I think Wellbred County was a fraud from the day the Territory set it up."

"I just want to see," No Name said.

"Should I worry about you coming back?"

"No. I want to see how this story ends."

"When I was a boy I wanted to be a Viking," Gran said. "Somehow life took me somewhere else."

No Name slipped into the late afternoon sun, noting the hollowness of New Dawn, and its empty streets. He walked quietly down the main drag, past the gallows, and across the bottoms to the bridge, a narrow one-lane affair that wobbled its way across the North Platte River. The bridge swayed with the current, which was fast just now, with snow-melt. The water was green. The land was hushed. He saw no birds.

He felt the bridge creak as he walked across the wide river. He reached the opposite shore, overarched by cottonwoods, and felt as if he were in a different country. Here was order and peace. Birds hopped from thicket to thicket. An ineffable serenity permeated the river bottoms, and the hills to the south. It was the same sort of country, same grama grasses, same sunlight, but here was something else. Wellbred was an open wound, but this place bore no wounds, at least none that he could feel.

He followed the two-rut road as it traversed a leafy lowland and then climbed out of the bottoms. The same views caught his eye, but somehow everything was different. There were no houses, buildings, ranches, branches off the rutted road. There was no settlement here, unlike Throatlatch and Wellbred County, but it felt safer on this side of the laughing river. He couldn't explain it. The road would take him south and west, through a land even emptier than the north side of the river. He settled in a bluegrass meadow dotted with sagebrush, and let his senses absorb this place. There were no revelations, and yet he felt he had learned something.

After a while he retraced his steps, crossed

the rickety bridge, and found himself back in a crucible of striving, and ambition, and fear, and loneliness. Especially loneliness. Did anyone in Throatlatch have friends?

CHAPTER THIRTY

A ten-wheel Baldwin pusher locomotive arrived, dragging a green baggage car and a coach of the same weary color. It pulled into the siding and stopped just behind the caboose at the station, where Gran and No Name watched.

Professor Rottweiler was on hand to greet the New Dawn arrivals, who stepped down gingerly for their first bewildered look at a decaying paradise. He greeted each one effusively, and designated assistants steered the couples, and families, and single males—there were no single females—toward their new allotment of heaven. Several working men, bound for the rail-head, stepped out, smoked, surveyed the barren country, and then climbed back into the coach. The engineer inched the train forward and coupled the caboose in front. It would take the caboose, with or without its passengers, to the railhead and back, and leave it on the siding once again.

Gran chose to go, and No Name went with him. There had been no sign of Judge and Mrs. Howard, but when the little train returned, things might be different. The train headed through peaceful flats, surrounded by vertical landscapes. Wyoming was a checkerboard of flats and peaks. A half hour later they pulled up behind the work train at the railhead, and settled down for a while. A horse and dray pulled up beside the baggage car and unloaded cotton sacks of flour, burlap sacks of potatoes, and sundry other crocks and crates of food for a male mob. Mick Malone collected the new workers, who stared about, wondering what sort of dry hell they had gotten themselves into. A few looked ready to bolt, but Malone, with his big smile and gift of tongues, put them at ease.

Next, half a dozen workmen, some injured, clambered into the coach. One had a broken foot and used a sapling pole as a crutch. The other had a heavily wrapped shattered wrist. Their working days were probably over.

And then, to No Name's surprise, Mitgang Schuster appeared, dragging a small sack of his possessions. Gran hailed him and helped him into the caboose. There would be time for some good talk.

"So it is you," Schuster said, assessing No Name. "You will have stories to tell me, so I hear."

"What do you hear?"

"A barber hears all things, and keeps very quiet about most of them," Schuster said. "I cook and I shave."

Gran and No Name did a quick tour of the

railhead, finding nothing unusual about it. A string of flatcars stood ready to unload ties, hardware, rails, and sundry other items. They boarded the caboose wordlessly about the time the Baldwin whistled a couple of times, and the little train began to back its way to New Dawn.

"So then, do you want a shave?" Schuster asked.

Both Gran and No Name did.

"Good. I always get more gossip when I have a razor at the throat," Schuster said, eyeing the available pots and spare water. "You might be getting a cold shave, but if you try hard, you can bear it." He whipped out his razor and stropped it, ran his finger along its edge, and seemed satisfied. Then he nodded to Gran. "You get the sharper blade," he said.

Gran enjoyed the little barber, and smiled.

That left it to No Name to tell the barber what had transpired in New Dawn. Magnificent Skinner's hanging, the Howards' interest in fleeing, the arrival of bewildered anarchists, and the sudden domination of the former sheriff, Clemson.

"Tell him about the jury business," Gran said, between razor scrapes.

"Mr. Gran is looking into the trials, the ones the judge staged, with the same six-member jury on every occasion, usually well dressed and utterly unknown to the rest of the town, Gus Glory tells me."

"Ah, the devil incarnate. I shaved them all. All six, and a few more, who came in for trims and shaves. They talk, just like everyone else. Now you are dealing with the darkest heart, the evil, the demonic in Throatlatch."

The barber paused dramatically, and scraped carefully around the back of Gran's neck.

"E Pluribus Unum Howard had some colleagues who lived in a sort of dormitory or wing of the judge's house. They called it research. Academics will call any fiendish thing research."

No Name wished the barber would hurry along, but the barber was taking his time and enjoying it. Even Gran seemed restless.

"They chose to gather at Throatlatch, the most remote and perverse and debased town in the country, so they could collect evidence about a new theory of theirs. It is called eugenics, and it's closely tied to evolution, and the purpose is to hasten the perfection of the human race by enhancing its intelligence. They would do that by destroying its misfits, its stupid members, its criminals, its cowards, and its sick and unhealthy and deformed persons."

"Am I descended from apes?" No Name asked.

"Enough of that," Gran yelled.

It startled No Name. He had never heard Torvold Gran raise his voice. Suddenly this was grave ground.

"I am descended from raccoons, myself,"

Schuster said. "With a little groundhog on the side."

Gran looked grumpy.

"One by one, in the barber chair in Throatlatch, they told me their story. Each a scholar. Each projecting the Darwinian theory of evolution, with is hard enough for most people to bear, into new turf—the deliberate improvement of the species. And how casually they considered the elimination—their polite word—of those who didn't make the grade."

Schuster wiped Gran's face and neck with a cold towel, and helped the marshal out of his caboose seat. Gran dug around for some change, but had none.

"Later," the barber said, and summoned No Name, who soon found himself being lathered with cold water. It was oddly uncomfortable, even ominous.

"Do you have names of these people?" Gran asked.

"Only first names. Elwood, Ambrose."

"What happened to them?"

"They stayed with the judge a while. It's hard to get here before this railroad. They had evening seminars and discussions—poor Mrs. Howard, she had to cook for a mob every night, and no one lifted a finger to help her. They talked, she cooked."

"Talked about what?"

"Throatlatch. The benighted trash who needed to hang to benefit natural selection of our species."

Something hard and sharp seemed to cut through No Name's soul.

"Say that again, and say it again," Gran said. "They had a plan to murder the citizens of Throatlatch?"

"The ones they deemed the dead ends of evolution."

No Name felt the razor scrape away stubble.

"I'm not sure these scholars were the jurors," Schuster said. "The jurors were dressed better than these scholars."

"Did these scholars keep records?"

"I wouldn't know. They came here, they avoided town, they experimented, and they left."

"The judge and his wife would know them all?"

"Certainly."

"What about the sheriff?"

"The sheriff never talked to me about it."

"Where did the money come from? The sheriff isn't poor, and the judge is comfortable and owns a lot of property."

"I get paid ten cents a shave. They do not share such things with a barber."

"Would you take a guess?"

"There are several things going on at once. Some of these men were buried in books. Other people came here to make a buck. Some of the hard-bitten in Throatlatch were on the run, and the law was far away."

The train slowed about the time Schuster finished scraping No Name's face. A brakeman jumped down and threw the switch to the siding, and the train backed in. The brakeman uncoupled the caboose near the station, rode the train forward a few yards, walked up to the switch and threw it back to mainline traffic so work trains could get through. There were no new passengers. The judge and Mrs. Howard did not board. A few people stood watching, and then the Baldwin ten-wheel engine whistled, belched smoke, and began to push the dull green cars toward Fort Laramie. It would be a long, hard trip.

No Name discovered the sheriff, quietly watching from a shadowed corner of the station. New Dawn might be an anarchist-non-government enclave, but Sheriff Clemson wore a sidearm. No Name didn't doubt that the anarchist sheriff had thwarted the will of the anarchist Howards.

"That's very interesting," Gran said. "I am getting lessons in anarchy every day."

"Is my old shop empty? I might move in. Even anarchists need shaves," Schuster said.

"It's empty but you might consult their leader here, Professor Rottweiler."

"I've met the man; a friendly fellow who believes in dog-eat-dog society."

"Mitgang. Be careful, and check with me," Gran said.

The barber nodded. No Name watched him step down, his barbering kit in hand, and head down the lonely street toward his old haunt, the tonsorial parlor, which stood abandoned in an empty town.

"He's my eyes and ears," Gran said.

The determined man made his way to his old place, circled the building, peered through a window hanging open, and then disappeared from view. No Name felt an odd fear. But then he saw the barber sweeping grit out of his tonsorial parlor, and thought that in time, Mitgang Schuster would return to his previous life.

"No Name, tomorrow go find a window in the old county building across from Schuster, and keep an eye out. Everything. Who comes by, who eyes the barber, who steps in and shakes his hand, all of that. You understand why, don't you?"

"Sort of."

"He's the last witness."

CHAPTER THIRTY-ONE

Lydia Howard eyed No Name darkly from her doorway.

"What a surprise. You've come to find out why we're here."

"I'd enjoy a visit with you and the judge."

"The judge is in his library starting a memoir. That's what scholars do when they're feeling out of sorts. His will be a big thick one, a thousand pages of grievances."

"Well, I wouldn't want to disturb him."

"He's been disturbed for years. I can tell you what happened in about one minute. The sheriff found out somehow that we were intending to take a long trip. So he showed up, told us we weren't going anywhere, not now, and then he walked right in, tossed everything out of our steamer trunks, and hauled them off."

"He could do that? In a place where there's no government and everyone thinks he's free?"

"He did it. And the revolver at his waist talked loudly enough to reach the deaf."

"So you're stuck? Are you going to complain?"

"Complain? We'd be talking to a tree stump."

"Could you buy a horse and wagon?"

"My backside can stand only so much abuse." She eyed him. "Have a seat. We can have a good confession. You get to be priest."

"I didn't mean—maybe I should go."

"No, you're a handy funnel. Anything I say will end up in the federal inspector's ears. So I'll give him an earful."

No Name eased into the wicker, and she took another. That veranda was built for good conversation.

"Well, what I'm wondering is why the sheriff stopped you."

She sighed. "Because word would get out and he'd spend the rest of his days in custody."

"What did he do?"

"What didn't he do?"

"You know, the inspector's debating his options. He can let this slide. Even the arrival of a lot of anarchists in federal territory. It doesn't amount to much. He's told me there's lots of groups and cults who've come west just to be alone and unbothered. He was inclined to do that, wind it up and leave, thinking that the cult would burn out in a few months. But then a former Throat-latch deputy was hanged yesterday—cruelly, with a lasso that choked life out of him and left him gasping. And now he's thinking about martial law. Put the soldiers in here for a while."

"Well, he's right. We need General Sherman or Sheridan around here."

"I've learned that you've had guests here."

"Guests? You mean masters. I'm the slave."

No Name waited quietly.

"Scholars. Colleagues. Visionaries. Three or four, usually. They came all the way here by wagon or horse or on foot just to see Throatlatch."

"Something unusual here?"

She sighed. "Pluribus is interested in a theory of human perfection, called eugenics. The idea is to breed more and more perfect mortals by eliminating the stupid, the misfits, the crippled, and the least successful. It's a bit radical."

"What do you mean by eliminate?"

"Well, the original idea was to control breeding, keep misfits from mating, and thus hasten evolution along. But Pluribus thought the process could be speeded up some, and more could be learned by studying the worst collection of dummies in the country. After asking a lot of questions, he settled on Throatlatch."

"To study human shortcomings?"

"Well, at first. But his colleagues thought maybe the whole thing could be spurred along."

"How does evolution fit in?"

"That Charles Darwin is an idiot. He's never going to get me to believe I'm descended from a gorilla." She smiled suddenly. "It's an idea that millions and millions of tiny changes, influenced by millions and millions of things, result in equipment we didn't pack around a few hundred

261

generations ago. These permit the best to survive and kill off the worst. Eugenics is sort of like that except it sails as fast as a Harvard rowing team."

"Are you a believer?"

"Well, there are times I'm ready to dip into the other world and scold my great-grandmother for giving me arthritis." She struggled for words. "It's why some lizards can turn into the color of the leaf they're sitting on."

"So E Pluribus Unum is a student of eugenics, and he's picked out a place that has the worst population in the country, and is far from anywhere, then what?"

"Then he writes his colleagues and tells them that he's discovered a perfect laboratory, where they can improve the population of the whole town, and drive off the misfits, and measure all this so it can be published in quarterly journals. They're interested. They correspond. They grumble about costs. Some decide on it, but most don't want to drag themselves overland to a remote and uncomfortable hellhole just to do some experimenting. But he did get them. They got most of the way by rail, and got themselves guided here by creepy males in animal skin clothing. And when they get here, there's Pluribus, a fanatic, eager to improve the human race."

"Aren't you avoiding certain words, such as execute, kill, hang?"

"Well, I'm delicate and female, so I get a pass on that."

"Were there other scholars who ridiculed him?"

"Yes, and that only made him fiercer, and it became his passion to show them what ignoramuses they are."

"And this sort of, well, infected the rest, your guests?"

"I was glad to get rid of them. Do you know how many pancakes I fried?"

"Who were they?"

She pondered that. "You know, I'm not sure. They were all Tom, Dick and Harry. They looked alike. Spectacles, suit coats worn out at the elbows, high-topped shoes that needed new soles, old goats with virgin wives, gents who camped in the outhouse for a half hour at a time, studying ladybugs."

"Were they professors?"

"Who knows? Most professors don't know how to dress."

"Were you in on it?"

"Actually, I heard plenty but they thought my ears were too tender, and conducted their policy seminars, as they were called, in the library while I was doing armloads of dishes."

"Policy?"

"Would a town improve if its mentally deficient were drowned like kittens in a bag?"

No Name got the whole story. These scholars

had started with an exciting idea—perfect the human race—and had gradually turned that upside down and were conducting criminal experiments. They were sitting as judge and jury, sentencing people to hang, just for the experience of it. It was an old story. Evil and cruelty done in the name of goodness and virtue. Something in this repelled No Name so much he wanted to run, flee, from this fancy home on a noble hillside.

"All of this happened before the anarchists moved in?"

"All of it, over several years."

"Why wouldn't the sheriff let you go?"

"Because he and Majestic Skinner were the executioners, the ones recruited—for a price—by the scholarly crowd. And now he knows he's vulnerable. Your inspector's looking into Throatlatch. And you are, too. And Clyde Clemson has to contain this, bury it, which will be easy to do if he can silence a few more witnesses."

"Where did the money come from? This is a large place, and so is the sheriff's."

She stared out upon the endless plains. "I inherited some."

"Where did the sheriff get his?"

"His wife has some."

"Wife?"

"Carolina."

"But . . . but . . ."

"He calls her his daughter, but she's not. She's

thirty, he's forty-two. It has to do with her inheritance. If she stays single, her money is hers. If she marries, her husband gets it all as a dowry. She wants to keep it. So she lives with him. She's a 'daughter,' so to speak. She confessed it to me one day over some Earl Grey."

No Name felt like he was crawling out of an avalanche, pounding snow away so he could breathe, and finally reaching air. Abruptly he bolted up and fled the veranda and the wicker, and stumbled downhill.

CHAPTER THIRTY-TWO

Torvold Gran folded his wire glasses and set his notepad aside.

"You've broken this open. With one good conversation you've given us the first real understanding of what's gone on here. We lack names, but we'll get them. We need to indict the jurors and get more testimony on the judge and sheriff. You've won your spurs, Nameless."

He stood, gathered a summer straw hat, put on a summer suit coat, and collected a notepad and sharpened pencil. "Time for me to show the badge," he said.

They found Clemson in the old Wellbred court-house, if the claptrap structure could be called that. The former sheriff was standing at the window, studying the tonsorial parlor, where Schuster was washing a window.

"Mr. Clemson, we've been looking for you," Gran said. "We'd like your help in getting this report done. I wear two hats, and my other one is United States marshal. You could be a big help."

Gran flipped open a leather folder, and let the sheriff take a good long look. Clemson's gaze flicked about, and then he nodded.

"Doesn't surprise me a bit," Clemson said.

"I'd like you to come with us to the graveyard and help us identify some graves," the marshal said.

"I don't know who's there."

"Well, you might remember when we get there."

No Name and the marshal led the reluctant former sheriff across the main road, up a side lane, to the graveyard, which had a few marked graves in the front, and a long row of unmarked ones at the back.

"All right, your testimony will be helpful, sir," the marshal said.

He didn't begin at one side, but led Clemson straight to the grave where Carolina had been weeping that long ago eve.

"Your woman visited here and wept. You must know who this is," the marshal said.

"Got me, I haven't the faintest idea."

"Was he Sioux, or part Sioux? Named Little something, I'm not familiar with these names."

"Might have been a breed renegade, Marshal. The name doesn't ring a bell."

"Why'd she come here alone at night and kneel here?"

"Who saw her do that?"

"I heard about it," the marshal said. "I gather this person was a half-brother of JimBob, who had the saloon in Throatlatch."

267

"No, that's crazy."

"Well, think about it. We could be misinformed. You've been in law enforcement, and know how you get things together piece by piece, and sometimes you walk down the wrong alley."

"I think we had a half-breed around here. He robbed someone and paid a price. You'd have to look it up."

"There are no county records worth the ink they're written with."

The sheriff smiled. "Well then, that pretty much ends that."

"What did your, ah, wife say to you about it?"

"Carolina? She just gets starchy."

"Didn't say anything?"

"Nothing that I remember."

"Well, all right, let's see what you know about the rest of these. Were they all hanged?"

"How should I know that?"

"We may have to disinter them and find out. I was hoping you'd save us some time. What are their names, and where are the court records?"

Clemson shrugged.

"I guess you pulled the lever, sir."

"No, that was Majestic Skinner. He was the expert. I just watched to make sure it was all proper."

"You never pulled the lever on the trap?"

"Well, not so much, anyway. A time or two."

"When the judge said so?"

"Yeah, I guess. This is history, marshal."

"Well, help me close this down, then. I've got to report what happened and why Wellbred County fell apart, and why it's now an ungoverned enclave that is not recognizing federal dominion."

"We'll get this solved, all right," Clemson said, his posture straightening.

"I've filed regular reports since the telegraph came in," the marshal said.

"Glad to help fix it up," the sheriff said.

"Judge Howard had his own half-dozen jurors. Who were they?"

"You know, that was a mystery. They were odd ducks, big spectacles, little chins, fussy sorts. One had a monocle he would put on and take off. I heard they were subversives, but I wouldn't know one from a rooster. They stayed with the judge, had noisy debates, and left after a month or two."

"You met them? If we found one, would you recognize him?"

"Me? No. They all looked alike, from Cicero or Peoria or some place."

"Weren't you curious about them?"

The sheriff squinted. "It pays to mind your own business with a judge like that."

"About the judge. Were you friends?"

"When it comes to words, he's a fast draw. He could shoot words at me faster than I could pull out my Smith and Wesson."

"Well, I have a project for you, one that can get me out of here and leave you at peace. Find out who those jurors were, names and occupations and addresses. And who's in the graveyard. Maybe you can get some help from your wife, eh?"

"I'll do it," the man said and hurried away.

The marshal eyed No Name. "More progress," he said. "You go visit your friend the barber, and see if any of those jurors told him anything interesting, all right?"

The marshal headed back toward the caboose. No Name decided he needed a shave.

"What did the sheriff tell you?" Schuster asked.

"You've been watching."

"I see the world go by my window."

"The sheriff, he said as little as he could. He couldn't identify anyone in the graves. Not even the one his wife visited."

"Daughter."

"Wife."

Schuster stared. "That demolishes a couple of my theories. I will tell you later."

The barber whipped up some lather in a cup, and applied it with a brush. No Name remembered that the scrape of the barber's straightedge had saved his life, turning a fleeing unkempt youth into a groomed man. He felt at home in this place, with a tradesman helping to clean up an evil town. Schuster seemed to live to heal a tragic world, and to have no large personal ambitions. There were people like that, rare and valued by any good society.

"The marshal hopes you can come up with more about those jurors, the judge's pals, who dropped in. Where they were from. What they talked about. They were part of a cabal of idealists gone perverse."

"How so?"

"Eugenics. They want to perfect the human race. But soon they were experimenting with killing some of it. They jumped from an abstract ideal to premeditated murder."

The barber scraped away, and wiped the lather off his razor.

"The judge brought them. He corresponded with them, invited them. It was a hard trip, and included overland wagon travel. But they came," No Name went on. "They are the key to it all, and we need to find them."

"We talked. Customers all talk. They had accents. East Coast, southern, Midwestern. They all kept silent about some things, but I've a way of sensing things, call it self-protection. I would ask who they were, and they would dodge it. I understood they were hiding things, in this case evil things, and doing a good job of it. They were smart. They steered the conversation. One of their favorites was to talk about Throatlatch's people, their weaknesses, their follies, their barbarity. Yes, they loved that. Even the judge, when he came for a trim, talked about that."

"Ideas can be dangerous."

"The darkest crimes begin with an idea. I'll see what I can remember. The very things the marshal needs, names, addresses, their correspondence or scholarly papers, these are what they kept from me. I wish I could help, but just now, I am blank."

"Were you afraid?"

"I never stop being afraid—of some people, who telegraph their inner selves to me."

A carriage drew up on the street. It was handsome, an ebony victoria, with two chestnut Belgians drawing it.

Schuster patted down No Name's face, accepted a coin, and undid the bib.

The gentleman entering the shop was Peter Dent, but No Name barely recognized him. This version wore a black silk top hat, a three piece suit, a cravat, soft shining shoes, and his fingernails were trimmed and polished.

"So, you've returned," he said to Schuster. "I claimed this. Abandoned property. In fact I own every lot in the town. A company of mine, New Dawn, my corporation. Abandoned, tax delinquent, it doesn't matter."

"You live here?"

"Across the bridge. This place has been overrun, which is useful for me. I'm charging rent. All these anarchists are a bonanza."

"What compels them to pay you?"

"They're good fellows. Just because there's no government here doesn't mean I don't own every scrap of land. I've worked out agreements with some, in greenbacks, not their imitation currency, and they'll pay or I'll evict. That's what I've come here about. I'm delighted to see you put my property to use, and wish to charge you twenty-five a month, in greenbacks."

Schuster opened a drawer and showed the landlord a few dimes. "I charge ten cents a shave, a little more for a haircut, and other items. Go ahead and pencil it out."

"I'm afraid twenty-five's my minimum, Mr. Schuster."

"How do I even know you own this place?"

"Easy. I have a record. I was the county clerk, Wellbred County clerk, and I possess the record. Every transfer to New Dawn is recorded and notarized in my own hand. All duly recorded when this was a county. I kept the record and can show you."

"What's your purpose?" No Name asked.

"Why, to make my fortune, of course. I have a knack for living well. Look at my rig out there."

The rig was impressive. The draft horses were checked by a carriage weight that Dent had placed on the ground.

"And that's just the beginning. This is my kingdom and it'll put me on Park Avenue. I'll buy out the judge and the sheriff, and bring in more of my family, and we'll be sitting pretty."

"I'm afraid I can't afford your rent. My small trade wouldn't even cover your rent, much less make me a living. But I might move to the railroad station. You don't own that."

"You're right, it's on railroad right-of-way, gotten from the government. But of course, I could always remove the station. The railroad doesn't own it. The town of New Dawn does."

The barber smiled.

Peter Dent lifted his top hat, and settled it. "I like you. I like having you here. New Dawn benefits from a barber. More anarchists are coming. Stay right here, and when you're making a living, make an offer."

"If I stay, I'll do that."

No Name intervened. "While you're here, sir, I have a few questions. I work for the federal inspector, who wants to know what happened to Throatlatch. What he reports may decide what the federal government will do. It might even send in troops to reclaim the lost county."

Dent absorbed that, and nodded. "There are always flies in the ointment."

"What do you know about the district court, and the jurors who sent so many people to the gallows?"

"Ah, there you have it. I like money, not power. I think this is worth some talk. People who don't make money the usual way, by milking it out of others, drive me crazy. That judge and his scholarly crowd, they were a greedy lot. Not for money, but for fame. They wanted to improve the entire human race, a proposition that reduces to war. Give me a trim, Schuster, at no charge of course, and I'll spill a lot of beans."

CHAPTER THIRTY-THREE

The ten-wheel Baldwin hissed to a stop at New Dawn, dragging the baggage car and coach once again. Several people were on hand, including the sheriff and Judge and Mrs. Howard. This time, Hannibal Rottweiler was on hand as well.

A conductor dropped a steel footstool to the ground and helped people off the coach, but most of them refused his hand. No Name found himself studying the newcomers, all of them a rougher sort than the previous batch. They were all anarchists fired from a Northern Michigan copper mine, and invited here by Rottweiler's organization. They stared around at the dry open country, a far cry from the shrouded forests of the north.

"Gentlemen, this way please. I'll take you to your new homes. We're pleased to have you, and eager to share a new way of life with you."

"Are you the government?" asked one.

"No, there is none here."

"That one there looks like a lawman."

"He's the former sheriff of Wellbred County,

but holds no office now. He'd be pleased to talk with you."

"What about that one?" the man said, pointing at Gran.

"He's an inspector, finishing up a report for the government."

"Yeah, and collecting our names to hand to the prosecutors."

"Let's get you settled, and you can ask all the questions you want at our meeting in the anarchist hall at five."

"Meetings of what?" the man asked.

"Anarchists. We need to agree on some things to make it all work out."

"Not me," the man said. "I make my own decisions."

The little professor bobbled about, and finally got his lightly burdened newcomers walking into town. These men were big, rough, poor, and scowling. No Name hiked along nearby, as innocuous as ever, barely noticed.

"Here are the houses. These streets. They're empty. They need repair. It's up to you to do that. Just choose one and it's yours."

A few of the earlier anarchists, along with wives and children, peered from front stoops and porches. Most of the newcomers looked about, wanting to see what was available, checking out the neighborhoods.

No Name heard the train whistle, and the

chuff of the engine as it started toward the rail-head, once again carrying new railroad workers and supplies for the railhead camp, now two miles further away. It would be back later, taking whatever was destined to return to Fort Laramie.

One house, whitewashed instead of raw wood, drew the attention of several newcomers. An elderly gent sat in a rocker on its porch.

"I want that one," the leader of the newcomers said. "It's bigger and better."

"That's taken by Mr. Brophy, sir," the professor said.

"Tell him to beat it."

"But it's his."

"It isn't anyone's. Now it's mine." He eyed the old lame gent. "I'm moving in. Take your stuff and beat it, or I'll throw it out."

"Now see here," Rottweiler said.

The miner grabbed the rotund professor's shirt and shoved. Rottweiler careened into the dust. Brophy rose, limped in, collected some stuff, and escaped.

"That's better," the newcomer said. "Call me Big Michigan." He pointed at some of his cohorts, five in all, and nodded. All five collected their duffel and walked in. Rottweiler dusted off the street grime, and watched. The big whitewashed place suddenly looked like a fort.

That was the only trouble. The rest soon

claimed quarters and spent the afternoon making them livable.

No Name corralled one of them, who stood on his new porch.

"What was that about?"

"What business is it of yours?"

No Name simply grinned.

"Big Mich runs his own show. At the copper company, they beat him, whipped him, kicked him off the grounds, and he just collected a few of us and busted glass, cut conveyer belts, tipped ore cars, and waved some sharp steel at the bosses. They finally got some cops to haul him out and promised him ten years locked up if he didn't get out of town."

"Big Mich. Is he gonna fight this place or help it?"

"Big Mich fights everyone, including himself. It's all his property now. He now owns this joint and everyone in it. Who are you?"

"I never had a name."

"Ah, one of us! You're a good man."

"We're going to enjoy you," No Name said.

He headed back to the caboose and shared what he knew with Gran.

"Go tell the sheriff. And the Howards."

He found Clemson and Gus Glory in the old public building and described what had transpired.

"I know the type," Clemson said. "But they respect a forty-five caliber bullet."

No Name wasn't so sure of that. "Well, I've told you, anyway."

Clemson nodded. "Looks like me and Gus will have to pack a little iron for a while."

No Name caught up with the Howards, who were starting up the hill, and told them to watch out. Not that two middle-aged people could do a thing to slow down Big Mich, but at least they knew what to expect.

"Is the sheriff going to let you travel when the train heads east?"

Lydia just shook her head.

"It'll be a chapter in my memoir," the judge said. He still was sour.

No Name located Gran at the barbershop. "You're in danger," he began. But Gran just shook his head. "I know the type. I can be the most reasonable man on the planet when I have to."

"You'll have to." He studied his employer a moment. "They know you're an inspector. That's as much as they need. They're capable of pounding holes in the caboose, prying windows open, and if need be, they'll line up along one side of it and tip it over. Especially if you're in it. They're from the copper mines near Lake Superior. They've gotten into big fights. They've been so violent the state's called out its National Guard."

Gran pondered that. "I have a job to do.

Thanks for warning me. My task has expanded suddenly. Now it includes protecting everyone here, including the dreamers, the idealists, who've thought that their belief was the key to a sort of paradise. These miners are dangerous, but less so than the ones with the bad ideas, the jurors and judge who sent innocent men, and troubled people to the gallows, all in the name of improving the human race."

He turned to Mitgang Schuster. "You're not safe here."

Schuster looked frightened, but he was seasoned in ways that would help him. That's how his life had spun out. "I know one thing. A building like this is like pasteboard against a crowd like that," he said. "But mobs don't form overnight. A few days from now, trouble for New Dawn, and maybe there won't be a New Dawn any more. The ones in the worst shape are the ones with the big houses on the hill. Big Mich would enjoy sitting on the front porch of either place, and seeing his power reach to the farthest horizon."

The little train returned from the railhead, paused to load anyone heading east, and then chuffed its way to safety. There were people around No Name who wished they were on it.

No Name left, and ate a light early meal at the saloon, which was filled with people who said not a word, and ate in eerie silence. As evening approached, No Name drifted to the meeting hall the judge had thrown together months ago. It was falling apart. But this afternoon it was crowded. Every one of the Michigan miners were seated, with Big Mich in the front row. Professor Rottweiler sat nervously on the podium. Others of the social radicals, the literati of the East, congregated around the rear, all of them behind the miners. And standing near the door were Clyde Clemson and Gus Glory, both well armed, with spare rounds lining their belts.

At the appointed hour, the professor stood, cleared his throat, and welcomed them all.

"It's a treat to have so many newcomers on hand, people who want to join a society in which there is only self-government," he said.

The miners looked puzzled.

"Now, we're here to have a discussion. We need to reach understandings, so people are secure in their lives and homes."

"Yeah, yeah, you've had your say," Big Mich said, standing up and shouldering the little professor off the podium. "Here's how it goes, understand? This here is no debating society. It's a revolution. We've got us a piece of ground and we're holding it, and we're going to take on any army that tries to stop us. We're the workers of the world, and the old ways are behind us, and now we'll get out the word, collect our people, and move piece by piece, Territory by Territory in the West, and state by state in the east. Got it? If you're not with us, take the next train out. I like that gallows out there. It's seen a little business. It hasn't seen a thing compared to what it's gonna see. You there, sheriff of Wellbred County, you and that scumbag deputy will be on the next train east, understand? Or you can turn over your little peashooters and join us. We need some manpower. For your information, there's no private property here, and I'll tell you where you can live and what you can do, and how you'll work. There's going to be a lot of work done around here, and you're all going to do it. Get the story?"

No Name got the story.

CHAPTER THIRTY-FOUR

No Name didn't like the idea.

"Are you sure you want to do that?" he asked Torvold Gran.

"You never know what you're made of until you try," Gran said. "You coming?"

No Name nodded, scared stiff.

They hiked through morning light to the whitewashed house where Big Mich and his cohorts had settled. No one walked the streets.

Gran wore his wire-rimmed spectacles, and a white shirt and dark pants.

The house lay silent. Gran knocked on the door. In time a rough-looking miner opened up, eyed the two, and yawned.

"I'd like to speak to your leader. I understand his name is Michigan, Big Mich."

"He's busy."

"I'm a marshal. I think he would want to speak to me."

The man vanished. In a few moments all the residents of the house appeared, Big Mich flanked by the others. They were a formidable wall of muscular bodies.

"I'm Torvold Gran, United States Marshal. I'd like to have a little talk."

"Get on the next train out," Big Mich said.

"I thought we could help you here," Gran said.

"I was told you're an inspector, looking over what's happened around here."

"I'm that, too. I wear two hats. The government hasn't enough people."

"It has too many, far as I'm concerned."

"Well, we're called peace officers for a reason. If there's trouble, our task is to keep people safe and unharmed, and protect property if we can."

"Get on that train when it comes. That's all I'm gonna say."

"You know, Mr. Michigan, the government has a relaxed attitude toward groups that want to be left alone. Big country, lots of people who just want to be free to do what they believe in. It's a free country."

"It's not my country. We're going to knuckle our way into a country of our own."

"Thank you for telling us," Gran said. "That makes it clearer. Meanwhile, I have a sworn duty to protect lives, including those here. Is it your plan to protect these people?"

"I don't have plans. I don't have anything but knuckles, and I use them. Like maybe right now."

"Yes, you could. You could do whatever you want with us. But it might not go well for you after that. There's four companies of infantry at Fort Laramie, led by Civil War veterans, and they're less than fifty miles by railroad from here."

"You threatening us?"

"No, I'm saying that what you do has consequences."

Big Mich looked like a tornado whirling on that porch. He jabbed a finger into Gran's chest, almost toppling him. "Here's the word. We'll rip that telegraph wire and wrap it around your neck, and then we'll tear up rail and wrap that around your neck, and while your infantry and its popguns are fooling around, we'll be in Fort Laramie, tearing the whole post down."

Gran smiled. "I like the way you express yourself."

No Name watched Big Mich's fists clench and unclench, and then, suddenly, the big miner grinned.

"Get your skinny butt outa here, and there'll be no trouble."

"What are your plans, sir?"

Big Mich smiled. "That army comes, we've got a hundred hostages, the tracklayers up a way. They croak as easy as anyone else. The infantry, it shows up, and a tracklayer goes six feet under every ten minutes. Got the picture?"

No Name marveled. He hadn't given a thought to the rail-building crew a dozen miles away. He marveled at Gran, who was collecting valuable information without even seeming to.

"Put that gallows to use, eh?"

"We're not hangmen. That's the first project around here. We're gonna tear that scaffold down and burn the wood. Too many good people got strung up. We got the story. That sheriff, he was part of it. And that so-called judge, he was part of it. We're gonna make this a better place."

"Amen to that," No Name said.

"Who are you?"

"An investigator. Any name will do fine. I work for the government. I hope you tear out that gallows. I almost got strung up."

"You too?"

"Yes sir. If you want justice here, tear it down."

"Who did that? Give me names."

"We're working on it, and I'll be taking them to court soon," Gran said. "They'll be my prisoners, and the railroad will carry us out, and you'll be free to live as you choose, so long as you don't threaten people I'm sworn to protect."

Big Mich stared. "I don't know whether you're another con man or you're a badge I can live with. You leaving here soon?"

"Soon as we can get a few more bits of evidence."

"You leaving us alone?"

"That depends on you, not me."

"All of you. Be on the next train." Big Mich

didn't wait for a response. He whirled in, followed by his muscle men.

No Name stared at Gran, thinking he had learned more about life in ten minutes than in all of his twenty-seven years.

Gran turned to him. "Go to the station. Wire the railroad to delay the next passenger train a couple of days. Any excuse will do."

"I was hoping it'd come in the next hour," No Name said.

Gran laughed.

"What's missing? What do you need?" No Name asked.

"The names of the judge's conspirators, all of them up for several charges ranging from premeditated murder to obstruction of justice. I'm afraid Lydia Howard is a material witness. We haven't found out who killed Majestic Skinner or why. And I need to look into the sheriff and his flunky. And his wife, Carolina. And I'm not done with Peter Dent, whose main failing seems to be greed. There's no law against it. But it needs checking out."

"In two days or so?"

"If you think I'm some Wild Bill Hickok who's going to clean up this mess in two days and shoot it out with a couple dozen toughs, guess again."

Gran was right. And he was staring straight at No Name.

"If you want to be a hotshot, then resign first," Gran said.

No Name felt bad. Gran was studying him.

"You'll be fine, No Name," he said with a sudden gentleness that was as close to a blessing as anything No Name had ever heard.

Back at the sunlit caboose, Gran heated some day-old java that had stained the mugs.

"I think we can get them to do our work for us," he said. "There's several groups, each with its own goal. The judge, the sheriff, Big Mich, Professor Rottweiler, and the clerk, Peter Dent. I want to leave Rottweiler out. He and his people are trying to live an impossible life. Big Mich and his fists might lead us somewhere fast."

No Name sipped, and spit out the foul stuff.

"Sometime soon the miners are going to find out where the judge and sheriff live. I'm pretty sure those big houses were built with prison labor. Those miners know how the world works. That will be interesting," Gran said. "Those Throatlatch people might suddenly be eager to ride out of town on the next train."

"It's like riding a bucking bronco," No Name said.

"What are your thoughts?"

"A lot of harmless people could be hurt. Mitgang Schuster, and all the idealists who came here with Hannibal Rottweiler. And Mrs. Howard. How could she turn in her husband, even if she wanted to? Crooked sheriff. Isolated town."

"That's a bad one, and we'll have to leave it to the courts."

"You have a plan?"

"Nope. We wait. If Dent comes to collect rent, that might start it. If Big Mich decides to move into the judge's and sheriff's fancy places, that might start it. If the sheriff tries to hide evidence, that might start it."

But Torvold Gran was wrong. The morning bloomed into a breezy summer day, with a bold blue sky lifting No Name's heart. He wandered New Dawn, alone at first, but soon people were stopping at the grocer or bakery. Mitgang Schuster was doing a good trade. Men vanished into his tonsorial parlor, and soon emerged trimmed, scraped clean, refreshed.

Then, midmorning, Big Mich collected his miners, who equipped themselves with pikes, sledgehammers, crowbars, and axes, and they walked quietly through the dusty precincts toward the river, until they collected around the gallows that were disfiguring New Dawn. Big Mich nodded, and his burly men swarmed over the structure. They headed for the most hated place, the trap, the treacherous floor that dropped from under the feet of living men, dooming them. This they pounded with sledgehammers, one blow after another, until the wood shattered, bit by bit, and the trap finally fell, but this time taking no life with it. The miners stood around the hole, peering in, seeing in their minds the ruin that had happened there, and then they continued their job. They shattered the trap, axed the lever that sent it plunging, and began chopping away the huge posts at either end, whacking away wood with each blow of the axe.

People collected, watching silently, as the work unfolded. An upright veered off at an angle, carrying the sturdy crossbeam with it. And then the other upright collapsed, while several axes whittled away at it. The whole structure slowly crashed down. The miners didn't stop. They chopped the uprights into firewood, and severed the crossbeam in several places. That wood would never serve again, would never be used in a building, and never would be another engine of death. It was good only for burning.

The sheriff and deputy arrived, unarmed, and watched. Their naked belts announced that they were private people, not lawmen. The miner stared a moment, and then continued with their job. They attacked the platform next, knocking holes in it, splintering wood, sawing off the corner posts, and shattering the little death-stair that led men to their doom. Sometimes the wood itself shrieked and howled as crowbars and sledges twisted the life out of it. By the time the great task was nearly done, much of the town had collected there. No Name well remembered that much of Throatlatch had gathered there for other purposes, and not so long before. What was the difference between those people and these?

When at last the gallows lay in ruins, the miners dragged chunks away, and piled it near the river, out of sight of the New Dawn. No Name saw no sweat upon these men. Their shirts did not drip. It was as if they were performing an anointed task, something like communion at an altar rail. Sometime about then, Judge and Mrs. Howard arrived, saw that the edifice that was shadowing New Dawn had been demolished, and they smiled. It seemed to No Name that the evil that had filled their persons and had darkened the new town, was lifted away, and New Dawn had become a place of hope, like so many towns in the great West, a place where a person could dream, and not be afraid.

But the miracles did not cease. Professor Rottweiler removed his hat, walked to Big Mich, bowed, bowed again, and walked away. Then, in groups, the idealists who had ventured into anarchy as if living a dream, did the same. They collected before Big Mich, bowed, and smiled.

He didn't smile. There was too much thunder in the man. But he nodded with each recognition. He acknowledged each person who approached him.

No Name waited to see if Clemson and Glory

would do the same, and in a way, they did. Clemson saluted Big Mich, and so did Glory. Big Mich did not acknowledge it. That seemed to be a public way of telling the two former lawmen to get on that train.

New Dawn had become a new town that morning. Only one incident marred it. Peter Dent arrived in his black carriage, saw that the gallows had been demolished, and went to Big Mich. No Name slipped closer so he could hear.

"You've done a good thing, sir, but I would like to be compensated," Dent said.

"What?"

"I owned it sir, and the land under it. Two valuable city lots. I value it at a hundred. I'm sure you'll want to make good."

Big Mich stared, thunderclouds lowering, and stared and stared at Dent.

"It's in the county register, sir, which I have," Dent said. "I'll donate it to the city for a memorial park. You can put up a statue."

"Get on the train when it comes," Big Mich said.

Something almost comic bloomed just then. No Name couldn't remember seeing anything so strange. People laughed.

CHAPTER THIRTY-FIVE

But Big Mich wasn't done.

"You got that county ledger, with all the titles in it?" he asked Dent.

"You bet I do. Right in my carriage. That's my goldmine."

"Get it."

Dent hurried to his carriage, collected the leather-bound ledger, and hurried back.

"Here. There's all the real estate in the county, deeded and notarized by me, and in my name, except for one or two."

Dent handed the ledger to Big Mich.

No Name expected the miner to shred the ledger, but instead, Big Mich pulled out some ready-made spectacles, and opened the ledger.

"There, you see?" Dent said. "Those two lots and the structures on it are deeded to me. I was the only one to claim them."

"Sure enough," Big Mich said. "Now what's this?"

"Oh, there are two other property owners in Wellbred County, not including the railroad, and the federal government. Clemson and Howard. They're outside of Throatlatch city limits, and both are old friends of mine, and both continue to occupy their land, so they have valid deeds. Each has a quarter section up there on the slope."

"The sheriff and the judge, eh?"

"You bet. Solid citizens of the county."

"You three, then."

"Oh, the railroad, of course."

"There's no Wellbred County, my friend. You understand that, do you?"

"It makes no difference. Owners are owners."

"And there's no government, right?"

Dent was looking unhappy.

Big Mich handed the ledger to one of his mining friends. And then he addressed the crowd.

"These men are hungry. Feed them, and we'll finish up what we started."

No Name had no idea what that meant, but soon enough, the crowd surged close, bearing bread and pastries and cheeses.

The miners wolfed it all down.

Big Mich nodded, and the miners collected their pikes and crowbars and sledgehammers, and followed him to the dilapidated county building. He nodded.

That brought Schuster to the door of his barber shop.

The miners swarmed the shabby structure, knocking holes in it, testing it, and then started with the roof, which they pried loose piece by piece, board by board. The crowd collected to

295

watch the show, plainly enjoying it all. No Name eyed Torvold Gran, who stared impassively at the spectacle.

The men with sledgehammers made quick work of the roof, ripping off squealing boards, shattering rafters, knocking timbers loose. They clattered to the earth, a rising heap of broken wood. Like the wood in the gallows, this would never be put to any other use.

The miners swung rhythmically, busting up the courthouse, while the crowd watched. Some of the bearded young anarchists saw the symbolism in it, and began hauling the shattered wood off to the heap at the edge of town. Big Mich didn't object. Schuster returned to his barbering.

The task actually was larger than demolishing the gallows, and the miners chopped and battered and pried the whole summer afternoon, until at last the building lay in pieces—except for the two jail cells, which stood nakedly in the sun.

Clemson looked stricken. Those cells meant power to him, but there they were, no longer his instruments of power. They meant plenty to No Name, who had endured time in one, time rattling the iron bars while the clock ticked toward that sunrise. He was flooded now with a strange euphoria, these last hated bits of Wellbred County about to succumb.

But Big Mich was in no hurry. He approached the former sheriff.

"You got the keys?"

"No."

No Name remembered he had thrown away a set; but stayed silent.

"Anyone got keys?" Big Mich asked.

"If anyone's got keys, the cells could be handy."

A deep silence lowered over the crowd. Big Mich nodded.

His men crowded in, assessed the iron work, and set to work. Some of it could be unbolted. Other parts could only be smashed into bent scrap. It was no easy thing to knock two cells down, and the miners lacked the proper tools, especially metal-cutting saws. But brute muscle sufficed. Bar by bar, they twisted iron into useless junk. No one took the pieces away; iron would have its uses in a frontier town. New Dawn had no blacksmith, but needed one, and soon.

No Name didn't much care for that. There was something meaningful about shattering the wood that had housed such darkness. He wished the iron bars he had once clenched and rattled could suffer the same fate.

The eager men and boys dragged the metal away, piling a heap of it on the edge of town. By the time the sun lowered, New Dawn had no governmental structures. Peter Dent was annoyed to see more of his real estate vanish, but it had finally dawned on him to shut up. The remnants of a stone foundation remained, but New Dawn had rid itself of another chunk of government. As a last act, several of the miners had roped the outhouse at the rear, and hauled it away, too.

The mood now was different than what it was earlier. When the hated gallows were ripped from the vision of everyone, there was release and joy. Now, with the county building with its cruel jail torn apart, the mood was contemplative. Even questioning. No Name knew what people were pondering. Could they live without a government?

No Name and the marshal retreated to the caboose, saying nothing until they were inside of it.

"I saw the look in people's faces," No Name said.

"That look will change tomorrow, or the next, and it won't be happy," the marshal said.

"I once was behind those bars, rattling them, helpless, hating it," No Name said.

"Big Mich would have kept those cells if he had keys."

"I once had a set, but I didn't tell him," No Name said.

New Dawn celebrated that evening. The weight of a thousand years had been torn from its shoulders. Even the miners, wary and silent, sat in the saloon, owning the universe. Professor Rottweiler toasted the Michigan copper miners, and they toasted him. No Name watched it morosely, unable to say why he didn't feel any joy in it. Peter Dent had climbed into his black carriage and vanished across the old wood bridge. Clyde Clemson and Gus Glory had vanished. The marshal had watched a while, and headed for the caboose, keeping quiet. E Pluribus Unum had long since fled to his big house on the slope. There were a lot of private thoughts floating around, and No Name was not privy to any of them. He headed for the abandoned livery barn, where he had found some old hay in the loft, and settled in for the night. He found himself wondering about Carolina, who she was and what her relationship with Clemson was, but No Name was clueless, and found himself not caring. If she knew about her common-law husband's conduct and did nothing, she was as guilty as he was. For one gentle moment he wished things had been different.

When he arrived at the caboose the next morning, he found Big Mich within, talking to Marshal Gran. The miner eyed No Name.

"Listen in, boy," he said. "We're going up the hill today, and we're moving in on those people. When the train comes, you'll be hauling them out of here, as well as yourselves."

Gran listened closely and then objected. "Those are legally deeded lots under the Homestead Act, properly recorded in Wellbred County records, and I am obliged under oath to defend that property."

"But not the criminals. Not the ones who hanged people by the dozen. I ain't gonna argue. I'm gonna tell you. Do what you want with them, but you're all leaving on the train whenever it comes. You want to come with us this morning?"

"No, I have no search warrant."

"Search for what?"

"The names of the six-man jury the judge was using. Every one of them was engaged in premeditated murder, among other things. And all to prove some thesis or other about cleaning the bad genes out of the human race. Of all the swine I've dealt with in my time as a lawman, those are the worst."

Big Mich stared. "If them names are in a ledger somewhere, you'll have them."

"For the record, I'll say you must heed the law."

No Name swore he saw a faint crinkle of flesh around the marshal's eyes.

"They can stay put until the train comes. We're gonna look that house over. Maybe I'll move in. A good anarchy needs a few knuckles around."

"You going to own it?" the marshal asked.

"Nobody's gonna own it. It takes a government for anyone to own anything."

"Truer words were never spoken," the marshal said.

No Name listened. What was it about this quiet federal marshal who got things done his own way? It was plain that Torvold Gran knew what went on inside of people's heads, and knew how to put that to good use. No Name wondered what Gran really thought about him. What did the marshal know of every misstep in a wandering life? No Name thought that as soon as they all got to Fort Laramie, he'd quit, and start wandering again. The marshal spooked him.

Gran was staring. "I hope you'll make yourself available for a while more," he said.

After Big Mich left, exactly nothing happened. The day drained away with no word from anyone. Torvold Gran and No Name toured New Dawn, and found smiling faces. The scaffold and the jail, those instruments of injustice, were gone. There was hope. They had a lively conversation with Professor Hannibal Rottweiler, who begged for patience. He believed that, if given a chance, New Dawn could be the laboratory of anarchy, the paradise devoid of coercion and cruelty. He had one of his family's dogs on a leash, and the dog sniffed amiably at the three of them as they engaged in sidewalk debate.

Then, late in the day, the judge himself showed up in town, full of indignation.

"Those subversives and barbarians marched right in, tore our home apart, looking for something they said we possessed, and told us to get on the next train and don't come back.

"My wife, Mrs. Howard, managed to get from

301

them what they were trying to find. A list of jurors. We have no list of jurors. We did have guests from all over the country, who overcame great troubles with travel, just to pursue with me a vision I have of a better world. None of them was ever a juror."

"But you're keeping their names private?"

"Absolutely. We're debating something so radical it could upend civilization. It's called eugenics, and it's in its infancy. It's about perfecting the human species with selective breeding and other measures."

"Who were your jurors?"

"They weren't my jurors. I don't own them. You're talking about the gentlemen who volunteered, as good citizens do, to hear these cases. Talk to Peter Dent about them."

"Dressed up. Dressed in suits and cravats, with gold watch fobs, felt hats, and all the rest," No Name said, remembering vividly his few moments before that polished group.

"When did you ever see academics looking like plutocrats?" the judge asked. "My guests can barely pay for a civilized suit of clothes. That's the fate of scholars."

"Tell me about eugenics," Gran said.

"We're just asking the first questions. What is a perfect mortal? Intelligence, Aggressiveness? Perfect health? Leadership? Social skills? Perfect bodies? Longevity? We don't know. We don't know how to breed for that, or whether there might be other methods, ah, it's all just scholarly talk. People breed sheep and cattle; why not humans? My guests and I talked all night, every night. It's the biggest idea in history."

"So who were your juries?" Gran asked.

"Peter Dent supplied them. He has a large family."

"Say that again? You seated jurors from where?"

"Putting a jury together in Throatlatch was impossible, Mr. Gran. As you can imagine. But our county clerk had a good supply of worthy citizens. He is a Mayflower descendent. Old Money. He lives across the river, you know. Big estate. More sheep than citizens of Wyoming. That's why no one in Throatlatch knew any of them."

"So why didn't you give Big Mich the names of your guests?"

"Because he and his hooligans were annoying me. On my shelves are folders full of monographs, papers, texts, magazines, with their names spread all over them. In plain sight."

"You sent a lot of people to their doom, sir."

"I did as the jury decided, sir."

"We'll see, Mr. Howard. We will certainly see."

Then, even as No Name watched, the judge seemed to diminish in size, until he was a crumpled old man.

"Mr. Gran," he said gently. "I await my fate. I hope you will spare Mrs. Howard."

"I can make no promises, Mr. Howard."

"You'll resolve this complex business swiftly, sir. There are a couple of things for you to know. One is the Dent family's ambitions. They have a complex across the river. You'll need to go there. I have a buggy and horse suited for that purpose. Don't consider it a favor; it simply is something I can do. And second, you should know that Carolina, who is more or less the spouse of Clyde Clemson, is Peter Dent's niece."

One jolt after another, No Name thought.

The judge walked Gran and No Name up to his house; he went out to his pasture, easily bridled a draft horse, brought it to a corral and harnessed it to a small black buggy.

"Cross the river, sir, and turn right on an obscure trail, the first you find."

"Will all those journals and papers still be on your shelf when we return?" Gran asked.

"Upon my honor, Marshal, what's left of it."

That was enough.

Gran and No Name boarded the buggy, and drove out, while behind them a broken man watched.

CHAPTER THIRTY-SIX

No Name drove the obedient gelding through a sunny, quiet town, across the rickety bridge, and into a silent wilderness beyond. Sure enough, a half mile up the road, an obscure two-rut road led off to the right, and No Name followed it. The road had been used. Iron-tired carriages had left their mark on the clay.

The road generally followed the North Platte River, but well away from the bottoms, staying on a bench that led to grassy meadows and rolling hills, somehow rare in a Territory of basins and ridges.

A mile or so in, they came upon something astonishing. A coat of arms, enameled metal, hanging from sturdy posts. No Name stopped. The shield had the word DENT across the top, in white, and below that a leopard rampant. At least that's what No Name thought.

"Am I seeing a leopard, with spots?" he asked.

"We're both seeing a leopard with spots on a family crest of some sort."

"Do leopards have any significance?"

"I suppose we'll find out. Or maybe not."

"Spots before my eyes," No Name said. "I'm a

man without a name. The Dents have nothing but name."

They traversed another mile or so, and then entered a groomed complex. The great house that No Name expected didn't exist, but there were several clapboard homes, gray and trimmed with white, probably kit houses sent to this wilderness and erected in this gracious yard.

Peter Dent himself emerged from a gray home and greeted them, almost as if he were expecting them. "Welcome to my family home," he said. "Let me show you about."

It all seemed rehearsed to No Name. Something planned, or at least anticipated.

Almost as swiftly as No Name stepped down, a Basque youth took the reins and led the horse and buggy to a white-fenced pen.

"We employ about two hundred Basques," Peter Dent said. "Best sheepherders in the world. We have over a hundred flocks. That is our business."

"Your entire business?" Gran asked.

"No, sir. We are landholders. My late father started it a decade ago, but he went to his reward and now I'm the senior Dent. There are siblings, cousins, uncles and aunts, as well as retainers here. To answer your question, sir. Our other business is land. We are well along toward becoming the owner of more land than anyone else anywhere. That's my father's vanity, and now mine also."

"And that's why you picked up every lot and plot in Throatlatch?"

"The miserable little town was a cancer that needed surgery, sir. We performed that surgery."

"How have you acquired all this land, Mr. Dent?" Gran asked.

"By every means. We've bought school sections from the state. Railroad sections from the railroads. All our employees are homesteaders who will sell their land to us as soon as it's proved up. We've also bought mining claims. And private holdings of any sort. And river frontage and water rights."

"Why do you keep yourselves out of sight?"

"That, sir, is the key to success. Invisible. No one has ever heard of the Dents."

"What does the leopard stand for?" No Name asked.

"Nothing at all. It's a family insignia invented by my father, for fun."

"Why have you placed a coat of arms there, on an obscure lane?"

"That marks this parcel, sir. We have about ten square miles in this parcel. It's what we call our estate."

Gran pointed at the man's suit coat. "Why, in the middle of nowhere, do you dress like that?"

"It's a family affectation, Mr. Gran. We all do. We all are properly attired at dinner every evening."

"Why here?"

"That's a matter of conflict within our ranks, sir. Some of us find it boring. But the train will ease that when it provides regular service. Meanwhile, we've set our sights on Wyoming Territory, as well as portions of Montana, Nebraska, and Colorado."

Gran seemed to harden a bit. "I have it from Judge Howard that your family supplied juries to Wellbred County district court. Is that the case?"

"Absolutely, sir. And I was county clerk there, the keeper of the records."

"Would you say these juries were sometimes a little hasty?"

"Never, sir. The guilt of the criminals was never in doubt. Anyone with eyes could see it."

No Name felt a rage ram through him, but Gran quietly touched his shoulder, and No Name contained himself.

"Did your family jurors have any private intent beyond serving justice, sir?"

"It was all public service, sir. We set out to rid the area of the rabble that had drifted into Throatlatch. Every last one. Clean that cesspool, and restore good order to the Territory. The West is full of riffraff."

"Well, did this serve any private purpose, sir? Dent family purpose?"

"Absolutely. When you clean out a nest of brigands, you find yourself in safer circumstances. We lost fewer of our sheep. Our fine Basques were not troubled. Instead of sending out vigilantes to clean up the country, my family chose to do it lawfully, using the Territory's own justice system."

"Are you done with all that, now that the place is called New Dawn and in the hands of cultists?" Gran asked.

"I'd rather not say, sir. But the family has a right to defend itself in all circumstances."

"By force of arms?"

"By whatever means is effective, sir. I can't commit."

"I gather that the sheriff's consort is your niece."

"That was her choice. We tried to stop it, but she's headstrong. At least she's kept her share of the Dent estate intact, and out of the hands of her consort."

"Is she restless, sir?"

"You'd have to ask her, Mr. Gran."

No Name peered into the afternoon sky, hoping to assure himself that the sun would set in the west. All the while he had been in Throatlatch, and then New Dawn, this place was thriving a few miles and one county line away.

"May we meet your family, Mr. Dent?" the marshal asked.

For once, Dent seemed undecided. "They generally prefer their privacy, sir. But perhaps a few. If you'll excuse me, I'll arrange for some to enjoy the pleasure of your company."

Peter Dent hurried off, and No Name found himself studying the compound. The grass was curried by several small bands of sheep herded by Basque boys. Twelve gray and white clapboard buildings sat in a semi-circle, but there were also white barracks and utility buildings apart, for staff and supplies. It looked to be utterly boring. A family obsessed with land and wealth and power could only be bored senseless here.

Eventually, Dent returned with half a dozen men and one woman. So the meeting would be out on the lawn, and not in one of their homes.

There they were, in suits and cravats, and the woman in starchy stiff attire. They oozed politeness and privilege. No Name thought that any one of the men had sat in the jury that had condemned him to death for no reason. But how could he know? He had been tried in a couple of minutes by well-dressed men in suits and cravats.

Peter Dent did the honors. "This is Marshal Torvold Gran, and—I'm sorry, I don't know your name, young man."

"Call me the leopard," No Name said. "I have spots."

They laughed. Dent did not introduce his family. "It's complex," he said. "But we're all a big family. Peas in the pod."

"Did any of you visit Throatlatch in its heyday?" Gran asked.

"Not if we could help it," one replied.

They laughed. Dent hurried them off.

A hawk circled over the distant hills.

Dent returned. "Is there anything else I may do for you?" he asked.

"Not at the moment," Gran said, "but I'll be back soon."

The Basque boy swiftly appeared with the buggy, and No Name took the reins.

They sat silently for the first mile, and not until they had passed the coat of arms dangling above an invisible line, did No Name venture to say anything.

"Two of those men condemned me to hang," he said.

"How do you know that?"

"I can't explain it."

"Could you identify them?"

"I think so."

"We need more, much more," Gran said.

He dropped the marshal off at the caboose and returned the horse and buggy to the judge, quietly wiping down the horse and freeing it. The judge's foothill home was oddly inviting, and he liked being there even though it overlooked a harsh, dry, cruel western landscape. He thought the Territory of Wyoming must have more dismal panoramas than any other territory in the country.

But it wasn't the scenery that was reaching out to him, it was something else he couldn't define. Thoatlatch's hold on him was as powerful as ever, and he couldn't break free of it. He did not welcome the train that would soon carry him away from this place of torment.

He walked along the lane, only to discover Carolina standing at the side, like a statue.

"May I walk with you?" she asked.

He reluctantly agreed. She confused him. She had once reached out, but had pulled back, and had even been icy toward him, all of which had shattered any little dreams that were percolating through him. But there she was, beside him, wanting to say something but unable to speak.

"The marshal and I, we're about done here," he said.

"Help me, please help me."

He stared, startled.

"I can't stand it here one more moment. Take me with you. Or help me run away, anywhere."

"Want to sit down?" he asked, pointing to a sandstone outcrop that offered a view of an empire.

She nodded and settled herself there, wary for a moment of rattlesnakes. She was in her starchy clothing, the same starchiness No Name had discovered out at the Dent estate.

"It was an arranged marriage. My family gave me to Clyde Clemson, only I didn't like him, in

312

fact he made me sick, and I refused. I wouldn't repeat any vow. So my family, the Dents, rewrote the trust. I don't know what's in it, but I know the Dents wanted a sheriff in their pocket, and they used me to do that. They never gave a thought to me, or my wishes, or my dreams."

"You're a prisoner."

"Worse. I'm a slave too. I do whatever . . . whatever."

"Have these Michigan miners told your husband to leave?"

"He won't go. He's about to slip back across the river and we'll be back on the estate."

"The Dent place?"

"It's the worst place in the world."

"Why is that?"

"Because they have only one thing in mind: they want to run with the Vanderbilts. There is nothing else in their heads."

"Meanwhile life whirls by," he said. "I've got the opposite problem. Something here tugs at me, entices me, as if this place had two arms to hug me."

"That's the strangest thing I've ever heard a man say."

"I grew up without a woman, without a wife. I never was hugged. Or had anyone to hug."

He thought for a moment she was about to hug him, but she eased away a bit. That would be a bridge too far.

"Is there some way I can help?"

"Hide me. Help me go. I have some gold coins. I can use them once I'm away, and they'll never see me again. You have to hurry. When he takes me to the Dents, across the river, across the county line, I'll be lost, with nothing but a grave to look for."

"What's keeping your, mate, ah, from taking you now?"

"He doesn't want to abandon his place here. The minute he leaves, those miners will move in. It makes him boil. They rule here. They're the government, even if there is none."

"He's like the others, then."

He glanced at her, and discovered tears welling up in her warm eyes.

"I haven't got a plan," he said. "But Marshal Gran is the best man I've ever met. He probably will just say it's none of his business. But I'll ask."

"Please do," she said. "My life is all that's left. And maybe I don't even have that any more."

CHAPTER THIRTY-SEVEN

Torvold Gran listened intently.

"There's official business and there's other business," he said. "The United States marshal must stick to official business, which involves crimes against the law and good order of the nation. But there's unofficial business, that doesn't involve the law, or the badge. That's something for the man, Torvold Gran, to weigh. This isn't my business. Helping a woman flee from her husband and her family might be considered the worst sort of conduct. It could even result in lawsuits. But let me think about it. I'll say this: she's caught in a dark web."

That wasn't the support that No Name hoped for. Marshal Gran was not the one who could heal the world, much less one lost soul in it.

"When's the train coming?"

"Tomorrow morning. They've wired me."

"Who's coming?"

"More railhead workers. The railroad doesn't know who else. But the coach is nearly sold out. It'll unload here, go up to the railhead, unload workers and supplies, and return with the injured, as before. That's when we get on."

"With prisoners?"

Gran smiled. "Let's call them volunteers."

"Judge and Mrs. Howard?"

"First in line."

"And Big Mich may add a few?"

"I haven't asked him."

"And our work is done here?"

"You can supply your own answer to that."

Not done, not by a long shot. But paralyzed by some violent miners.

"Half done," No Name said.

"Half started," Gran replied.

"When I read those ten-cent novels, some hero rides in with a pair of six-guns and sprays some lead around, and everyone lives happily ever after, except for a few bad ones."

"Not a bad idea," Gran said, which puzzled No Name. He had the feeling that the marshal wasn't saying what he knew. He'd been demoted to a lackey.

"I'm gonna get cleaned up," No Name said.

He headed for the tonsorial parlor, which now sat across the dusty road from the remnants of what had once been a county courthouse that had hidden endless cruelties within its clapboard walls. The courthouse was gone, but the cruelties lingered there, and No Name hated even to step onto the barren lots where it stood.

He entered the barber shop, and that clanged a

bell. Schuster emerged from his private quarters, swallowing the last of a hasty supper.

"Ignoring me, as usual," Schuster said. "You need a shave, haircut, tooth cleaning, and a spit bath. And I don't accept blue notes. They're pure junk."

"I get paid in greenbacks. The marshal hands me an envelope."

"You're a mess. If we had a hot springs around here, I'd send you there first. You announce your presence well before anyone sees you."

No Name didn't like that. First the marshal was hiding stuff, and now his other friend was needling him. Worse, Carolina had endured his stink all the while they had talked.

"I'm leaving."

"No you're not. Sit." The barber stabbed a finger toward the chair.

No Name settled sullenly, and the barber started out with a wet towel, soaking No Name's grimy hair. No Name shut up. He was tired.

Schuster worked hard, lathering up the hair, rinsing it, scraping beard, while saying nothing at all. Sometimes the barber scrubbed so hard it made No Name uneasy.

"You'll be on the train when it leaves tomorrow?"

"Big Mich says I will. The marshal isn't fighting it. He told me he's no Wild Bill."

"Then I'll lose the only friend I've got here.

But maybe that happened long ago. I hardly see you."

No Name sank down inside of himself and wished he could escape.

"If there's more than one coach on that train tomorrow, expect some surprises."

Mitgang was shaving, so No Name kept his trap shut.

"The government can live with a cult, like Professor Rottweiler's bunch, but it can't live with a hostile mob at its western border. To answer the question you're about to ask, I talk to railroad people on the work trains. And a few commissioned officers in civilian clothes."

"So?"

"We'll see what tomorrow brings."

The barber scraped loose hair from the back of No Name's neck.

"There's more. You haven't seen Gus Glory around, and he won't be on the train when it heads east. He's now employed by the Dents. He'll do the sort of things that are beneath the Dents, and he'll be in Dent attire—dressed up as if he were attending a funeral. He'll also be armed, discreetly, Dent style."

"Is there some reason?"

"Peter Dent doesn't like the miners, and he doesn't like Professor Rottweiler's dreamers, and he doesn't like the marshal and you, and anyone who was around here when Throatlatch was

318

roaring and the cemetery was growing every few days."

"Meaning you."

"Gus tells me these things. The Dents told him to clean up, so he's a regular customer now. His job requires some attentions from his barber. Now then, tell me what you and Carolina Clemson are doing."

"What . . . what?"

"No Name, there are times when I make assumptions, and this is one. Forgive me. She came here quietly one eve, desperate for help. Would I find men's clothing for her, complete, and would I quickly, when the moment came, shear off her hair and turn her into a young gent? I said that would be like taking the butcher knife to the Mona Lisa, but she didn't laugh. She was hurt. She said you men are all alike, and fled." He sighed. "I invited that, I'm afraid."

"I told her I'd help her if I could, but I don't know how," No Name said.

"You aren't alone," Schuster said.

No Name paid, and stepped into a quiet summer's eve. A band of red light lit the western sky. His restlessness was worse than ever. He slipped into a side street, not yet named, and hunted for Professor Rottweiler's house, which he understood to be the biggest on that street. He felt driven by needs he did not understand. But there was the house, and on its porch sat the professor and his family. No Name turned in.

"So you have come for a visit, at last," the professor said, a faint rebuke in his tone.

"I understand you'll have more of your people arriving on the train, and I thought to tell you so you can settle them."

"Nothing is being done about New Dawn," the professor said. "Why aren't you doing anything?"

"Uh, sir, I'm an investigator for the government inspector who's looking into the collapse of this county."

"But that's unimportant. What's happening now is important, and if we don't get relief, we may leave. This is intolerable. We are people of good will, and seek to live peaceably with other people of good will."

"I'm afraid I have no power to do anything, sir."

"If things don't improve, fast, we'll start over. We'll move west and find some unsettled place where we can be alone."

"The West is a big place, sir."

"We don't want to do that. We came here to settle. But then the Michigan miners, all of them brutes who know nothing about our ideals, moved in, pushed us out of our homes, took over, refuse to honor our blue scrip, and now are about to form their own government."

He had a point.

"Have you sat down with them and worked out a compromise, Professor?"

"They don't sit down. Their leader, Big Mich, is no more an anarchist than Queen Victoria. He'll move into Judge Howard's estate before the train is out of town, and begin making laws and rules."

"I gather you expect my employer, a United States officer, to resolve this. But he has no power to do that. He's looking for violations of federal law."

"If not him, what are we to do? Anarchy is a delicate arrangement that requires perfect virtue in all citizens. If there's to be no government, then all of it must lie in the bosom of each person. If he can't govern his ambitions and hungers, then he must leave us. These miners, Big Mich and his hooligans, haven't any self-governance in themselves. They're just another mob. They need to recognize they aren't fit to be anarchists, and leave us."

"You'll need to take your case to Washington, sir. I have no power."

"Washington! Washington!"

No Name hadn't the faintest idea what to say, but finally settled on one idea. "In Fort Laramie, about a hundred miles away, there are four companies of infantry. If you need to restore order here, on federal land, you can ask the commanding officer there."

"This isn't federal land; this is a new enclave broken away from the Territory of Wyoming."

"It's up to you, sir. You can catch the train tomorrow, and by evening be talking to the commander."

"We don't use governments, sir. We'll decide on other means. But thank you for your counsel."

No Name nodded. There really wasn't anything to say. Governments were given a monopoly of the use of force for a good reason, that was apparent right there, on this side street of New Dawn.

"Frankly, you and your superior, Mr. Gran, have disappointed us, young man."

No Name nodded. The man annoyed him. The professor was leading a cult built on madness; the sort of madness that seems real in one's mind, but falls to pieces in a cruel, harsh world.

There were two groups here, both calling themselves anarchists, and neither one of them would survive for long. No Name had the advantage of them. He had grown up without parents.

He headed for his nest in the hayloft, wondering what tomorrow would bring.

CHAPTER THIRTY-EIGHT

The next day began terribly. Marshal Gran yelled at him from the door of the livery barn.

"Hurry up," he said, and let No Name stew as he laced his boots.

The marshal was curt. "We have work to do," he said.

He led No Name toward the tonsorial parlor, which stood silently in the early light.

"He's not there. They took him. And there's more. There's no one up the slope. Clemson's gone, with his wife and their horse and carriage. Judge and Mrs. Howard are gone, too, also with their horses and carriage."

"Where?"

"Do I need to tell you?"

"Dents. Do you think Clemson forced the Howards to go?"

"Yes. The judge left all those journals he promised to give me. He'd given up, and was awaiting his fate. He was a weak and in the end miserable man, but there were some threads of decency in him."

They entered the silent barber shop. The

barbering tools rested neatly on a shelf next to the barber chair.

"He didn't take them. That means he was coerced."

They peered around the empty quarters at the rear, innately tidy because Mitgang Schuster was an orderly man. He had dressed tidily and they had hauled him off.

"Clemson?"

"Who else? Now there are no witnesses in town. Schuster was the last. What happened in Throatlatch is now hidden away."

"All sorts of people fled when the place fell apart, Torvold."

"Drifters. You happen to have any names, occupations, forwarding addresses?"

"Clemson, then. And he's got Gus Glory, the Howards, and Peter Dent, if that's where they went. Nearby. I'm assuming they took Schuster. He saw it all. He's a hostage, unless Clemson kills him."

"Throatlatch is gone. But I'm not done. If they're at Dents' place, we can bring them back."

The marshal headed upslope to the Clemson place, and showed it to No Name.

"Some instinct told me to take a look, so I did. It was still dark. This is what I found."

The horses were gone, barn empty, house forlorn and abandoned. Carolina's stuff lay about, mostly abandoned. He must have had a bad time forcing her to dress and go with him. No Name could almost read the story from the chaos of her wardrobe.

The marshal led them to the Howards' place, which was much the same. Horses and carriage gone, house silent. Lydia, unlike Carolina, took most of her clothing. But there wasn't much to see. Did Clemson use a weapon? Did the judge cooperate? Who harnessed the horses?

There wasn't much of a story here, but the rest of it wasn't far away. The Dents' property would probably be housing a hundred secrets.

The judge had packed a bag too. His several pairs of shiny shoes were gone, along with his suits and cravats. It looked like a leisurely effort, maybe prearranged with Clemson. But who could say for sure?

"What do you make of it?" Gran asked.

"Preplanned. A conspiracy that included a few others. Both the judge's buggy and carriage are gone. All horses gone. Same for Clemson. The only problem was Carolina, who probably was dragged out and maybe gagged."

"You're hired," Gran said. "We need a deputy marshal."

"So what's next?"

"Keeping the peace in New Dawn. Those anarchists are going to need a little law enforcement when the train arrives. After that, we'll head for Dent's place. We won't find much. The ones we want, Clemson, the judge, they'll be spread out among the Basque sheepherders and flocks, all over the Territory."

"Then what?"

"Oh, marshals have their ways," Gran said.

They hiked silently into New Dawn, which rested quietly but could fall into tragedy whenever the train pulled in. They prowled the eateries, looking for Schuster just in case they had misread what they saw in his business. But Mitgang Schuster was gone, and so was Throatlatch, and the past, with all its brutal crimes.

They did find Big Mich, who eyed them sourly. "You're gonna be on that train when it leaves. You and those relics around here."

Gran smiled and nodded. No Name thought the marshal was being too agreeable.

But the quietness was an illusion. New Dawn was as taut as an over-wound watch.

A little after ten, the wail of a whistle drew the whole town to the track, the little station, and the nearby caboose. The same Baldwin ten-wheeler huffed around the bend, spitting steam, belching smoke, and then slowly squealed to a stop. It pulled a baggage car and two coaches, all of them dull green.

Two coaches. Big Mich growled something, and his men spread out.

A brakeman jumped down and addressed the silent crowd. "Anyone going to the railhead?"

No one was.

The baggage car door slid open and several expressmen began unloading crates and sacks and casks, as well as personal luggage. The grocer in New Dawn rolled a handcart to the track and began loading it.

The brakeman uncoupled the coaches, and hopped aboard the baggage car, even as the locomotive blasted steam, and eased forward, its bell clanging.

No Name watched all this unfold, curious about the second coach, as was everyone else. The conductor opened the coach door, slipped a stool to the gravel, and invited the passengers to depart. They were some of Rottweiler's anarchists, mostly ethereal young men in combed beards, eager to participate in a great revolution. No Name could almost read their minds: they had come to launch the future of mankind. A dozen or so of these were followed by a few families, mostly adventuresome young husbands towing uneasy wives and children. Professor Rottweiler welcomed them, while the Michigan miners watched warily.

Then the conductor opened up the door of the rear coach, and a lieutenant, dressed in a mustard uniform, stepped down.

"I'm here to make an announcement," he said, unrolling a scrolled document.

"Be it publicly proclaimed that the Territorial

County of Wellbred is now under martial law, and will remain so until the United States government and its ancillary entities have established federal sovereignty and good order."

With that, two platoons of armed soldiers stepped down, each carrying a repeater rifle, a bandolier with ammunition, and a knapsack. Each rifle bore a bayonet.

The miners stirred, and looked to Big Mich, but the tough copper miner held his peace. The two platoons, each commanded by a sergeant, lined up in battle order, their attention upon the miners, not the dreamers.

The lieutenant, who seemed well briefed, approached Big Mich. "You are the leader of these men, sir?"

"They lead themselves, sir. That's what they believe in."

"Very well. You have the option of staying here if you pledge your allegiance to the United States and agree not to take up arms against it. Or you may leave here without hindrance. Or you may return with us to Fort Laramie, and disband."

Big Mich absorbed that.

"I will say, unofficially, sir, that the copper mines of Butte, Montana Territory, are looking for experienced miners. If on your parole you wish to go there peacefully, we will not interfere."

"The hell with that. We've come a long way. We wore out boots. We've spent our last dime.

We've been beaten by government thugs for trying to organize a union. We've been caught and whipped. We've been starved and our wages stolen from us. The mining companies, they got ahold of the politicians and blood spilled. We buried some of our men. They had the militia, we had nothing but fists. They had laws enacted, and we had only brotherhood. They had the press, with headlines calling us criminals. We had only the facts. They had thugs who beat up our children and threatened our wives. We had fines to pay, judges to lecture us, jails to cage us. They had copper ore, and we had labor, and they said the ore was what counted. Labor, the sweat of our brow, didn't count. There was plenty more of it. We're here, and we're staying here."

"Think it over and let me know," the lieutenant said easily. "The train will be back in an hour or two, and we will proceed to Fort Laramie. I will need your decision before then."

Professor Rottweiler's crowd absorbed all that, plainly alarmed.

"Come along now, and I'll get you settled," Rottweiler said. "These houses need some attention, but that's the future, and we're here to create a new world."

"I don't think I want to stay here with these hooligans," one young man said.

"We never coerce anyone. You are free to

live your life as you see fit," the professor said.

"But that officer said this is going to be a county again. We can't have that," the youth said.

Rottweiler nodded, and headed over to the lieutenant. "We recognize no government, sir. Where do we stand?"

"This is United States territory, sir. If on you choose to stay, you will need to swear your allegiance and agree to abide by the laws and authority of the United States."

"But this is a free land. We've claimed it."

The lieutenant simply shook his head.

"These people have endured great hardship, come vast distances, to create a new world here, and with a wave of your hand you're demolishing the hopes and dreams and research of courageous people."

"I appreciate that, but it's beyond my power to change any of that, sir. I can do this much. There's not room enough on these coaches to carry you away. If you cannot abide by any of this, make your plans to leave, whether in a week or a month. Meanwhile, Wellbred County will remain under martial law. These decisions have come down to us from high up the chain of command. Let me add that the only legal tender here will be the United States dollar."

The groceryman steered his laden pushcart toward town, resupplied with foodstuffs for a gaggle of people who might not stay to buy it.

We're back to Wellbred County and Throat-latch, No Name thought. He wasn't sure whether that was a good idea.

CHAPTER THIRTY-NINE

The crowd drifted apart. The miners collected above the railroad station, and the professor's crowd simply gathered in the main street. No Name could see some of them talking. Most just stared, sometimes glancing toward the soldiers, who were relaxed along the railroad track.

The lieutenant and the marshal were caught up in conversation. The lieutenant looked much calmer than Torvold Gran, which surprised No Name. The soldiers dug into their knapsacks and pulled out field rations. Sometimes, they stared up the shining rails, looking for the train that would soon return to New Dawn. It would be backing, baggage car first.

No Name joined the marshal and lieutenant.

"Lieutenant Griswald, this is my deputy, who calls himself No Name."

"That's the best name of all," the lieutenant said. "What do you make of this, young man?"

"I have no opinion, sir."

"No name and no opinion," the officer said. "That's safe enough."

That irritated No Name.

"I suspect that my deputy's view is my own. These people won't budge, and you've got more of a problem than you realize."

No Name didn't add what else was on his mind: he found himself sympathizing with those who were about to be herded like cattle. A swift glance at Gran told him that the marshal was sharing the same thought.

Gran peered about. No Name did too, discovering that the crowds had diminished. He saw no miners, and few of Rottweiler's people.

When the train did finally show, with the baggage car leading and the brakeman hanging onto the steps and handrail, the soldiers leaped to attention and gathered their weapons. The lieutenant peered into the silent town. Gran was staring up the slope, and so was No Name. He knew where the anarchists had collected. They might well have a few rifles now, if the sheriff hadn't taken them all with him.

After some careful maneuvering, the baggage car's coupler knuckled into the coach's. In another minute the train would be ready to return to Fort Laramie.

But there was not anyone in sight, save for a pregnant woman with a child, watching from the main street. It seemed oddly peaceful there, just a woman and child and a black dog that looked like a Rottweiler.

"Looks like we'll have to round them up," the

lieutenant said. The man was a civil war veteran, but this wasn't war.

Marshal Gran nodded. "They're up here a way," he said.

The officer barked some orders, and the platoons spread into small groups and followed along. They hiked beyond the railroad right-of-way, and climbed a lane toward the sheriff's big house. The officer peered ahead. The place was occupied. Several miners stood on the large porch. No Name saw no weapons poking from any window.

The lieutenant, a brave man, headed toward the house, after waving the rest back.

"All right, it's time to board the train," he said. "Come along peacefully and there'll be no trouble."

He turned to his own men. "Hold your fire," he said.

In turn, a woman appeared, and began walking toward the lieutenant. Behind her, Big Mich came along. The woman was not being manhandled, and she voluntarily was providing cover.

"We're staying here," Big Mich said. "You don't need more reasons."

"The miners and the professor's group?"

"We're in this together."

"You realize that I am empowered to do what I must, under martial law."

"Then do it. This is more important than life."

"If anyone there wishes to take the train, and wants safe passage, now is the time to come forward. You will be safe."

That met with a deep hush.

Lieutenant Griswald tried again. "Listen closely. That train can be out of here in an hour, with my men on it, and you can be in your new homes, building your life here, if you'll agree to one thing: Tell me you are a citizen of the United States and will abide by its law. That's all. We'll be done. If you won't do that, then we'll remain in a state of martial law. My men and I will stay on. In short order you'll be starved out of your refuge here, having gained nothing. It's up to you."

No one responded.

"I guess we'll starve to death," Big Mich said.

No Name could barely imagine feelings, or ideals, that ran so deep.

Marshal Gran's face had hardened into a furious frown.

"All right, I'll send the train on its way."

The lieutenant sent a corporal to release the train. No one moved. Eventually, the corporal returned, a whistle blew, and the train, hauling a baggage car and empty coaches, puffed eastward, rounded the bend, and vanished. They heard a last wail of the whistle a moment later.

Big Mich and his protector walked deliberately back to Sheriff Clemson's comfortable house.

The lieutenant posted his men, and arranged for rotations. There would be soldiers on duty night and day.

There was not a bird in the sky.

The lieutenant took his off-duty men to the railroad station and set up camp there. He wired something or other at the station, and sent two of his men to requisition flour and coffee and other supplies from the grocer.

No Name supposed another train from Fort Laramie would arrive soon, with supplies for a long-term occupation. He didn't like any of it. He could see that the marshal didn't either. They still had work to do; bring several criminals who had destroyed lives in Throatlatch to justice. That meant a trip to the Dent estate across the river. And evidence, more evidence. And there was one task even more urgent. Find Mitgang Schuster or learn what happened to him. Maybe the marshal and he would go about their task, and leave this other trouble to the army.

"What are your plans?" Lieutenant Griswald asked the marshal.

"We will continue to pursue our tasks."

"Well, there's martial law now, and you'll need permission from me. You'll keep me posted and do nothing without approval."

Gran's face flamed, but he contained himself.

"I'm going to find out who's in this town. There

was a pregnant woman and a child with a dog, earlier. I want to make sure they're protected," No Name said.

"We'll do that," the lieutenant replied.

The marshal glared and No Name knew enough to keep silent.

The lieutenant smiled. "Of course you know that until martial law is lifted, I'm handling all responsibilities here. But don't worry; I'll keep you posted. If you don't mind, I'll make that caboose my headquarters."

"I'll collect my papers."

"There's no need, Marshal."

"They are legal evidence and records, Lieutenant."

"Well then, trust me to take care of them."

Gran ignored the man, headed for the caboose, collected the files and ledgers and a few personal items, and walked out. The lieutenant watched, but didn't block him.

"What next?" No Name asked.

"A missing man and valuable witness. This is a good time to check out the town."

They started with Schuster's tonsorial parlor, but it told them nothing more.

"You could stow your papers here," No Name said.

"Not here," the marshal said.

They began a systematic search, working up and down streets, checking every building thoroughly, calling Schuster's name just to make sure. They found nothing.

At the big house appropriated by Professor Rottweiler, they found the young woman and child and dog. Her name was Maria. Her child was Socrates.

"You all right? Need food?"

"Where are they?"

"Up in one of the houses on the other side of the tracks. I think they'll be free soon."

"My husband Caesar is there."

"I'm a marshal. I'll watch out for him, and for you, Maria."

She hugged her child and nodded.

They continued their search, house by house, not neglecting any shed, but the town yielded nothing to them other than a sense of knowing where the barber was not.

"Are there some burlap bags in the livery?" Gran asked.

"We can look."

They found some, and Gran slid the county records and a few other papers into it.

"Put this up in the loft, where you're sleeping."

No Name climbed the ladder and slid the Wellbred County records into a corner and scattered a little hay over them.

"Safest place I can think of," Gran said.

They returned to the caboose, and found the lieutenant cooking a stew for himself.

"The woman and her child are all right, have food, and seem to be safe. Her husband is missing, and probably with the rest. We'll check on her frequently."

"That's our business, Marshal."

"Then do it."

"Are we bothering you, Marshal?"

"You've got a hundred unarmed, harmless people bottled up with armed guards up there. They aren't criminals."

"They're engaged in insurrection against the United States, marshal."

"Civilians, women and children. Send them back to their homes."

"They're rebels, Marshal. It's called treason. Sorry."

"Send food and drink. Even prisoners of war are entitled to that much."

"Sorry. These people are traitors, and will be dealt with according to the rules." He paused. "And let me remind you that it's your duty to support us. And I've instructed the telegraph man at the station to show me any correspondence to or from you."

The marshal absorbed that with more self-discipline than No Name could manage, and they left the caboose into the welcoming night, with brilliant stars scattered across the heavens.

CHAPTER FORTY

A shout and uproar jolted No Name out of his sleep in the loft. He yanked on his brogans, tied them, and headed into the dawn. He spotted the marshal, also hurrying ahead, and the lieutenant, clawing his coat on as he left the caboose.

Ahead, a silent column of people, two abreast, walked steadily to the river, letting nothing, including the bayonets of the soldiers, stay them. The infantrymen were waving their rifles and jabbing their bayonets, but not shooting.

"Stop them," yelled Lieutenant Griswald.

But there was no stopping these people, who had reached the old wooden bridge and were marching across it. No Name thought he saw Maria, the pregnant woman, and her child among the crowd. He spotted the dog, and was sure of it.

"They're safe now," Marshal Gran said quietly as the column reached the other side of the North Platte. "Let them alone."

"What are you saying?" the lieutenant asked.

"That's another county across the river. The boundary runs down the middle of the river. Your martial law covers Wellbred County. Now they are free."

"This is hot pursuit, criminals, and we'll bring them back."

"Hot pursuit? You've just ended the disorders here. Every anarchist is gone. You don't even have grounds to continue your martial law."

"You're crazy, Marshal."

Gran suddenly seemed larger than himself, radiating some sort of power that caught the officer's attention. "Your superiors will enjoy the show, Lieutenant Griswald."

Griswald watched his men, still badgering the column with their bayonets, even on the other side of the river.

"You can wound and slaughter those people and bring them back, and then you'll have grounds for more martial law. Right now you have none. I think your superiors would enjoy that, as they decide on your early retirement."

"They're criminals, escaping."

"They're in another county. Wellbred County no longer has any. Not one. Unless you consider me, and my deputy here, fodder for your martial law."

"I should have forced them onto that train."

The marshal was enjoying this. "Wire your commanders. You've succeeded. There no longer is an anarchist in the county. You can proceed to restore Wellbred County and Territorial control. Good job, Griswald. Maybe you'll become a brevet captain."

"What's in that county? Who's in charge?"

"Let your commanders handle that. Those people are without food or clothing. They have a long walk toward nowhere. They need rescuing."

Griswald sent one of his off-duty corporals to round up his troops and return them to New Dawn.

"They're gone, sir. They said it's Wyoming Territory," one soldier reported.

"I'll send for an engine," he said. He hiked to the station and sent the wire to Fort Laramie.

He turned at last to Gran and No Name. "You still have business here?"

"Several premeditated murders, obstruction of justice, and more, Lieutenant."

The lieutenant looked like he was about to say something conciliatory, but then turned sharply away.

Four hours later a bare engine arrived. A brakeman coupled the passenger cars to it, while the two platoons loaded themselves and their gear. Then it huffed away, leaving a station man, two federal men, and a railhead crew in Wellbred County. New Dawn was a ghost town. And Throatlatch before that was a ghost town. The West produced ghost towns faster than it generated new towns. There were more dead dreams than live ones in the West.

"It's sort of lonely around here," No Name said.

"We've got to find Mitgang Schuster, and fast. He's not in town."

There wasn't a horse and buggy or wagon in sight.

"All right, let's get settled, and then we've got something to do," Gran said.

The marshal moved back into his caboose, and No Name settled in a nearby house, vacating his hayloft. Then the two walked up to the Clemson place, which needed to be examined for damage.

A handsome coppery saddle horse was tied to a hitching rail in front.

"Anyone here?" Gran yelled.

For an answer, Clyde Clemson appeared at the door.

"You must have gotten word fast," Gran said.

"I came to look over the damage. I'll say this: the place is clean enough. Hard to believe a few dozen people spent the night here."

"May we look?"

Clemson nodded. No Name and Gran toured the homestead and found that it barely showed heavy use. But the outhouse stank.

"That's what I needed to know," Gran said. He turned to Clemson. "What brought you here?"

"One of our Basques saw a bunch of people, asked some questions, and told the Dents. I saddled up for a look."

"Who's at the Dents' now?"

"Oh, a bunch of us."

"Is E Pluribus there?"

"I imagine. Hard to keep track. They come and go."

"We've been looking for the barber. Is he there?"

"We've been looking too. Half the Dents want a shave and a trim. They've got a Basque boy who can do it, but there's nothing like a good barber, and he's the best."

"Is Carolina with you?" No Name asked.

Clemson smiled. "She got the vapors and we've shipped her out. Dent's Basques took her in a wagon. She must be in Casper by now."

"She's ill?"

"No, just full of complaints. Say, was that the army you had here?"

"Martial law for a few hours," Gran said. "They're gone. Hardly anyone there."

"That's what we heard. Peter Dent bought out the grocer for his stock, and the grocer left with the rest of those radicals. The railroad's gonna add wire up to the railhead, and move the station man up there. They need a telegraph handy."

"You know more than we do," Gran said.

"The Dents are well informed," Clemson said. "They got word that the county's on its way out. The Territory's gonna wipe Wellbred from the map, combine it with Converse County."

"So what's left?" Gran asked.

"A railroad siding, that's convenient and might help some ranching outfits some day."

"Two ghost towns one after the other," No Name said. "A lot of blood was spilled over nothing."

It was the wrong thing to say. Clemson clammed up instantly. "Guess I'll head out," he said.

"You moving back here?" Gran asked.

"Hell no. It's desert. Chicago, maybe."

"The Dents, are they staying there?"

"You'll have to ask them," Clemson said, unhitching the reins and smoothly climbing into his saddle. "I'll let them know. And you might want to wire the Justice Department. There's nothing around here to investigate."

"Except a long line of new graves, all unmarked," Gran replied.

They watched the former sheriff ride off on that fancy copper horse, trot through the ghost town, and across the rickety bridge. And then he faded from sight.

"Dents know more than I know," Gran said.

"Maybe they own the station man and his telegraph."

"They own more than that. They own a few informants in Cheyenne, a few more in Fort Laramie, and a few dozen eyes watching sheep, and people, in the back country."

"I don't know what I'm here for now. A ghost town," No Name said.

"We've got work to do. A bunch of Dents on a fake jury sentenced you to death, along with a fake judge. You and a dozen more, casually strung up. And our friend the barber's missing. I'm afraid for him, and I'm going to track that down. And your friend JimBob, dead too." Gran stopped for a moment. "I've found that ghost towns tell their tales."

"So it's us against the ghost town?"

"No, us against the suspects, who are alive and well, a few miles away."

"You got any ideas?"

"The judge's place, next door. Normally I'd need a search warrant, but we're miles from a functioning court, we're in a dead county, and I have a hunch if there's anything of value there, it won't be around for long."

"What will we find?"

"That's the big question, No Name. But if we don't look now, we won't find anything at all, because that place is likely to burn down."

"I never gave a thought to Peter Dent. He was the Wellbred county clerk," No Name said.

"That's how he wanted it. And now E Pluribus Unum is his houseguest."

CHAPTER FORTY-ONE

A hard look at the judge's house and grounds yielded nothing. There was no hidden wall safe stuffed with double eagles and finger-pointing contracts. Somehow, both No Name and the marshal knew it beforehand, but there were rituals of detection that had to be followed, so they methodically did the required search.

When they returned to the caboose, they did encounter the only surprise of the day. Peter Dent sat there in his elegant victoria, waiting for them.

"There's nothing there," Dent said. "The real crime is bad ideas, the sort that lead to bad acts."

"Yours?" Gran asked.

"Not in the sense of violating any law. My bad conduct is moral and ethical, but entirely within what is allowed by statute."

No Name had never heard such talk, and he gaped.

"I'm the eldest of the Dents," Peter said. "I'm sixty one. No Dent male has lived beyond sixty-two because we are born with a bad valve in our hearts. So I have a year or so. My brothers are younger, ranging through the forties and fifties. They have a little time."

"Are you going to tell us about their innocence?" Gran asked.

No Name marveled. The marshal had already turned this encounter into a confession.

"Come sit in the carriage. These quilted leather seats are comfortable. It's breezy, so you won't be baked. We'll talk. It's always easier in a moving vehicle. And while we talk I'll drive us through this dead town, once a thriving place that was conquered by bad ideas."

Gran nodded and climbed in beside Dent, while No Name slipped into the cramped rear seat. He marveled at the elegance, leather upholstery, shining ebony hardwood and iron. Dent flipped the lines gently, and the obedient draft horses lumbered into a slow walk that took them down empty streets, piled with tumbleweed and old cans and broken jars. Doors swung on their hinges. Windows allowed the passage of daring birds.

"There, a dead town. It will burn away someday. I own every lot, but it was a worthless quest. You can't buy cities or ambition or dreams."

"You thought this would be worth something someday?"

"Yes. The railroad would make this a marketing center for ranches. But I was defeated by bad ideas. Who would have thought that a scholar full of bad ideas and a theory called eugenics would settle here and wreck this town and corrupt my brothers. I was entirely whipped by an idea that seems seductive but actually perverts good into evil."

"What's eugenics?" the marshal asked.

The marshal already knew; he and No Name had discussed all that.

"The idea that breeding can perfect mankind. First you determine what's excellent, and then you breed for it, much as you breed cattle for weight, or hardiness in cold weather, or ability to forage in one or another climate. Breed humans into perfection. Perfect intelligence. Perfect bodies that don't sicken. Perfect virtues. Select the mates and get rid of those who don't fit the model."

"That was the judge's ideal, was it?" Gran asked.

"It was. And it was much debated in his parlor, the one you just tore apart looking for crime. The crime was there, all right, but not recorded. Right there in that parlor, evil scholars with evil dreams debated what to do and how to do it, and the infection grew until it invaded my family and ruined a town and county."

The draft horses pulled them to the end of one clay street, and Dent turned them through an alley to the next. The alley was melancholic, littered with shattered glass, mostly whiskey bottles, and antlers. There was no wood; it had all gone into stoves.

"Why was that evil, this business of perfect-ability?" Gran asked, and No Name wished he had asked it.

"Because it denies us the value of our unique-ness. We are imperfect, and thus to be treasured for ourselves."

"I don't get it," Gran said.

"I don't either," Dent said, which startled No Name once again. "But it wrecked my brothers."

Dent stared grimly ahead, avoiding the eyes of his listeners. "All of us who aren't perfect are worthless. I'm not religious, but I would think we are all worth something or other."

"So the judge and a crowd of boozy people put a noose around a humble little woman's neck and killed her," Marshal Gran said, an edge in his voice.

Dent chose his words carefully. "The judge, influenced by drinking a bad idea, laughed and pointed to a slow-witted woman and all that followed was the darkest chapter in the brief chronicle of this Territory."

"And were you guilty of this?" the marshal asked.

"No, my addiction is property and my sin is greed."

"Why? What inspired it?"

"A name, a reputation. Let Peter Dent be larger than J. P. Morgan. Let Peter Dent own a whole Territory. Let Peter Dent be known to school children a hundred years from now. It's all in my name."

Ice water rose in No Name's veins.

"Maybe it's better not to have a name," No Name said.

"A name is nothing but a courthouse record," Dent said.

He turned the team onto the main street and stopped at the empty lots where the Wellbred County courthouse once stood.

"I was the clerk here. Clerks keep records. The real purpose of public records is to hide what really happened. You can read pages of my records and not know what happened in this county, who paid taxes and who didn't."

"So your name is a record of what didn't happen?"

"We shape our stories to fit our names," Dent said. "Your name is the front cover, but only you know what's in the record."

The marshal was growing restless with all the abstractions. "Over there. The parlor. What happened to Mitgang Schuster?"

"I wish I knew."

"Is he dead?"

"Probably."

"He's been called the last witness."

"The last who was not a party to the crime. There are several witnesses who could testify against one another. The judge. Sheriff Clemson.

Gus Glory. There's others, such as those railroad men. Mick Malone, their foreman, is a witness. No, not the last witness."

"Where do you think he is?"

"Up a gulch somewhere far away."

"Who killed Majestic Skinner?"

"Someone who was his friend. He would not be an easy man to hang."

The driver snapped the lines, and the ebony carriage started down main street, past forlorn shops, including the grocer.

"You own that now?" the marshal asked.

"I do, and what little was in it. The anarchists managed to get most. He was one of Professor Rottweiler's idealists."

"Where are they now?"

"One of my Basques, herding a large flock, ran into them. They held him at gunpoint and selected a dozen rams. They didn't touch the ewes or their lambs. They took the rams, which wasn't easy, but miners are big and literally carried them off."

"Not much food for a crowd that size. Did they say where they're going?"

"They did. The miners are separating. They'd decided that Butte, Montana, wasn't a bad idea. There's plenty of anarchy in Butte, and a living wage. When they reach the Union Pacific, they'll become boxcar hoboes and if they do it right, they'll ride all the way to Butte."

"And the others?"

"The desert draws them. Rottweiler said that the prophets headed for the desert to sort things out. I doubt that any of them will make it. That's all I know. All my Basque could find out. I have good, loyal sheepherders."

The victoria pulled up at the place where the gallows had stood. It had a hollow, desolate look under the hooded sky.

"Here's what we came to see, all of us. This is where most of it happened," Dent said.

"Would you like to confess now?" the marshal asked.

"I can honestly say that I was not a part of it. I was engaged in my own misconduct which happened to be legal."

"What of your younger brothers, those well-dressed gents who comprised E Pluribus Unum's jury?"

"They were careless of life, weren't they?" Dent asked. "Most will be dead within three or four years, thanks to our family malady."

"They didn't give their victims three or four years. Where are they now?"

"On Union Pacific trains running in all directions."

"Are you a conspirator?"

"No word was ever said to me. But I'd bet my bottom dollar none of them will be there when I return."

353

"It's a long way to the Union Pacific anywhere from your estate."

"I believe the baggage car that came through here two days ago took them away."

"And you didn't report it?"

"Worse than that, Marshal. I didn't know it."

"What of Carolina Clemson?"

"My niece? A sad case. No female complaints at all. The sheriff railroaded her into a virtual prison where she will be regarded as slightly demented and very sad."

The marshal eyed the barren clay where the gallows had stood. "Who did the hanging?"

"The sheriff and Majestic Skinner, the jailer, vied with each other for the honor."

"Of the living, Clemson took the most lives?"

"Maybe the judge did. His words, condemning them to hang by the neck until dead, they did the killing even if a pair of lawmen did the work."

No Name remembered those words, applied to himself, and remembered the sheriff and the jailer pitching him into a cell. What he couldn't understand was why he rather liked both men.

"Why did the jurors, your brothers, dress up? Coats, waistcoats, cravats, trimmed beards, spectacles, clean fingernails?"

"They were Dents, Marshal. And when they're laid out in a few years, they will be dressed just like that."

"Are you married?"

354

"I was, briefly. Childbirth, you know. Most of the Dents don't marry; it's the bad heart business that does it."

Dent drove them through the last shabby streets, and back to the caboose.

"This was a bad investment, Marshal."

"Will you sell it?"

"I can't even give it away. When it was Throatlatch, I thought I'd make crime pay. There's no greater magnet than a town full of crooks and killers. But that didn't work out. Even worse, was a town full of cultists and idealists. I could argue that bad ideas were the doom of my dreams of getting rich."

"What are your plans, sir?"

"Get out. Turn this into a large ranch, hire a manager, keep the flocks and the Basques, and go somewhere lively. Friends are a greater joy. If I live a while more, I'll enjoy good company."

"Would you come into the caboose and write out the names and ages of your brothers, sir?"

"Oh, I suppose. They're guilty, not because they're criminals but because they swallowed a lot of bad ideas from the judge. If you want to hang the guilty, then hang all the scholars who are fevered by eugenics."

That struck No Name as a novelty, and also a slick way of shuffling off responsibility.

Peter Dent and Marshal Gran vanished into the caboose, and soon returned.

"You'll be out at your estate, sir?" the marshal asked.

"When there's a ticking clock in your chest, home is wherever you're alive."

They watched the eldest Dent climb into his ebony victoria, and send his perfectly paired horses toward the old bridge. The sounds of shod hooves and iron wheels echoed from the planks of the bridge.

The marshal headed for the station, intending to wire his superiors. They might catch a few Dent brothers if they moved fast. But when they got to the little station they found it locked. There was no station man within, nor was there a telegraph key. But a note on the door said the telegraph would reopen in a week, after the line was extended to the railhead fourteen miles up the right-of-way.

"One could argue that Peter Dent thought of everything," the marshal said. "But sometimes luck is an accident."

CHAPTER FORTY-TWO

There they were. Stuck in a ghost town. The marshal had no way to wire his superiors either to convey news or obtain instructions. They had minimal food. The marshal had his handgun, but it wasn't much use for hunting. They could hike fourteen or fifteen miles to the railhead, or they could wait for the next work train to come through, which happened every few days.

"Looks like we wait for the train," the marshal said. "Meanwhile, let's see what more we can manage. There's no physical evidence in this tumbledown town, but there's a lot of impressions. Dent told us more in an hour than we've gotten from seeks of hunting down enough evidence to do some justice."

"You mean argue about what Dent said?"

"Yes, I do."

"You mean, try out theories?"

"And propose ways and means to catch criminals. And we have one more mystery that begs an answer. Who killed Majestic Skinner, and why?"

"We don't know where Mitgang Schuster is."

"We can't stray far if we hope to catch that work train, No Name."

"I want to find him."

"We can go out, one at a time, and look, and stay in touch."

"I'm good at looking, and no good at debating," No Name said.

"You're good at both."

"I've been thinking: Peter Dent's trapped by his name. I'm not trapped because I'm not a person."

The marshal laughed. "I'm stuck with being a Norwegian."

But No Name was weary of it. "I'm not any good at checkers," he said. "I'll go for a hike."

"Go have your walk. I'll be making notes on everything that I can remember. Dent said a lot, and it leads in all directions."

That was a relief. He stepped into an airless, sunless afternoon, in a dead town haunted by ghosts. There wasn't much on his mind except an urgent need to get out. To hit the road. Drift to wherever he was meant to go.

That strange urge to return to Throatlatch, to be here, work out an ending to a strange story, had passed. He was ready to leave. The sagging buildings, already turning silvery in the summer heat, now were repelling him. He wondered what had drawn him back. When the work train came, he'd go with the marshal to Fort Laramie and resign. He lacked cash, but it didn't matter.

So he drifted, down a haunted thoroughfare, down to the gallows, and was glad to see meadow-larks plucking at the weeds. The ghosts had gone, and the birds were finding a home there. Some ghost must have left him, too, because he could gaze at that spot and feel nothing at all. Forgetfulness was a kindness.

To his surprise, a buggy drawn by a single horse was crossing the noisy planks of the bridge, and within it were E Pluribus Unum Howard and Lydia, both dressed up in party clothes.

The judge lifted his hat and reined the dray horse.

"We're going home. Tell the marshal, and come visit us. Give us an hour to refresh."

"I'll do that, sir."

He watched the horse and laden buggy turn up the lane and vanish in the distant driveway.

He hurried back to the caboose, and saw the marshal frowning.

"Was that who I think it was?"

"They asked for an hour to refresh, and asked us to come then."

"I'll finish my notes. Come by in an hour."

No Name devoted the hour to exploring Professor Rottweiler's house. He understood the miners well, but had no idea what drove the professor, and all his fragile idealists, to think the world would be better without any government. But the house offered no clues. He decided he had the intuition of a billy goat, and headed into the cloudy afternoon. He sat on the caboose stair while the marshal scribbled, and then the two of them hiked upslope. Neither ventured a guess. No Name had run out of guesses.

The judge, with great bags under his eyes, welcomed them with a thin smile. Lydia didn't rise, and sat motionless.

"We thought we'd save you the trouble of coming to get us," the judge said.

The marshal nodded.

"Have a seat, and we'll try to help you along. As for ourselves, we've decided to take what comes."

That was a surrender.

The marshal sat, and No Name sat nearby in a wingback upholstered chair.

"You'll want to know where people are, I suppose," the judge said. "And after that, all the details."

"Mind if I take notes, sir?"

"It's your duty, Marshal. First, most everyone's flown the coop. Sheriff Clemson and Gus Glory loaded a wagon sometime in the night and headed for parts unknown. The Dent brothers slipped out several days ago. I don't know where. Their wives have now left, in wagons driven by the Basque retainers. The sole person of interest to you is Peter Dent, and I gather he's been in touch with you. He believes he's done nothing unlawful, and is staying to put the estate there on a new basis, with a paid supervisor. When he leaves, there will be no Dents, and no guests."

"And the telegraph line is down," Gran added. "Maybe not coincidentally."

"Mr. Dent is a man of probity, and were it not for conversations with us, we might have taken the same path. There's good fishing in the Gulf of California, I hear."

"Oh, nonsense, Pluribus, we're both guilty as sin," Lydia said, deflating her husband.

"Yes, a lot," the judge said. "Condemned to hang, or killed in some other manner. A dozen or so transients innocently passing through, although one young hooligan got away. Nameless in hasty graves. A few locals, including a retarded little woman. Some railroad men, Marcus Penn, Martin McGee, Wallace Parson; a deputy, Majestic Skinner; a saloon man, JimBob something or other, and one other—I think. The barber. But that's only been a whisper. No one says much. The Dent estate's a living graveyard."

"Why, sir?"

"Bad ideas, Marshal. You know all about that. This place, a den of ordinary frontier evil, was transformed into something much worse by scholars like me and my friends, and by cultists

361

and visionaries, like Professor Rottweiler, whose visions defy human nature—and the value of persons."

"And what do you expect me to do?"

"Take us away."

"Who did the hanging? You sentenced, but someone pulled the lever."

"The sheriff and the jailer."

"What did the railroad want?"

"To get its right-of-way back, and not contested."

"They lost three men. Why?"

"The railroads are not paragons of virtue, Marshal."

"Who hanged Majestic Skinner?"

"Gus Glory, after doping him with a spiked drink. Majestic was becoming repentant. The fewer witnesses to what happened here, the better."

"I'm weary and I'll lie down," Lydia said.

She rose, made her way out of the room, and they heard a door click shut.

"Where are Gus Glory and Clyde Clemson going?"

"They'll split up as soon as they reach a railroad. I'm not privy to much else, but I'd say that Clemson will go to Casper and try to get Carolina out of the asylum she's in. She has money, a trust, and he wants it. Gus Glory, who knows? I'd guess he'd try to stay on the right side of the law and become a deputy somewhere, especially some country county."

"Who killed the railroad foremen? They were murdered."

"I don't know that, Marshal."

So it went through the overcast afternoon. The judge was forthcoming. Some decency, some conscience in him was guiding him toward complete, open confession. His voice was thin and reedy. This was gallows talk. He had condemned innocents to death, all for the sake of a theory of human perfection—if that. By the time he had performed this odious task a few times, it was no longer motivated by any theory at all.

No Name knew he was far from being a true detective. Gran was steadily opening one page after another, and recording the answers. Somehow, the marshal had constructed a framework and was fitting events into it. It was macabre work, and it was persuading No Name to escape this profession.

The muffled shot rattled them. It came as a thump, like a pillow hitting something. The judge blanched. The marshal sprang up, raced to the bedroom door, and opened it slowly, carefully, while the judge and No Name followed, not wanting to see inside.

She lay upon the bed, her lips flooded red. She had put a revolver to her mouth and pulled the trigger. No Name sagged, a loss so deep he could not bear it. He had once wished she had been his mother.

The judge stared and then turned away.

"It was time," he said.

EPILOGUE

Judge E Pluribus Unum Howard died of natural causes a few weeks later. There never was a trial. No one could find any suspects or come up with witnesses or solid evidence. The younger Dent brothers had vanished, but there were rumors in the East that some of them were enjoying a life of wealth under other names. Peter Dent remained in Wyoming, and was watched a few years, but had no contact with his family, and no one could pin anything but greed on him. Local historians argued that Throatlatch had engaged in more murder than any other place in the country, and no one was ever convicted of it.

No one ever found Mitgang Schuster's body or grave. Throatlatch gradually decayed into silvery wood that caved in year by year. The little grave-yard was hard to find, but near one edge of it was a short, dark obelisk with an inscription on it: *MS, Of Blessed Memory*. In time, the monument faded and the legend became impossible to read.

Some of the Michigan copper miners ended up in Butte, worked for the Anaconda Company, and caused as much trouble as they could. Professor Rottweiler's group reached Arizona Territory and vanished. Some say they wished to ally themselves with the Apaches but the Apaches had other ideas.

Torvold Gran became a celebrated United States marshal, operating from Denver. No Name resigned from federal service. He never chose a name, and remained No Name all of his days, because that was how he wanted it.

ABOUT THE AUTHOR

Richard Wheeler has emerged from retirement to write one more novel. He retired a few years ago after a career in genre fiction that won him numerous honors. He began his fiction career in midlife and wrote over eighty novels, some under pseudonyms. His western and historical novels have won him Spur Awards, starred reviews, and inclusion in the Western Writers Hall of Fame.

He chose as his current project to write a western, but it turned out to be much more, and defies categorization in any genre. He does not know whether this is his swan song, but he does know that this is unlike anything else he's written over four decades as a novelist. It is his tip of the hat to countless friends, reviewers and readers.

Center Point Large Print
600 Brooks Road / PO Box 1
Thorndike, ME 04986-0001 USA

(207) 568-3717

US & Canada:
1 800 929-9108
www.centerpointlargeprint.com